# Praise for *Daughter*

"bandele writes about family grief and  ring immediacy. . . . This powe~~r~~ ~~~~sks for: it breaks the silence."

*list*

"If silence is the cancer that kills our dreams, then asha bandele's *Daughter* is surely the cure for what ails us. As real and as terrifying as the news stories we don't want to read, *Daughter* forces us to look behind the headlines and see the human beings who live there. bandele's truth creates almost unbearable pain on the page, but her great gift is that she is able to find a path leading us out of that deadly quiet and into a song of sisterhood."

—Pearl Cleage, author of *What Looks Like Crazy on an Ordinary Day* and *I Wish I Had a Red Dress*

"At its heart, this beautifully and sparely written tale looks at one woman's escape from her own emotionally locked-up life. By the end, you may be pondering your own mom's life pre-you."

—*Elle Girl* (Reader's Pick)

"Rather than making her novel into an examination of political and racial issues or police brutality, bandele turns it into a eulogy for motherhood lost, a plea for tenderness and the kind of storytelling that resurrects lost family history. . . . bandele's background as a poet serves her well."

—*The Washington Post*

"[A]n eloquent message about the tragedy of dreams—and life—deferred."

—*Kirkus Reviews*

"bandele's low-key take on a grim aspect of the urban black experience stands in refreshing contrast to more sensationalist renditions."

—*Publishers Weekly*

"Thanks to vivid flashbacks, the story that unfolds is searing, passionate, and intense. This urban coming-of-age tale grapples with difficult material, centering on the fragility of the mother-daughter bond. Highly recommended."

—*Library Journal* (starred review)

"The silences that injustice feeds are so intricate and mutable that the mere possibility of expressing them is risky. Gloriously, in *Daughter*, asha bandele speaks from this impossible place. Let her take you there."

—Adrian Nicole LeBlanc, author of *Random Family*

# daughter

## A NOVEL

# asha bandele

*SCRIBNER*

New York   London   Toronto   Sydney

SCRIBNER
1230 Avenue of the Americas
New York, NY 10020

First Scribner trade paperback edition 2005

SCRIBNER and design are trademarks of
Macmillan Library Reference USA, Inc., used under license
by Simon & Schuster, the publisher of this work.

For information about special discounts for bulk purchases,
please contact Simon & Schuster Special Sales:
1-800-456-6798 or business@simonandschuster.com

Designed by Colin Joh
Text set in Aldine

Manufactured in the United States of America

1   3   5   7   9   10   8   6   4   2

The Library of Congress has cataloged the hardcover edition as follows:

bandele, asha.
Daughter : a novel / asha bandele.
p. cm.
1. African American college students—Fiction. 2. African American
families—Fiction. 3. African American women—Fiction.
4. Mothers and daughters—Fiction. 5. Police brutality—Fiction.
6. New York (N.Y.)—Fiction. I. Title.
PS3552.A47527D38 2003
813'.54—dc21
2003045536
ISBN 978-0-7434-1798-3

For my grandmother Harriet,
my mother Dolores,
and my daughter Nisa.

*Speak, so you may speak again.*
Zora Neale Hurston

# Part 1

# 1. Eight Manchester Place: Wednesday, 7:15 A.M.

It was a morning thick with winter and a surprising sun. And the light was early. It was gliding down the two-block road, down the stripped-down street, down past where the old frame houses wore their paint like rags and did not concern themselves with frivolities like manicured front lawns or usable porches. The light coasted until it came to the corner where the small brick two-family house stood, stiff and alone.

Eight Manchester Place. That was the home. Well kept and clean, it was a reminder of what this neighborhood, this street, had once looked like. Here had been a community born during the migrations of the 1930s and 1940s, organized by the push and power of the 1960s, rocked by the horse and recession of the 1970s, asphyxiated, cut, cast out, and cracked in the 1980s. Still, there was light somehow. Even in this final decade of the century, with all its bruises and deep-set abrasions, there was light somehow, and this morning it was coming in early.

It was coming in and Aya Rivers, who lived on the second floor of 8 Manchester Place with her mother, Miriam, was trying to sit up under it. Cross-legged in a chair at the dining table, beneath the window and furious spider plant, Aya was reading from an anthology of poems for her Black women's literature class. She was particularly fixated on a Sonia Sanchez verse, when she called out to her mother. "Mom, you gotta hear this," she said.

Miriam answered in that same mild voice she always used no matter what the circumstance, "Okay, okay, but quickly. I have to leave a little earlier than usual today. There's a big meeting at work."

There was *always* something whenever Aya wanted to talk to her mother. All the trouble she had caused and now, finally, at nineteen, Aya was doing what her mother had asked of her. She was in college and was making excellent grades. She'd been off probation for seven and a half months, and hadn't done anything that would raise an eyebrow with anyone, anywhere. She was trying so hard to be that thing, that neat and perfect thing her mother always wanted her to be.

But it always came back to, *how?* Not how to become, but how to forever be that thing? With all the swerves and wild twisting that the day could bring, how? That question had never been sorted out clearly for Aya. Her mother would tell her to get proper rest, to eat, to study, and to be on time. But she never told her how to make sense of the confusion and all of the hurt stacked up inside her, stacked and cluttered, chaotic, and dusty.

As much as she could then, Aya relied upon the judge, her probation officer, and even her mother when they said, Just follow the rules. *Please,* her mother would plead. Just do what they say. Which Aya did. But it didn't help that no one ever said what to do when the rules didn't make sense, when the rules were stupid.

That's where Aya had always stumbled. When she came across a rule that didn't fit into her life. But for the last seven and a half months, and even before that, back when she still had to report to Mr. Wright, Aya had followed the rules, even when they seemed ridiculous. Like the curfew that was so crazy it almost dared her to violate it. The year Aya was turning eighteen years old, she was supposed to be in the house by six o'clock on weekdays and by eight o'clock on Fridays and Saturdays.

Now, with probation over, she no longer had a court-ordered curfew, but Miriam still insisted that Aya be home as early as possible: eight o'clock Sunday through Thursday. The weekends were negotiable. But not by much. Every now and again, Aya would push, though lightly. She would mumble something about wanting to hang out—*just* hang out—and Miriam would not only remind Aya of the girl's own troubled history "just hanging out," but she'd also make a cryptic reference to Aya's father. Something about how he learned the hard way about running the streets. "What do you mean, Mama?" Aya wanted to know.

She wanted to know because these vague remarks Miriam made from time to time about Aya's father countered the image she had in her head of the war hero. Miriam never explained though, beyond remarking with an almost imperceptible measure of sarcasm that he didn't spend the whole of his life in the military, and when he was out in these streets, he didn't always make the right choices. Once, during a stilted, four-sentence conversation about Aya's father, Miriam wandered out of the room muttering something about the need to always buck authority. What was she talking about, Aya wanted to know, but there was no way to know. Not from this woman, not from her mother.

Besides, the last thing Aya wanted to do was upset anyone, which is why she always let her questioning go, she usually made it home even before dusk settled in, and she concentrated on her schoolwork. Because her grades were so high, she told her mother that she hoped to get a scholarship for graduate school. "To study what?" Miriam asked one morning as she made herself a cup of coffee. "Psychology, I think," Aya answered matter-of-factly. "I want to understand people so I can help them." Miriam had just looked at her daughter and nodded. She said nothing. Aya had looked at her mother that day, waiting for engagement, but it did not come. And when it did not come— it never came—she slipped, Aya did, back into her mind, back into her plan of finishing school, getting a job, moving out, doing her own thing, really living her life. For now though, she'd have to tolerate this life, as constrained, unclear, and frustrating as it was.

There was one thing Aya found completely unfair, nearly intolerable. It was the mandate about Dawn: She was not to hang out with her. As if it had been Dawn who was the bad influence, as if it had been Dawn and not Aya who would fight anybody, try anything, go anywhere. As if it had been Dawn and not Aya who had mastered the art of lying. Dawn and not Aya who had the courage to get all hooked up, and make fake IDs, and go out to the clubs, and flirt with men twice their age.

Dawn would never have done any of that. If anything, Dawn was the one who would say, "Aya. Let's just go to the movies, girl. I don't want to get caught up in all this mess." And it was Aya who would push and cajole her friend until the girl gave in, which she always did eventually. They would leave Aya's house, and tell Miriam that they were going to the movies and to sleep at Dawn's. Miriam did not know that Dawn's mother, the only parent in the home, worked nights. Miriam would say, as she said every time, "Okay. All right. I'll give you a ring before I go to sleep to say good night."

"Okay, Mom," Aya would say before bouncing out of her house with a smirk. She knew Miriam would call by 10:30, and sometimes when she called, they would have the television turned up as though they were watching a show. Sometimes they pretended to be sleeping. But by 11:00 P.M. the girls were dressed and made up, their nails were done, their hair was done, and they were heading out to the club. And despite the fact that when they started doing this, neither girl was yet sixteen, makeup, fake out-of-state IDs, and especially Aya's confidence convinced people that they were twenty-five.

They would get in the club and begin dancing immediately. Even though they had to start out dancing together, in almost no time a couple of brothers would come over and join them, and Aya, dancing and winding sexy, would always talk men into buying them drinks.

On the night that Aya still replayed in her head, there had been these two men, friends, who were such excellent dancers, so generous, so *fine,* and sweet, that when one of them asked Aya to come back with them to their apartment, she had agreed to it, and then she had convinced Dawn to come along, that it was going to be fun. Together, the girls went with the men to a building that was just over the 138th Street bridge. The men lived in a loft at the edge of the Bronx, where Aya imagined she would be taken to the edge of her fantasy, her secret Prince Charming fantasy. It was the one she had had for the whole of her life. The one that had her being claimed by somebody, claimed and cherished.

This dream, this hope, coursed through Aya like a sudden and brilliant and convincing hallucination when she looked at Robert, the man who had been talking to her, dancing with her, buying her drinks and making her laugh. And Robert, who was carved, beautiful, deep brown, thick, and shining. Aya thought maybe this was him, the man who would love and take care of her. The man who would make her feel as though she belonged somewhere. There was something in the way he stared all the way into her when they danced, the way his hand confidently touched her hip as they moved together in the beat and dark. He opened her up there, on the dance floor where everybody became their own universe, and everybody became the same universe. She still remembered thinking how it seemed crazy to want this man in an instant, but then again, you had to meet the great love of your life somewhere, somehow, didn't you?

At the club that night, Robert was the one who suggested it. He said he wanted to get out of there, to go back to his place where they could really, really talk and get to know one another, away from crowds and noise. Robert said he didn't want Aya to be just some girl he danced with in a club who disappeared after the music ended. And it was after this plea, this sweet plea that made Aya feel desired and hungered for, that she took Dawn into the ladies' room and said, "Come on. Let's go with them. We'll have fun! They're *really* nice. Plus it's perfect timing since your mother is in Atlantic City for the weekend. Come on!"

At first Dawn had said, "No, Aya. We don't know them. I don't want to." She'd said, "Aya, I *don't* want to do this. Please. *Please.*"

But Aya had pushed her. Aya had told her not to be so damn afraid of everybody. "They're *so* nice," she'd whined. "And *so* cute. *And* they bought all the drinks. This is fun. We're having fun. So come on. *Come on.*" Aya stared into Dawn's immobile expression. "Listen, this *feels* like it's going to be fine. There's something about Robert. And I'm sure if you talk to Marcus more you'll see he's sweet, too. Plus we're together. There's two of us."

"And there's two of them, too."

"I know. But I *really* like him. You know this isn't usually me, girl. I never even give out my number. But these guys are different. Can't you see that?"

"Not really," Dawn argued.

But finally she relented and the two girls fixed their makeup and headed out of the ladies' room to meet the men who quickly steered them out of the club, out onto a wide and fast late-night Manhattan street corner where they hailed a taxi and sped uptown.

≋

Robert Small and his friend Marcus lived in an expansive loft that was once a factory where chickens were packaged. It might have been beautiful-looking, this building, but the owner didn't have the money or the inclination to renovate it the way they did the old silk factory building downtown, and all the others like it in SoHo. Here, there were no bright parquet floors. Here, there were no clean and glistening walls. There were no shimmering brand-new fixtures. Here, nothing shone. Any beauty that existed in this building was brought to it by the tenants, many of whom also had the converse effect.

So what it was, where these two men lived, where barely sixteen-year-old Aya and barely sixteen-year-old Dawn went to, was an old building with sixteen-foot ceilings that was cut up into spaces where people could live in or squat, whatever you wanted to call it. It was, and this briefly occurred to Aya, like walking into an old black-and-white photo. Walking into a photo you saw in a book about war. It was something like that. Something like devastation. Nevertheless, and never having been much of anywhere, the girls were impressed.

"Excuse the mess," Robert said, as the foursome walked in. "I'm a designer," he explained, picking up an unfinished pair of pants. "I work in leather. See?"

All over the apartment were jackets, coats, and other garments in varying states of completion, but mostly there were scraps and bits of things that were unidentifiable. Robert quickly cleared off the couch and chairs, and asked the young women to sit down. It occurred to him as he looked at the girls here beneath his track lights that they definitely didn't look old enough to be in that club. Dawn's dimpled cheeks were still puffed by baby fat. Her hair was set in Shirley Temple curls. Her skin looked new, and her waist was still only barely defined. And Aya, pretty Aya with her close-cropped hair and almond eyes, the full sensuous mouth and the long shapely legs, the round breasts and stand-up nipples, even with the makeup and the tight body, even she looked very young. But so what. So what, he thought.

Dawn had plopped herself heavily onto the worn black leather sofa, but Aya sat down slowly, the way she saw women do in movies, crossing her legs *just so,* the certain curve of her thigh enough to hush an assembly of men. It hushed these men, and Aya knew it. She knew Robert was watching everything she did. Even Marcus was, but she didn't really care about him. He ought to be paying attention to Dawn. That's what she was thinking as she reached over to Robert, bending in such a way that hinted at her breasts.

And Robert looked at this girl who was trying to pass for a woman and thought how she looked like something to be eaten. Something to be bitten into. He thought about all the things he was going to do to her, how he was going to turn and twist her so he could get into every part of her. He imagined her on her knees. He imagined her screaming.

But his face gave none of this away. His face was, the whole time, easy, smiling, reassuring. He made light conversation, talked about being a designer, and told Aya she was pretty enough to be a model. "Both of you are," he said, and Dawn blushed.

"Marcus," Robert began, "why don't you go open a bottle of champagne so we can celebrate making new friends?" Marcus got four glasses and a bottle of Perrier Jouet and poured the drinks and toasted to friendship. Excited and nervous, the girls drank their champagne down, but the men only took a small sip of theirs.

The girls did not notice this, how little champagne the men drank, any more than they noticed how Robert and Marcus did not smoke much of the blunt that was suddenly being passed around. And because neither Aya nor Dawn had much experience with getting high, they also did not notice the minty taste of angel dust that was mixed in with the weed.

Today, three years later, on this February morning, it all seemed so stupid, so foolish to Aya. The way she went to their house, how she encouraged Dawn, how she sat there and got high in that foreign place. But that night it had all made sense, it had felt so comfortable. Aya still remembered how the high did not hit her or Dawn immediately. She remembered how at first they were just sort of stunned by the weed, but certainly not disabled by it. She remembered Robert taking her by the hand.

"Come here," he had said in a voice that was wet with sweat, a sticky voice that stuck to the inside of Aya's brain, where everything was beginning to slip into itself. Everything was slowly becoming indistinguishable, sloppy and useless. Aya walked toward Robert, and he led her into his room.

"I have something I made. I want to give it to you." In his room Robert closed the door, and motioned for Aya to sit on the bed, which she did; she almost stumbled onto it.

Robert opened his dresser drawer. "Here," he said, pulling out a leather halter top. "See if this fits. Put this on."

"Okay," Aya agreed, clumsy in her examination of the skimpy burnt orange top. The drugs and alcohol turned her voice against itself, but finally she managed, "Where's the bathroom so I can change?"

"Girl, don't be crazy. You can change right here. I'll tie it in the back for you."

"No. That's okay. Really. Where's the bathroom?" Aya insisted, despite the fog that had settled into her mind.

"I know *you* ain't shy," Robert challenged, and then, *"Are you?"*

"No. No. I just, umm, want to, you know, surprise you. You know what I'm saying?" Aya wished the debate would end. It was getting so hard to keep finding words.

"All right. Okay," allowed Robert, apparently relenting. And then, "I'll turn around. Tell me when you have it on."

Tired, defeated, Aya reluctantly agreed to those conditions. "Okay. Turn around," she said softly, and then she turned around, too. She began to unbutton her shirt, which was a sleeveless, cropped silk-like vest that you could not wear a bra with.

Even now, as she recalled that night, Aya once again felt the sudden, tight grasp of fear, the instant wash of anxiety that had spread across every part of her. Even now her heart raced madly and she became queasy. That night, when she was suddenly naked from the waist up, Aya was shaking, but not so that anyone watching could see because it was inside of her, this shaking that had her feeling as though in the very next second she was going to collapse, that her bones would come apart, that they would just crumble.

And Aya could remember how she wanted to scream, but then she'd thought, what has he done to make me scream? Besides, screaming took energy, and she'd felt as though the high had taken all of hers. She remembered calming herself down. He's only given me a gift. This is what she said to the inside of herself. Just calm down, relax, stop acting like a child. She thought, the best thing I can do is simply to relax, but even as she thought it, she knew that this was frivolous advice.

It was impossible for her to relax because as she was standing there, partly undressed, telling herself that everything was fine, she could feel him. She could sense Robert's movement, his beat and his breath close, close, which is why she was not surprised, although nevertheless horrified, when she felt his hands slip around her naked waist, and then travel up until they were grabbing at her breasts.

Aya tried to say no! But her brain was now unwound by the alcohol, the drugs, and the unanticipated turn of events. Her voice was a small broken staccato of sound. If she could have sorted through and spoken aloud the jumble and chatter in her head, Aya would have said that this is not what she wanted, that she understood how it looked, but she wasn't ready for this. She would be ready, but not tonight. Tonight was too fast. Aya wanted to say these things, and if she could have, she would have.

Just as she would have said, had she been able, something about wanting to be in love, and about wanting someone to be in love with her. She would have talked about how good and warm and important it would be if, for once, she could feel claimed. If she could walk down city streets with someone holding her hand. Like they belonged to each other. Aya wanted to say that, from the way he had been talking to her at the club, the delicate sweetness of his voice there, she had truly believed that he wanted these things, too.

Aya would have told Robert about being a virgin, and she would have told him all the things that her mother had taught her about "giving it away." How it meant the years after of being alone. That was always the implication. A child without a father. A life without a pulse. Aya had learned this from her mother, who always had herself as a living example of bad choices, though Miriam never did say what those bad choices were.

But none of those thoughts came out as words. They came out instead as a beggar's look that Robert found easy to ignore. And then what happened after, everything that happened after, was too dim, overcast, blurred, and murky for Aya to ever remember it in a way that was meaningful.

What she remembered was being there naked from the waist up, feeling the melting and chaos inside her head. She remembered her back being turned, and his was supposed to be, too, and how she was getting ready to put on a burnt orange leather halter top, and then his hands coming around her waist, her breasts, and then what, what?

How did she get on the bed? She had never been able to recall that. Only how he was on top of her, and how his kissing was not kissing, but really biting, and also how, trapped beneath his weight, she could not get any air. She remembered that. How there was no air, but not how, frantic for oxygen, she was able to dive deep inside herself and pull.

Aya could not remember how she pulled deep down from the center of herself, how she reached into the place where her strength was stored, how she yanked and jerked until it was all free, every bit of it. Aya could not remember or understand how she shoved that man, like this, *Bam!* with both her hands and he went flying. Robert hit the dresser, and groaned, and as soon as he realized what happened, he looked at Aya with eyes that pushed hate, and demanded,

"What the fuck is wrong with you?"

Robert did not yell this—indeed, he nearly whispered it. And it was no question, this was a demand. Aya did not answer. She could not. Where was her voice, where was her sound? She still could not find them. Her mouth was open, but nothing. Nothing.

Enraged, Robert moved toward her.

"I said, what the fuck is wrong with you, girl? You better relax. You better relax and get back on that muthafuckin bed and stop tripping. You hear me?"

But she didn't hear him. Aya didn't hear anything. She only saw things now:

The man moving toward her.

The door.

The knife.

The knife there on the dresser.

And she grabbed it, the knife. Robert stared at her. He glanced at the knife but he stared at the girl. And staring at her, he saw it, the measure of her youth, the width and depth of it.

He saw all the things she did not know, and had not done, and could not yet understand. He saw all the things she still feared. He saw that she was a virgin. But this seeing did not elicit any sort of sympathy or calm. In fact, it made him very, very angry. As a man. He was very, very angry.

To be set up, to be teased in this way by this girl, this virgin, this bitch who had *his* knife in *her* hand. Why had she wasted his time? She was *not* going to waste his time. She was *not* going to play him. Robert looked at Aya and said in a voice so menacing it astounded her, it made her bite down on her tongue, "Let me ask you something. Who you think you fucking with? What the fuck is wrong with you? Put the knife down. Now." Robert's voice was low, and really, you needed to lean into it to hear it clearly. Aya did not do that of course. She only knew he was moving toward her. Aya was fixed, motionless, and then Robert was in front of her.

"I said put the fucking knife down, little girl." But she did not, which was when Robert pinched Aya's nipple violently, and she opened her mouth to cry, but still, nothing! Not a word, not a phrase, not a yell, not a whimper. That Aya remembered—the pain and also the silence.

But when did she drive the knife into him, and where? His shoulder? That's what they said later, but she could not remember. When had she twisted the knife around, the way they said she did? She could not remember. Not that, and not if he screamed or didn't scream. Not if he pulled the knife out, or if she did. Aya could not even remember running out of Robert's room half dressed, clutching the leather top, leaving behind the one she had come with, leaving behind her bag, and for some reason, on her way out, grabbing his wallet, fat with cash.

She could not remember telling Dawn to, "Come on. *Come on!* We got to get out of here." Or Dawn, not even hesitating, but running out the door with Aya, and stopping her in the stairwell only to help her get the halter top on. Dawn yelling, "Girl, what happened, what happened? Oh my God, there's blood! Are you bleeding? What happened? Oh my God!"

Aya could not remember the police stopping them fifteen minutes later as they ran through the unfamiliar Bronx streets looking for a train station or cab, something, anything, to get them the hell out of there. She could not remember that, or later, the handcuffs, or the ride to the police precinct, the holding cell, or her mother coming to get her.

But Miriam did get her. She posted the $1,000 bail and took Aya on a long, silent train ride home, where Miriam very quietly told her daughter to go take a shower and then explain to her *exactly* what happened. Aya tried to explain, but nothing came out right. Not one part. It all seemed so stupid now. None of it made any sense. Miriam never said that to her daughter, but after each statement Aya made, Miriam, staring intently, would repeat it as a question. And so the conversation went like this:

"We went to the club at about eleven."

"You went to *the club* at *eleven* o'clock?"

"Well, Dawn's mother went away, so then it just came to us because everybody at school had talked about this place and we wanted to go, too."

"Dawn's mother *went away*? It came to you to go?"

"Mom, let me just tell you what happened."

Miriam did not respond. She just kept staring at Aya. Staring and frowning. Aya tried to talk, but she stumbled over her words because saying what happened out loud made things all seem like her fault. Made things seem crazy and incomprehensible. How could Aya convey to her mother that she just wanted to have fun, she just wanted to feel good. How could she explain that getting all dressed up and going out dancing made it seem as though she was part of someone else's life. And being in someone else's life, someone who was fly and sexy, someone who people wanted to know, was intoxicating.

Aya looked into the unblinking stare of her mother, the hard line that was her mouth, and knew there was no way to say what it was about the man, about Robert. No way to explain the initial sweetness. No way to talk about her hunger for love and touch and loving touch. No way to explain what she did not understand herself. She could not do it.

She could not do it and so she did not try to do it. Aya told her mother a whittled-down story about how she had been drinking and it was her first time and the man had gotten the wrong idea and reached for her and she'd panicked and that's when she picked up the knife and did it. But, she said, she never meant to hurt him. She just wanted to get away. Where was Dawn, Miriam had asked calmly.

"Umm. In the other room."

"Uh-huh," Miriam had responded. "You were in a bedroom alone with a man you just met? What wrong idea could he get?"

Aya opened her mouth to answer her mother, but Miriam put her hand up. "Stop. No more. Listen to me. I don't want to hear any more of this. I'm very disappointed in you, Aya. And very ashamed of your behavior. I raised you to know and do better than this. Lying, sneaking around, going to some man's house you don't even know, going into a room *alone* with him."

"I'm sorry, Mommy. I know it was stupid. I know."

"I don't think you do. I heard the charges against you. I don't think you understand the seriousness of what you've done. But you will."

And those were the words Aya remembered as she listened to the judge say two years, one to be served in the Division for Youth, one to be served on probation. It was supposed to be a deal. It didn't feel like one. But the lawyer Miriam hired said they could have sentenced Aya as an adult. They could have even gone for attempted murder.

She was convicted only of assault and robbery and the lawyer told Miriam, who borrowed against six months of salary to make the first payments to the attorney, that they were lucky. The judge said the case was treated with unusual leniency because Aya was a first-time offender. But of all the emotions that coursed through them that day in the courtroom, neither Aya nor Miriam felt lucky. Not then, and not once during the interminably long year that Aya spent locked up. The year that Miriam spent alone and helpless to rescue her child.

There was no luck in going without visits, which Aya did since Miriam had been forced to take a second job in a diner on the weekends to finish paying off the attorney. And Dawn, who was only given probation, and whose mother had snatched her daughter up and transferred her to a different school, had disappeared. Besides her, there really was no one else who would have made the four-hour trek upstate to see Aya.

Miriam came once, when Aya first got to the Hall. She told Aya that she was going to have to get a second job, but even if she didn't, on principle she wasn't going to be the kind of mother who would "run up here every weekend. Some children seem tracked for places like this. Some have no parents. You didn't have your father, but you had me. And I have done nothing that wasn't for you. I have tried to give you whatever you needed. I haven't had a day off since you were born. If I wasn't changing a diaper, I was changing a file, changing the coffeepot, cleaning, clearing, whatever, whenever. I can't believe this is my reward. I didn't deserve this from you, Aya. You didn't deserve this from yourself. You think about that. About what you had, and about what you threw away. And maybe when you come home you'll appreciate things."

"I'm sorry, Mommy. I'm really, really sorry," Aya said as reality began to break her face down into a flood of tears.

"Show me," Miriam whispered to her sobbing child. "You do this time, and don't give these people any problems, and come home and be the daughter I raised you to be. Can you do that?"

"I can do that, Mommy," Aya whimpered. Miriam held her daughter, not for very long, but she held her and she kissed her and she told her it was going to be fine, everything was. She went in her pocket and pulled out a tissue and wiped her girl's face, and she stared at the child she'd borne, the child she was going to have to get up and walk away from. Which is what she did. When the time abruptly came, the guard said visiting was over and Miriam stood up, embraced her daughter quickly, and said to no one, "Okay. Okay." And then she was gone.

For one year. Four times, not including her birthday or Christmas, Miriam sent Aya cards. And once more she visited. Right before Aya was about to come home, Miriam came to see her daughter's progress, and Aya impressed her. In the year she'd been locked up, Aya had gotten her GED, and taken alternative to violence and drug programs. She'd behaved perfectly, and her institutional record reflected this.

"Mommy, I just want to come home and go to college and be normal," Aya said and then leaned into her mother's chest. Awkwardly, Miriam patted her daughter on her back and said, "And I want you home, Aya. I do. I *have* missed you." She paused, and for the first time, her voice could not hide the weight of her emotion. "I really have. I just want things to be right."

"They will be, Mommy. I swear." Aya's eyes went wide with promise, and the two lapsed into a conversation about college. Miriam had picked up an application and financial aid forms for Aya, and Aya talked about the classes she wanted to take. She said she was excited, and Miriam nodded, quelling her daughter's energy. "Just come home and do well," she whispered, adding that doing well required a specific kind of discipline. "Right. I know," Aya assured her mother. "I know."

Now, at home, it was the rules. It was everything restricted. And it was hard, but Aya did want to succeed. She definitely didn't want to go back to where she'd been. So here and now, away from her old life and into her new one, the one where she was a neat and combed college student who got all A's her first two semesters, what she tried to remember was the advice about slowing down. A social worker had said this to her, that she needed to consider all the possible consequences of her actions. Think about them *before* she made a decision. What were the possible risks, and were they worth it? When and where she was able to, Aya put this advice to use. Like this morning.

This particular February morning, when it was one month into the new semester, and when Aya, excited over what she was learning in class, tried to talk to her mother about a poem by Sonia Sanchez. It was a poem that made sense, a poem that made her feel human and connected and understood, and when Miriam clearly was uninterested, the hurt Aya felt made her want to curse, to lash out, and say, "I hate you! You never have time for me! You never have anything for me!"

But she did not. Aya breathed back her anger and said, "Okay, okay, okay. I'll read fast." Aya began to read while Miriam continued on with what she had to do: first make the coffee, then put the bread in the toaster, then pull out the grapefruit, slice it in two, get down the plates, set the table.

Finishing her preparations, Miriam sat down to eat as Aya triumphantly concluded the poem,

*I shall become a collector of me / and put meat on my soul!*

"Isn't that beautiful, Mom?"

"Yes. Uh-huh. It is." Miriam said this as she tried to figure out how many packets would be needed for the meeting that day, how many pens, how much coffee, how much tea. She did not look up at her daughter, and so her daughter looked away from her.

Miriam finished her breakfast, and across from her Aya let the words in the book become an intimate dance against the silence. She let the words become an embrace, full on and complete, and gradually her sadness and anger began to dissipate, though not entirely. Miriam rose, cleared the table, kissed her daughter on the forehead, and said, "Don't sit here reading all day. What time is your first class?"

"Eleven-ten."

"Oh. Well, don't be late. See you tonight."

"Bye."

And Miriam said good-bye. She called it over her shoulder, pulled her coat out of the closet, and picked her purse up off the kitchen counter. Miriam walked out of the door and headed up the block, up along the route she took every weekday. She thought about how proud she was of her daughter. All A's!

But she also thought, don't get too excited. You never know what's coming around the corner with this girl. Never know what's coming around the corner, period. Quickly moving toward the train station, for some reason Miriam thought about when she had first moved to this neighborhood, the hard mean days that had brought her and her baby girl here. As fast as the thought came, however, Miriam let it go. Without even trying, and without a break in her step, Miriam let the thought go, and she just continued on, and she did not look back.

Aya sat at the table for another thirty minutes. She sat there and thought about her mother, a woman she had lived with all her life but a woman she still did not know. Miriam was a woman who added up only into fractions of a number. She was fractions of a woman, of a mother, a parent, a person. That's how Aya saw it, and didn't want to be that way, too.

Small tears collected in the sides of Aya's eyes, and she wanted to know how to make her mother see her. See her growing, glowing, and needing more than hot meals and fall school clothes. More than homework reviewed, and admonitions about chores and responsibilities. If things are changing everywhere every day, why couldn't they? Why couldn't they be closer, have intimate talks, do silly things, mother and daughter things? Why did her mother make mothering seem like a chore, like an unwelcome assignment from an unfair boss. Aya felt like an item on a to-do list. How could she become more, to her mother, to herself?

Aya remembered Dawn's mother, the nights at their house. She remembered the way the rooms filled with the wall-shaking sound of her laugh. She remembered the bid whist games and beers, the times she slipped and cussed, and Aya and Dawn heard her and giggled. Mostly Aya remembered all those times she saw Dawn's mother kiss her daughter. The times she hugged and cracked bad jokes with her, and she wondered, have you ever told me a joke, Mommy, or kissed me just because? Did you do it when I was baby, did you stop just when I began to walk? I miss you, Mommy. I miss the mother I never had and I don't think it's fair. I already don't have a father or grandfather or grandmother or cousin. I have no one and am lonely, Mommy. I am reaching for you. There is no one else.

Do you know I hate living in such a quiet house, Mommy? Mama? Please listen to me. There are things I want to say. Aren't there things you want to say, too?

# 2.

Aya Rivers was a runner. Running helped smooth the rough places inside of her, if only temporarily. There were times she would just walk, and there were times she would jog, but mostly what helped Aya sort things out was a fast hard run. As if by that movement she would stumble onto something that had been lost or taken away, or more likely, something that had never been given. Never even lent.

Running was also the one thing that Aya did against her mother's wishes. The first time Aya donned a sweat suit and headed toward the door, Miriam stopped her and in an uncharacteristically sharp voice demanded to know where Aya was going. "Just for a run, Mom."

"Dressed like *that*?" Miriam asked, referring to the black pants and hood Aya was wearing. "You look like a man."

"Mom, I'm just going for a run. It doesn't matter what I look like."

"It always matters."

Aya shrugged and headed out the door, mumbling she'd be back soon, and from then on, Miriam never quite said don't go running, but she would complain about it all the time. She would remark about the damage it could do to the body, that running was also an invitation to be chased, especially since Aya wouldn't join a gym and run on a treadmill, "where it was better," Miriam offered. "What do you mean," Aya wanted to know. "Well," Miriam would explain halfheartedly, "you know. Better for your feet. Why don't you take up dance or something," she would suggest, and Aya would say she'd look into it but never did, and finally Miriam gave up trying to convince her daughter with the same old arguments that never seemed to leave an impression anyway. "At least run when it's light out, Aya," Miriam would admonish, but with no further explanation.

It had begun, Aya's addiction to running, when she'd gotten locked up. Not at first. At first when the judge said she was going to have to spend twelve months in the Hall, and they put her in handcuffs, and started to lead her out of the court to what she knew would be a bus waiting to drive her away to who knows where, and her mother was just standing there looking blank, Aya felt all the air leave her body.

Then, in that terrible moment, Aya could not imagine ever having the strength to move herself, let alone move herself with speed and determination. Then, even her blood and the smallest of her cells seemed forever stopped. Aya felt as though her neck had been broken, her neck and her back. And so even though there, in the court, as she heard the sentence, and she was standing, she was upright, Aya was certain that this was only because she had been set there, stood up like a prop. In that moment Aya was convinced that she would never return to her body again.

And really, she didn't care. Not then. Then she had no fight. Then she just allowed herself to be taken away. Handcuffed and shackled, limp with defeat, Aya allowed herself to be led onto the bus that ambled and bumped its way up the New York State roads, through winding paths until it finally, hours later, reached a clearing. And in that clearing there were several buildings surrounded by a fence. The bus pulled in and the kids, aged twelve to sixteen, stumbled off. Aya remembered that moment. Trying to get herself off the bus with leg irons on, and while cuffed to another girl. It was insane. She knew she wasn't dangerous.

Actually, no one on the bus seemed dangerous. But Aya kept hearing her attorney say how there were girls in the Hall who weren't like her, girls who truly meant to harm people, and so she had to be quiet and careful at all times with all people. That advice meant something until Aya actually got to the Hall and saw how the majority of girls here were loud and carrying on, just like in school. You could disappear, she figured, in the noise, disappear with the noise.

Indeed, the one girl who stood out did so not because of what she said but because of what she never said. Never a good morning, never a what's up, never any gossip or threat. Nothing. Her name was Karen and she didn't speak, and like everyone else, Aya used to watch her, this girl with the voice kept secret. She reminded Aya of her mother.

At first Aya watched Karen and talked about her the way all the girls watched and talked about her. "She's crazy," the girls would agree. "She ain't crazy. She just stank. Fuck that bitch," said another girl, and everyone nodded. But slowly, Aya began to notice something. She noticed that despite the way people stared, whispered, and wondered about Karen, she had this ability to walk with an impenetrable shield. And Aya knew, even after being in the Hall only a month, that this was what anyone trapped in there truly wanted: to be able to get through the day without being hurt by it, by the biting loneliness of it.

So Karen was shielded here in the place where everything was or could be, at any moment, extracted from you. Extracted, snatched up and out, and put on display for police, and for counselors, and for other residents to see and touch and judge and kick around or laugh at. In this environment, Karen had made herself inviolable, unlike the rest of the girls, unlike Aya.

Once, in a small group, Aya tried to offer this alternate view of Karen. She said that perhaps Karen was just trying to do whatever time she needed to do, and get out with the least amount of drama. But that theory was met with aggressive arguments fueled by all of the crazy rumors that persisted about Karen. "Everyone know that girl out her damn mind," insisted Lisa, who had been in the Hall longer than any of the others in that group. Lisa, who therefore had authority, went on to talk about how Karen had cut her own father into a hundred pieces and scattered them in garbage cans across the city. "She even had a baby for him," Lisa said, her face crunched up in disgust.

"I heard she stabbed some bitches up in here. But that was before I got here. 'Cause you know I wish that bitch would bring some of that shit to me," Lisa continued with a false bravado that no one dared challenge. Yet as passionate as Lisa was, as convincing as she tried to be in her characterization of Karen, all Aya could think was how it didn't ring true. She never saw any of that in the mysterious girl. She never saw the violence. If Aya had to tell the truth, she'd say she never saw the madness. She only saw the quiet determination.

She saw and she saw the control. And she wanted to become it. She wanted to stop all the questions in her head. Who did she belong to, and where? That's what Aya wanted to know. Her people could not only be the impermeable mother who had somehow figured out how to hug without touching, how to laugh without smiling, how to care for a child whose heart she refused to know.

Who was Aya's father, what did he look like and how did he love? These were the most persistent, the most haunting questions. These, and also, was he really dead or was that just something she'd been told?

Once when Aya was still small, about eight maybe or nine, she could not remember, she'd gotten into a fight with Yvette, the girl who lived in the fourth house on the block, the one that had nearly fallen down around itself. Yvette hated Aya. She hated everything about her. The neat brick home she lived in and the extra-proper way her mother always acted, as though they were better than the other kids. Yvette even hated Aya's name.

On that day, the day of the fight, Aya was walking to the store wearing pants that were a little too small. But why wear her good pants to run up the street, her mother had asked. "Put these on," Miriam had said. Aya did, reluctantly, and began to plod up the block to the bodega, where she ran into Yvette, who started screaming and laughing, "What the hell you got on? Damn. How you come out your house like that?" The other kids who were there started laughing, too, and Aya wanted to die. She wanted to vanish. Right then, right there. But since she could not, she did the next best thing. She punched Yvette. Out of nowhere, she clocked her dead in the face. Yvette, who didn't expect this from Aya, never had a chance. Aya beat her ass for anything and everything that had ever hurt her. She punched her and punched her and did not stop until the police came and broke it up and took Aya home.

They told Miriam that Yvette's mother wasn't going to press charges, but that was this time. Miriam, disguising her shock, humbly thanked the officers and sent them out the door. Afterward she turned to Aya, shook her head, frowned, and asked, What was wrong with her? Had she lost her mind? Did she need to be locked up? Was she some kind of animal?

Aya tried to say what happened, but she couldn't make sense of the thoughts in her head. She could only cry and say "Yvette always picks on me," to which Miriam wanted to know, "Why can't you just ignore these stupid people? Just ignore them. Do you think you're the first person to be picked on? What would happen if everyone who got picked on beat people up? Think, Aya, think."

Miriam told Aya for the next month, no phone, no television, no nothing. Then she sent Aya to her room and said she did not want to discuss it anymore. In her room Aya cried and cried and pulled out the one photograph she had of her unknown father and she asked him to come to her because she was certain, one hundred percent, that he would understand and protect her.

It was not the first time Aya had called on her father, whoever he was. It would not be the last, though by the time she'd gotten to the Hall, Aya had pretty much determined that no father was coming on his white horse to rescue her. Or more appropriately, in his black BMW, and so she knew she had to develop ways to protect herself. Not that she had any idea how, which is what made her turn to Karen. Turn to her so she could move like her, act like her, be protected like her.

That's how Aya started running—watching Karen, who ran from 2:00 to 2:45 every afternoon, no matter what the weather. Biblical rains, or heat that was the apparent fire this time, Karen always tore down the air with her speed.

The first time Aya ventured out onto the track, she didn't make two laps before it felt as though her heart was coming out of her chest. It was late afternoon, and Aya had barely eaten anything. She didn't stretch, and took off at top speed. That lasted less than sixty seconds. Her run slowed to a jog, which quickly slowed to a walk, and then to a stumble. The next day, while pretending to talk to another girl, Aya watched Karen. Karen stretched for a long time and then walked around the track once, slowly picking up speed. By the second lap, Karen was running, and by the third lap her pace was fast and steady. She ran for forty-five minutes. And after she ran, Karen walked.

Aya followed suit. Not running at first for forty-five minutes. There was no way she could do that. But she was able to walk and jog for about twelve minutes at first, and after a month of jogging five times a week, Aya was able to go half an hour. After two months, she hit an hour—an hour of running—and in that hour, she always felt free.

Aya never allowed anything to interrupt the time she spent on the track. Her friends thought she was bugging out. Lisa said Aya was tripping. Acting like that girl Karen. Aya laughed and just said, "Girl, you don't know when running is going to come in handy." And they joked about getting away from men and police, but the truth was Aya ran not to get away from but to get closer to the perfect world that existed inside the expanse of her imagination.

When Aya ran, there was no more fence and lock-in time. No more terrible food. No more visits and letters that didn't come. No more loneliness or sense of displacement. No more attack in a nasty loft apartment in the Bronx. No more missing her father. Running, Aya could hear her father's voice, she could feel him, as though he was there, encouraging her around the track. Her father, with a stopwatch and whistle. Running, there were so many fantasies though they didn't seem fantastic.

Aya could work her imagination so thoroughly that the line between real memories and false ones slipped out of sight. Indeed, had she been asked, Aya could have described the father she'd never seen, imitate a voice she'd never heard, mimic a walk she'd never studied. Running, Aya's life was not defined by what was missing, but by what was in abundance. She became addicted to it, and that addiction did not change when she came home.

And so on this Wednesday evening in February, Aya after class, alone, unable to contact any of her few friends, prepared to run. From the second she had walked back into the apartment, she had immediately felt an aching to be out again. She wanted to be anywhere but here in this apartment, in this place that echoed and limped. To live in this apartment, Aya felt, in the stilled way her mother lived, was to know life only as a hollow thing. Life as a disabled thing. Life fixed and life stalled.

When she'd first come home from school, Aya had waited an interminable hour for Bakar, her sort-of boyfriend, to call. He had said he was going to call at three, but it was fifteen past four and she couldn't take it anymore, the silent phone, the being alone. She began to go through her phone book looking for anyone who might want to hang out, go to a movie, go get something to eat, whatever. Whatever. She began to dial.

"Peace, Kim. It's Aya. Give me a call when you get in, okay?"

"Hey, Monique. It's Aya. Call me when you get in."

"Wassup, Chaniqua? It's Aya. Wanna hang out? Call me back."

And finally, with no one else to reach out to, Aya broke down and paged Bakar. She didn't want to do it. If she paged him it meant that he would probably not call back. So many times he did not call back. She knew she was setting herself up but could not stop. She punched in her number when the pager beeped, and waited for him to call. She turned on the television and tried not to look at the phone or clock.

She could not help it though. Two minutes passed, four minutes, seven. Thirty minutes passed. Thirty-two minutes. No call. Of course. As usual. It was five o'clock.

Aya closed her eyes and thought about this man, this Bakar with the tight cornrows, the tight abs, the tight expressions. Bakar, who could dance fluidly, kiss intensely, and have you believe that you were the first, the last, the only, the forever. He could convince you of this just before he turned, walked out of the door, and yelled over his shoulder,

"Ima give you that call, aw'ite?"

Bakar who most often didn't give Aya that call. Not until days and days and days had passed. Bakar, whose every hello felt like the prelude to good-bye.

Aya loved him. She loved the beautiful young man she'd met in a political science class who was so smart, always challenging the teacher, always bringing in the Black perspective. Bakar, who it seemed could hold court anywhere, attract all the women, and even the men. Everyone wanted to be caught up in his vibe. And three months ago he had chosen her. Asked her to walk with him, talk with him. Bakar, who called Aya to him, and then turned away. And then back to her again. And then away.

Bakar. He existed in the brief moments the two of them shared, the moments full with touch, moments so wide that Aya forgot, each time, what it would be like after. After, when he left and took a week to return her call and acted as though a week was an hour. After, when the separation and aloneness came and bit down at the core of her until Aya screamed.

No one ever heard her, but Aya screamed, and with no one to hear her, no one to respond to her, she would fall into the narrow lines of her journal. On this day, this particularly cold day, when she came home from class and called everybody she could think of but nobody was home, and watching television could not distract her from a phone that did not ring, from a visit that did not come, Aya screamed. And like her mother, she screamed an inside scream.

She thought about how many times Bakar was supposed to call but didn't. Supposed to come by, but didn't. What was it that kept her following behind him, crying his name? Crying out from the distant background of his life. How had she learned to want so badly someone she couldn't have? Aya wandered in and out of the four-room apartment. Looking for what? She looked out of her bedroom window, and watched the night beginning to press against the sky. She picked up her journal and began to write.

*Dear God,*

*I hate B. I mean I love him but I hate him. Why won't he just love me back? Why won't anybody? I don't want to end up like my mother, God. She's so beautiful, but I've never seen her with any man. Don't know how she could go through life without a man. I think the last man she had was my father. She never says anything about him, and sometimes I wonder if he really loved her, if she really loved him, if their relationship was great, if he wanted me. Maybe he was glad to go to Vietnam, glad to get away from us, from me. Why doesn't she talk about him? She says nothing and he was my father, and there hasn't been a man since. Why not, Mommy? Who are you and what do you feel?*

*You know what's weird? I miss him so much. I miss you, Daddy. God, how can I miss something I never had?*

Aya stared at her words for a long time, and then finally closed her journal. She could not stay in the house anymore looking over at the phone, trying to will it to ring. "Fuck you, Bakar" she thought as she pulled T-shirt and long johns out of her drawers, a black sweat suit out of her closet. It was 6:30 and Aya knew her mother would be home any moment, and so she scribbled a note—*Going for a fast run, Mommy. See you no later than 8. Just really needed to get out. Love, Me.* Aya dressed quickly, laced up her sneakers, put her headphones on, rushed out of the door, and down the steps of her apartment building, nearly knocking over Dante, who once lived here. He was her neighbor's nephew. The old lady who lived downstairs.

"Oh! Sorry!" Aya exclaimed apologetically.

Dante, getting his balance back, laughed. "No problem. But you should come with a siren." Aya smiled shyly, and Dante looked at her. Was this the little girl who'd lived upstairs from him? When had she grown up? He'd been gone from his aunt Althea's house for a few years now, and although he lived right nearby, he'd been wrapped up in his own life, and hadn't come by much since he'd moved out. So he'd missed it, the blossoming, those little-girl eyes now a woman's, almost seductive, certainly inviting. And that body she had—even a sweat suit could not disguise it, not from his trained eye. She was *fine*. And he couldn't resist saying it. "Wow. You have grown into a beautiful woman."

Aya blushed. "Thanks," she whispered, and the two looked at one another, and then away.

"I mean it."

"Thanks," Aya whispered again.

"So, what you doing? Going out for a run or something?"

"Yeah."

"Wow. You committed as hell to be running in this cold-ass weather."

"Makes me feel good."

Dante hesitated, and then decided to go for it. "Anything else? You know . . . make you feel good?" He asked in a way that was sensual without being vulgar, and Aya laughed nervously, beginning to enjoy the flirtation. Dante was, after all, a good-looking brother. But how old was he?

"Sure," she said, making that one-syllable word sound like four syllables.

"What?"

"Guess you'd have to get to know me to find out."

"A'ight. A'ight." Dante was grinning wide and hard now.

"So call me sometime," Aya said as she put her headphones on. She called out her phone number to Dante, who tried to lock it in his brain as soon as each number was yelled out.

He looked at her and remembered when he had first come to live with his aunt. He had been just fifteen years old and trying to make sense of his life. His mother, Althea's middle sister, Mary, had been dead three years, her life shattered by obesity and alcohol. A life shattered by the man, Dante's father, who'd left the moment he found out she was pregnant. When she died Dante had gone to live with Cynthia, the youngest of the sisters, but she was still raising her own boys, and tension crowded the house. Then Dante began hanging out in the streets with boys Cynthia called thugs, and everything blew up. "You got to go," she pronounced one day, and then suddenly he was living with Aunt Althea, who refused to allow social services to get any of *her* family.

Life with Aunt Althea was boring and restrictive, but at least Dante felt loved, and at least in this home there was stability. Every morning his aunt had breakfast made, and when he would leave for school, he'd see her, the little girl who lived upstairs, coming down the stairs looking so put together, all pressed and starched. She always smiled; she always said good morning. Aunt Althea said she thought the woman upstairs was a little strange, not much of a talker. Not much of a neighbor. Dante never noticed any of this. Mrs. Rivers was polite to him, and the little girl, she was always sweet.

Now she was sweet *and* grown. Dante smiled to himself and watched Aya run down the block. He wondered if she really wanted him to call her, just as Aya, nearly out of his sight now, was hoping he would. She was thinking, Fuck stupid Bakar. I hope Dante does call. She pulled her hood up over her head, and picked up speed.

*If you watch you will see*
*my dreams split the night*
*in the place where the sky*
*holds color in secret and spills it*
*hot*

*although it is cold I don't feel cold*
*although I am alone I don't feel alone*
*it's you and I know*

*you bringing warm*
*air blowing onto*
*my face      which is yours*
*isn't it?*

*Daddy these eyes sitting wide bordered with memory*
*my blood seeks to know*

*I am running and are you?*

*I am scared and are you?*

*I choke back songs*
*and stumble over dances*
*I edge and crawl and kneel and beg*
*like this and*
*like this and*
*like this and*
*like this and*
*like you?*

*am I*
*like you, Daddy?*

*what about the night when I was a day*
*did you hold*
*me of the same skin and breath?*

*did you lick my tears away or swallow them?*
*did I hear your heart, curl up to it,*

*feel your chest rising and me*
*there*

*did I make you smile?*
*did I make you proud?*
*did I make you love?*

*imagine us running these streets      mmmm*
*imagine us holding hands      mmmm*
*imagine us belonging to ourselves      mmmm*

*imagine playgrounds the swing the monkey bars and ice cream*
*the first day of school and if you had taught me how to fight (I learned*
*anyway) would you have done that, Daddy? taught me to fight, would*
*you have taught your girl and if not then what?*
*what would you teach to me*
*your daughter?*

Eight and a half miles and Aya is still running at the same speed.

Her breath is not labored.

It is steady and even, like her.

This is the girl who can traverse these dark, broken-up Brooklyn streets in worn sneakers, and appear as though she is running on a brand-new track.

Her Walkman is blasting Public Enemy calling for *Black Steel in the Hour of Chaos.*

She hears nothing but the gravel and insistence of Chuck D's voice, the fight and pound of the drum machine, the bass and words winding hard through her blood. She cannot imagine what could ever stop her, what could even slow her.

And now she is losing her pain/herself in his voice.

The questions, the confusion, the sense of loss, the rage, the sadness:

They have all stepped aside for the moment and it's the music, the music, until just now.

Now the song is over.

She reaches inside the jacket to rewind the tape, and does she hear a voice behind her?

Aya's right hand reaches over into the left side pocket as she turns to look behind her.

She is thinking, I want to hear that song one more time and then, stop!

## 3. Lincoln Avenue: Wednesday, 7:42 P.M.

*The sky is rolling counterclockwise, and Aya is wondering if she is somewhere inside a dream. She can see the night filled with breath and dance, and wants to go to it. She wants to run again, she wants to sprint or leap, but her legs seem to have just now vanished. Where have they gone, she wonders but does not say.*

*Reaching to see if any other part of her has disappeared, Aya feels places where her skin is cold, and wet, and coming loose. But somehow these are the very places where she burns, internally, outrageously, incomprehensibly. She is burning. It comes to her that the world is a cacophony of opposites. And why is that?*

*In a language that she can only speak through the eyes, Aya demands to know, How did I get on fire and why is nobody coming to help me?*

*And there are voices not so far from her. She hears what could be two or five or eight or even ten of them. But it could also be thirty or forty or fifty of them. Aya is confused and thinks, Why won't just one person come over and help me?*

*Mama, she cries from deep down inside herself. Mama, she cries, and her terror is palpable. Mama, she cries but no sound or tear.*

# 4.

It could have been any urban war zone, and the hospital could have been a MASH unit. This thought passes through Miriam as she approaches, in a daze, the old brick building. A building that had become, years ago, tired, weather-beaten, desperate for retirement, or at least a long rest. But it stands here, somehow, it stands. Stooped over and sagging, it stands, in the center of Brooklyn, only a bridge away from the spit shine and plenty of Manhattan, Wall Street, City Hall, the skyline of make-believe gods. Still, as the mayor boasted at a press conference recently, this hospital has one of the two best trauma units in all the five boroughs. Shootings, stabbings, car accidents, burn victims, the hospital administers to victims of these injuries all the time. And practice makes perfect. Everybody knows that.

Some, though Miriam Rivers is not one of them, remember days when this hospital was a premier facility. But those days are forty, sixty years in the past, and they belong to a different people. They belong to the World War I and World War II people, the people of easy physical assimilation, the people of immediate citizenship.

Now the hospital belongs to those who speak in voices that are thick with a poverty that has repeated itself for too many generations. They are voices thick with being last in line, sometimes never in line. They are the carry-the-most, accept-the-least voices. And the languages they speak are rarely taught in grammar or high schools. The English they speak is spliced down the middle by Selma and Kingston, Port-au-Prince, and Stone Mountain.

On this brisk Wednesday night, with its usual emergencies and nods at death, Aya Rivers should not have been in here, in this part of the hospital, not in a room alone. But the circumstances surrounding her shooting dictated a measure of privacy, or more appropriately, isolation. Still, the room was far from palatial. It was what was referred to as a transitional room. Supplies for the floor were stored there. Nurses shuffled in and out all day long scooping up cotton balls, garbage bags, and rubber gloves.

Miriam tried to pull the curtain around her daughter's bed in an effort to block them out and blunt the fluorescent light that punched through the thin window that ran the length of the metal room door. No barrier, no curtain, no wall, however, could silence the chattering of the nurses, or the phones that never seemed to stop ringing. And the chattering and ringing as though the world had not spun off its axis. As though life were normal.

Miriam closed her eyes and tried to understand why she was in a room where God and air and tomorrow and small dreams and big ones had apparently slid sideways, out through the window, down the old brick wall, into the nameless street where they could hide in the rush and crowds forever and ever. Nevertheless, betraying no emotion, no tremble, Miriam placed one thin brown hand against her daughter's face. She tried to warm it, her daughter's cheek, but her own flesh and blood, like her child's flesh and blood, was so very, very cold.

A nurse walked into the room and pulled the curtain back. She saw Miriam, she saw Aya, but said nothing. She went back out of the room and left them alone.

And them: the child, almost a woman with the new, cropped haircut and with the smooth, easy honey-colored skin (was it now graying around the edges?). And she with an earring missing somehow from her right ear. She with the strong one-hundred-thirty-five-pound, five-foot six-inch body. She who could run distance, and do fifty push-ups in a clip. She who hated cigarettes, being alone, and rules. She who loved poetry and the way Bakar took his time when he kissed her. She who never knew her father, who was never told about her father. She who always knew not to ask. She with questions. And she without answers. But always more and more questions. She who had been working so hard to come meet herself in herself. Now suddenly she who lay here, stilled, unnatural.

And them: the mother who held tight on to herself, and who spent the last twenty years breathing as lightly as possible. She who had worked in the same office for eighteen, almost nineteen years, and she who, despite her talents and intelligence, still hovered in a position somewhere near entry level. She who did not challenge flying low. She who, when asked, always said she was fine. She who always said she was making do. She who paid every bill on time. She who prayed. She who appeared eight or ten years younger than she really was. And she who could still turn the heads of even very young men, though no man ever seemed to be able to turn her head. She whose current pain, whose sudden fear had been seen by this hospital far too often to be soothed or even recognized as what it was: a searing and slow burn, a branding, a scarification.

These are the people from whom the nurse turned away, and they were alone again in the odd way hospitals can leave people alone. A mother and child at once interlocked. A mother and child at once in parallel universes.

After a long silence, and after a long time when there was no movement, Miriam slid her hand down from her daughter's face, down to Aya's hand. Their hands looked alike. Miriam noticed this. She had noticed this before of course, but had never said anything. In this moment alone though, Miriam whispered,

"You have my hands, Aya. Look. Our hands are the same. So are our feet and so are our eyes. Did you know that? Everything else is your father's, but your hands and feet and eyes—they come from me."

Aya did not stir. She did not give any sign of acknowledgment. Still, Miriam held her daughter's hand lightly and began to kiss it, to caress it, to whisper into it. "Baby, baby. Aya, Aya, Aya. Mommy loves you. Mommy loves you so much."

And then for the first time in eighteen years, Miriam Rivers began to cry.

Space, sound, air, light, time, movement, sound, light, space, time. Which was not unknowable, or abstract, or amorphous? Did anything make sense, did anything take on meaningful shape, anywhere? Anywhere? Miriam sat in a chair by her daughter's bedside and it could have been midday or night, evening or dawn. Who knew, who could tell? And what was the difference anyway?

All Miriam wanted to do was clear out her mind so she could concentrate her energy on Aya. On Aya coming back. On Aya getting whole again. Like before, like when she came back from the detention center. Miriam tried to force herself fully into this bizarre and terrible reality in order to beg, to demand that Aya come back. But as hard as she tried to clear all else out, to focus on this unfathomable now, old times, long ago confusion, came back and came back screaming. Why? She let it go then, why is it bothering me now? Miriam raged silently at the distraction.

Where does a woman who has never questioned begin to

look for answers? And how does she recognize answers as such, even when they line up before her, imposing and unavoidable? How can a woman know what she has never been taught to know? Miriam Rivers had been raised by an ethic and a people who did not believe in the past, who thought that looking over your shoulder would most certainly turn you into the defenseless pillar of salt that gets blown away forever by the first current of air to come through. Her own mother had warned her of this.

The childhood Miriam Rivers recalled was one that was punctuated by a mother regularly admonishing her that "You can't look backward and forward at the same time." And sometimes Mama would add, "Listen here when I tell you. You can't change what happened yesterday, but you got a shot at tomorrow if you position yourself in the right direction."

Miriam had always tried to face the right direction, and the right direction was always the direction Mama pointed toward. The one time in her life that she had strayed from Mama's compass, Miriam's life—the neat and order of it, the clean and predictable of it, the tranquil and simple of it—vanished fast as the winter sun over the New York horizon.

From that moment on, despite all external appearances, despite all the followed rules, despite every minute she had spent facing forward, the neat and the order, the clean and tranquil never did come back. Not in the way she had once known them. But because she had managed to get by with the life she had created after she veered from her mother—and get by if not peacefully then at least quietly—sitting here in a black vinyl chair beside her child who was laying in a room that was becoming somehow, exponentially, smaller, Miriam thought it had to be impossible. It didn't make sense. It had to be some mistake.

Perhaps this was not her daughter lying here! Perhaps this

girl was an extraordinary look-alike. Urgently wanting to convince herself that it was not Aya here and broken, Miriam determined that this must all be an evil joke. And although she tried and she tried, she could not convince herself of this. The girl laying still before her was of course her child, her baby, her girl. When she finally accepted this cruel reality, Miriam was overcome by an immeasurable sadness, one that exists beyond definition or border. And that sadness was compounded because it was all mixed up with a dense confusion, a violent burst of inquisitions.

This is what Miriam wanted to know. How could she be here, in a place she had already traveled to, a place she worked so hard to never ever see again? After all the rules she had followed and all the reconstructing she had done, why were days and years long gone, long dead, pushing up out of the earth? Why were bones coming back and coming back like this?

Miriam began to cough, to choke on her questions. But then she looked over at Aya, and said, "Enough!" She laid her hands back on her daughter's body, and she stared as hard as she could into Aya's beautiful face. "Live, live, live," Miriam said out loud, trying to will movement into her child's body. "Live, live, live, live, live, live, live, live." Miriam chanted this over and over, until the chanting transformed and transported her, back and back and back. She could not stop it from happening, although she would have given nearly anything, an arm, sections of her heart, all her dreams and wishes, to keep from looking back, falling back, thinking back. She needed to be here, all the way here in this moment with her daughter. But this was then, time was collapsed, all yesterdays and todays meshed together, and there was nothing Miriam could do. The visions came.

And she could see herself now—her once-upon-a-time self.

The self she had abandoned. And standing before her old self she could see how she was everyone. Everyone, and no one. She was her daughter. She was her daughter's father. She was her mother. She was days and nights that had not been recalled for nearly two decades. She was rules that had been repeated again and again. She was years of Bible study. She was words that had never, ever been spoken. She was the woman who existed behind the woman who went forward into the world, and raised the child, and worked the jobs, and attended the funerals, and denied the men, and deferred the dreams, and prayed every night of her life for just one thing: that she never break.

*Please, God, don't let this life break me.* She was that prayer, and she was the woman before the prayer. The woman who had once been a girl of seventeen taking prayers for granted, and then she was the nineteen-year-old genuflecting, quoting passage and verse. She was that, and also she was sounds she had not made in twenty years. She was a jagged moan, a careless mix of screaming and sobbing, and she was the woman who once bound her tongue in the middle of the night. The woman who taught herself to live with the binding, to ignore the discomfort, to exist just alongside it. Miriam Rivers saw what she did not want to see: that right here and at once, she was the woman she had herself conjured forward; she was the woman she terribly feared—the woman who would eventually come and rip all bindings to shreds.

# 5.

Room 902 smelled bitter. The stench hit Miriam suddenly, and she was back again, back from the nasty claw of memories, back and praying over her daughter. Instinctively she covered both her nose and Aya's, and looked around for the source of the odor, but did not find it. There was such a bad sense in here, it coursed through Miriam, and as much as she could, she draped her body over Aya's, wanting to protect her from it. But the bad sense, the bitterness, was in everything. And it made everything wrong. Stench hung off the pale green painted walls, which were chipped in some places, gouged out in others. It clung to the crusty windows that were lined with chicken wire. It made the white sheets go pale gray. The room went limp from the bitter odor that carried with it a hopelessness that weakened all who entered. Patients, doctors, family members, and nurses. Everyone felt it, and Miriam was trying to block it out.

But she was trying to block it from a place where what was, is. What will be, has always been. Bitter were the truths that Miriam Rivers had spent the last twenty years of her life trying to disprove, and they were all in that room. In that room that had not been prettied up, covered up, or made cheery for any person; the only thing that could exist was stark and undistracted reality. It was there and pulsing. It was there and stinking and leaving Miriam no place to go and this terrified her.

Here was a woman who had spent the last twenty years of her life trying to reorder the first twenty. It was possible, this reordering, if you applied prediction to your life, if you rejected caprice. Miriam believed that. Indeed, she believed nothing else. This is why she had no weapon, no means of protection when she had first stepped inside that echoing hospital room with the complex of wires and machines gone silent. She was there paralyzed with fear in a room that kept getting smaller and tighter and tighter and smaller. Miriam was there, staring at her child, and she was at once immobilized, but she was also somehow being violently tossed back and forth over the lines and barricades that held yesterday in the past, and today in the present.

Even as she desperately attempted to grab hold of the sides of her life, Miriam knew her efforts were and would be absolutely, completely futile. In fact, she was in large part responsible for her own undoing. It was the questioning that did it, her questioning. What went wrong, what went wrong? How could this be my baby here like this? How? Not my child, not mine, *not mine!*

Miriam gritted her teeth as the questions and the demands banged on inside of her, and as she did a police officer was suddenly there, standing in the room, standing over her. The officer asked if he could speak with her a moment.

Miriam turned and stared at him but could not really see him. His wide girth and odd complexion, the color of alabaster, were all stretched out until you could nearly see through it. She did not see the stripes on his shoulder, or the gleam from his shoes. She did not see his baton, or his handcuffs, or the way his pants, nearly a size too small, bunched up in the crotch. She only saw his gun.

"Pardon me, Ms. Rivers," the officer began. "My name is Chief Conners. I'm one of the division heads at the precinct, and if it's all right, I'd like us to step out here in the hall so you and I could have a talk."

Miriam continued to stare at the officer and his gun.

"Ms. Rivers, if we could just step outside."

Was he talking to her? Miriam wondered this. His mouth was moving but his words were incomprehensible.

Already tired, Chief Conners resigned himself to the fact that Miriam was not going to leave the room just yet. He began to tell her the little bit he was authorized to say.

"We don't have all the facts yet, and so what I'm going to tell you is very preliminary. Details may change as more facts emerge. But the police department wanted you to know something right away."

Miriam blinked. Who was this crazy man standing over her, speaking in a language she could not understand? Who was this man in a uniform, carving a ragged hole in the space reserved for just Aya and her?

"There was a robbery at the convenience store, the aaahh bodega, on the corner of White and Jefferson, and the owner was shot at."

But by this time Miriam had turned away from the officer. She leaned close into her daughter, close against her daughter's cold face, and began to hum very lightly, nearly inaudibly.

"Ms. Rivers? Ahh . . . please. The owner was shot at but he wasn't killed. He gave a description of the suspect. The suspect was a male, Black, in his early twenties. He was reported to be a relatively small man, about five-eight and one hundred fifty pounds, wearing a black hood and sweatpants. Like the ones your daughter has on. Had on. From the back there was no way to tell if your daughter was male or female. From the back she looked like the suspect. Same height, same weight. The officers who saw your daughter asked her to stop, to give up. They asked her to stop. She did not. She reached inside her jacket and began to turn toward them. At that point the officers reasonably concluded that they were being threatened, and moved to defend themselves."

Miriam was rocking herself and, as best she could, she was rocking her daughter.

"I'll come back a little later, Ms. Rivers. We can talk later," Conners finally said, and then he turned, and left. Miriam didn't notice. He stepped outside the room, people were beginning to gather. Nurses, doctors, police officers. They were staring, trying to figure out what next.

A nurse leaned over to another and softly commented, "I mean if it was, God forbid, my daughter . . ."

Chief Conners murmured to one of the other officers who were present, "Jesus, I hope this doesn't become nothing crazy. I'm gonna keep the fucking reporters away as long as possible. I don't wanna deal with this shit while we got Charlie dead and Brian barely hanging on." Conners was referring to two officers who'd been shot three days ago, allegedly trying to bust a suspected drug dealer. The dealer hadn't been apprehended; one of his top detectives was dead, and one of his youngest might not, the doctors said, make it through the week. The thought of now having to defend his men to the media when *his* men were the ones putting their lives on the line every day for scum, was enraging. The shooting of the girl was a tragedy, yes, but his men were targets in a war. That's how he felt.

Conners walked over to the hospital psychiatrist who had been called, just in case. "How much longer before we send somebody in there?" Conners asked. "I mean, I don't want to be insensitive, but the mother is not responsive and I need to talk to her, and I need to get back with Officer McBride's family—"

"Give her a little more time," the psychiatrist answered, as he walked over to consult with the other doctors.

"You think she's losing it?" Conners turned to another officer and whispered, "I think she might be a little crazy. I mean . . . I understand how hard all this is. But she was making strange sounds in there. I mean . . . I seen a lot of these people lose their kids, and I never heard sounds like that."

"Uhh . . . I hear you boss, but I'm saying, you know, it *is* her daughter in there."

"I know. But still. It's a little more than what I think is, you know, normal. Understand what I'm sayin'?"

"I guess." The young officer who had only two years in, shrugged his shoulders and thought about his wife who was home with their child, a girl, seven weeks old. He wanted to call them, just to talk to them for a second, but now was not the time.

"And I know this sounds cold," Conners continued, "but to be honest, they see their kids shot all the time. And it ain't usually like this. Know what I mean? You'd think they'd be used to it by now. You know? Think they would almost prepare themselves for the eventuality or something."

Conners looked at the officer, and the officer looked at him. After that, nothing. Neither said another word.

≈

*If you are born a woman you must always remember to walk with your own things.*

*Money, keys, change for the phone, the bus schedule, a train ticket.*

*A woman has to be prepared even more so than a man.*

*She must never forget that.*

*There will always be a woman to take care of a man, but there won't always be a man to take care of a woman.*

*A woman has to be ready to be her own man sometimes.*

*She has more to protect.*

*If you are born a woman you must never lend any more than what you can afford to lose.*

*This includes your heart.*

*You cannot live if you give your whole heart away.*

*Don't give it all away, and don't even look like you might want to give it all away.*

*That is why you sit like this.*

*Why you cross at the ankles like that.*

*Why you keep your clothes ironed and neat, and wear nothing to attract too much attention to yourself.*

*And wear panties and bras that are very, very white and without holes.*

*And always make sure you are very, very clean.*

*Everything makes a statement about who you are in the world.*

*When you have nothing else, you have your appearance.*

*If you are born a woman more work will always be expected of you.*

*Less time will be given to you to complete that work.*

*This is why you must learn the art of efficiency and of being focused and disciplined.*

*This is also why you do not ask for help. You do not give to someone else what is your responsibility. It will not be done correctly, and you will be blamed.*

*Just do your work, and do it quietly.*

*Then go home and rest.*

*Don't waste time dwelling on how unfair this may be.*

*You cannot make a revolution alone.*

*Just try to live as peacefully as possible.*

*Go to church. This will help.*

*Honor God. This will help.*

*Mind your manners. This will help.*

*Mind your business. This will help.*

These were the rules, at least in part. The rules that Miriam's mother had given to her. They were the rules that Miriam had passed on to Aya. They were the rules to live by. Weren't they?

Miriam had lived by them nearly all her life. Which is why it made no sense—that these same rules, replaying themselves in her head here in this hospital room, had turned tyrannical, had turned into a vicious, biting laugh.

After the phone call, Miriam had arrived at the hospital armed with an insurance card and her rules. Even as the doctor said there was nothing else that could be done, Miriam sought to negotiate.

"Please," Miriam had said. "Not her. Not Aya. Not us. You don't understand. It's impossible. The way we live, who we are. It can't be her. My baby can't have been shot. It's impossible. Listen to me. Please." It was the verbal equivalent of a mother on her knees. She grabbed the doctor's arm. He was a small man, gentle, with shining black eyes. He did not jump when she grabbed him. Instead he placed his thin, deep brown hand over hers. He stood there for a moment and let the pleading fill the space, let the pleading have a proper hearing.

After a small while, the doctor said in a thick Indian accent, "Come with me, Ms. Rivers." Miriam nodded. She allowed the doctor to direct her because what else could she do? And together they made their way down one long terrible corridor, around another, arriving finally at the room where Aya lay motionless. Where Aya lay with bullets still inside of her.

Now Miriam was moving toward her child, her baby, her Aya. She didn't know how she was moving, but she was moving. Moving to a place a mother is never meant to move to.

And the more she moved, the closer she got to her daughter, the more Miriam felt herself skidding inside herself. Every year, every month, every hour, every day that had brought her to this day. Every experience that had made her who she was, and who she was not—they sloshed inside of her.

Miriam touched her daughter. She stared at her daughter.

She whispered and she whimpered. She begged. She begged and she begged: For Aya's eyes to open. For the girl to stand or smile or curse or kick. For a poem or an argument. For anything. Miriam begged. But it did not work. Aya did not respond.

Which is what made Miriam desperate and confused. It's what made her go into a place she thought she had locked away forever. And from that place, she began to call on Bird, Aya's father, gone now for nineteen years. Miriam called on him to come, come save their baby. *Come save her. I need you, Bird. I. Need. You.* She called and called and almost did not even know she was calling. She called, although of course he could not hear her. He could not come.

But in calling on Bird, Miriam Rivers—a woman who had tried to invent herself as an entity who needed no one; who never had to reach for anyone; a woman who could sleep alone any night, every night; a woman who never had to share a meal, a laugh, a joke, a memory with anyone—this woman did something she never, ever thought she would do again. She admitted, albeit silently, that she needed someone. She needed someone now. She needed Bird now. Again.

And this unsettled her. It alarmed her. How could she still need him? So many years later. How could she? It made no sense. It was all some kind of deranged babble.

And the questions in her head: They stagnated her.

The answers in her head: They tortured her.

The reality she was about to face: It dismantled her.

And the God in her heart: He coughed and walked away.

# 6.

Once there were days that never seemed too long or too short, and once there were days that were not bordered by terror. There were days when the air was not like some wartime ration: thin, insufficient, and unfair. There were mornings, afternoons, evenings, and nights uncomplicated, planned, and at times, even sweet. Sweet as the every now and then gifts a father coming home from work would have for his children. Daddy who could pull magic out of a pocket: butterscotch candies, or chocolates with a cherry in the middle; a fifty-cent piece or multicolored marbles; a purple felt-tip pen that cost the same as ten regular blue ballpoints; a book you stayed up to read under the covers when you were supposed to be asleep. Magic.

Once there were days that were simple and sweet like that, and once there was a girl who was entirely protected, entirely surrounded by parents who feared her disappearance, and so they locked her into themselves. But then because she had been protected, surrounded so, this girl . . . she didn't ever have the chance to know what to do if that protection failed, and her spirit was tested. Tested and then narrowed.

Her parents named her Miriam. Miriam from Mary, but with an interesting twist they thought. Still, for all the thought that went into the naming, Miriam's parents, Maud and Frederick Rivers, called their girl Miracle. Five pregnancies, five miscarriages, and then, almost unbelievably, Miriam.

Maud Rivers, a preacher's daughter, had had people to pray over her, pray for her, pray with her. And when people said they didn't know why she was being forced to suffer as she was suffering, Maud didn't have to work hard to figure out what it was or why. She remembered the day things changed between her and Fred. The day of the church picnic when they went for a drive and the sun started to drop and it was getting darker and darker, but her parents knew she was with Fred, and Fred was known to be a good young man, and Fred's people had some money and his mother played the organ for the choir, so it was fine that they were out so late and that now it was night.

It was night and warm and close and they were young, and almost in love, and the touch was good. More than good. It was defining. His hand beneath her skirt. His hand strong, determined, rubbing and pulling away the garments and finding its way. His hand. She could not stop him. Would not stop him. Did not want to stop him. That was the truth. She wanted the touch. She enjoyed it.

Weeks later, when Maud discovered that she was pregnant, her good young man married her. They eloped, which only caused a minor scandal because everyone had seen them together, known them to be a couple for the last year. Yes, there were rumors that Maud had married him because she was pregnant, but when there was no baby seven or eight months later, people, even their parents, just accepted that this here was the genuine thing. Here was real love.

But no one was there on the day Maud bled alone on the kitchen floor, expelling the small clot that should have been her baby. Only Fred knew and she swore him to secrecy, and he cleaned up the blood and took care of his wife who lay in mourning for two straight weeks. She ate only when he forced her to; when he could no longer stand the smell, he bathed her.

Then two weeks to the day the baby left her, Maud got up and announced, "Enough with all this." She rose and cleaned the house, and cleaned herself, and as she did she spoke out loud to God and promised to be the best. The best wife, the best worshiper. No more going against His will. Never, never, never, never. And through each pregnancy, and each lost baby, Maud made more promises, negotiated longer with God, begged, cajoled, read the Bible again and again and again.

Until finally Miriam. Born at home two weeks and three days early.

Maud Rivers used to say, "The girl came into the world almost like she wanted to be a secret." If she, Maud, felt close to someone, or else if it was one of those rare occasions when a hard slap of memory knocked words out of her mouth before she could gather her bearings, she would go on to explain that "Maybe it was me. Maybe I made the girl feel like she needed to sneak into the world. I kept so quiet about her. I tried to stay around the house mostly. Needed to keep people from seeing me. It wasn't that I was ashamed of her. Oh, no, no, no. That was never it. Never. But after all my babies that had gone, it was too hard to have people looking at me wondering if this baby was going to leave me, too.

"So I did my best to keep company with myself, and love that baby who was growing inside me, without getting lost in that love. It was a hard balance. Mostly I tried to be the same, act the same as if I wasn't pregnant. Of course that didn't work too well, but it didn't keep me from trying.

"Anyway, what happened was that I felt something damp between my legs sometime before three in the morning. But after I checked and saw it wasn't blood, I paid it no mind. I turned over on my side and tried to pray myself back into sleeping, but it wasn't meant to be. I couldn't drift off. I couldn't get comfortable. My back started hurting so bad. I couldn't breathe right. Finally, I woke Fred up. Told him to get me some water to drink, and a cool rag for my head. I was so hot. I got out of bed, but then all of a sudden I felt this pain so sharp that I nearly fell down. Well, I did sort of fall down.

"I fell onto my knees and grabbed onto the edge of the bed and rested my head and tried to breathe. So if you can imagine this, I was kneeling down, holding on to the bed, hot as I don't know what and the pain was—I can't describe it, but it was so big that I couldn't even scream.

"I opened my mouth and nothing came out. Then Fred came rushing back into the room. He had the rag and water. I told him I couldn't drink the water but please, please get the damn—yes I cussed—get the *damn* nightgown off me. I was so hot.

"So he pulled the nightgown off me. I told him to put the rag on my head. Put the rag on my head. He did. I said rub down my back, Fred. Hard. Rub down my back. He did and I started to cry. I was crying and heaving and I was pushing. I didn't even realize it. I was pushing. And just when I was about to tell Fred to call an ambulance, something is happening with the baby, and I didn't understand what it was.

"All of this happened in the space of about ten minutes. So I didn't realize right away that I was in labor. Plus I'd never been in labor before. But as soon as I realized what was happening, that's when she came. It was Fred who saw first. He was on the floor beneath me, and he was saying, 'Oh my God! Oh my God! I see something, Maud. I see something.'

"And I was saying, 'What? What?' And before I knew it, Fred was grabbing a pillow from the bed, trying to shove it down on the floor between my legs. And now I was screaming. I screamed one big scream, and I guess it mixed with a push, because the next thing I knew was that this beautiful, messy baby girl lay on the pillow between my legs.

"And for one second I was terrified. I didn't know what a living, breathing, just-born baby looked or sounded like, and she was just laying there. She was bloody and still, the worst thing was that she was silent.

"And then as fast as that terror invaded me, it left. Because my baby, my Miriam, my miracle started crying. Not crying like you see in the movies. Not loud. Just a slow, soft whimper. You could almost miss it if you weren't listening for it.

"Of course you know there wasn't anything else I was listening for."

Maud Rivers always took a long, deep breath at this point in the story. This point in the story was always when she needed to remember to compose herself, an act she never failed to do. She would breathe, and then tell everything else quick, fast.

"Fred ran across the street and got Mrs. Peters, the retired nurse, to come over. She came and checked the baby who was still attached to me by the cord, and then she called Dr. Washington—a Black man—who she once worked for. The doctor came rushing over, and checked me, and checked my baby (*my* baby!!), and everything else was a blur, except this.

"Dr. Washington said me and my baby were fine. He said I was fine. He told us to go on and check into the hospital for a couple of days rest. He smiled, and promised he would check on us once we were there. And then, before disappearing from the bedroom, the doctor, for extra reassurance I guess, added, 'Looks like the girl just had her own time line. And that's nothing to be worried about. This girl is fine, and there's no reason to think she's not going to stay that way. Remember that children been coming and going on their own schedules since the beginning of time.'"

~

Just as the good doctor had predicted, she was. Fine. Miriam Miracle Rivers. The girl who slipped into the world early would dawdle her way through childhood, mostly at her parents' insistence, but Miriam clung, too, grabbed at the frayed edges of what she'd come to know as safe. There was a part of her who wanted to hold on to each day of her youth, and in general, wanted to pace her way into womanhood. Indeed, had her body not ignored her mind's slow walk to maturity, Miriam could have been nine, or twelve for years and years.

But it wasn't as though Miriam had some picture book childhood, no. She was loved, yes, but hers was a childhood defined by the church, and by her mother's restrictions and protection. Growing up, Miriam had few friends; Maud Rivers shrouded her daughter. No one was *really* good enough for her miracle child. Other children, Maud Rivers used to say, would be jealous of Miriam.

"You are so pretty," she would say and run her fingers through her daughter's long hair. "And we have things, dear, lots of things that others do not. Your father makes money that many of these people could not imagine. Most of them don't even have fathers, Miriam. And you come from a line of children who had fathers. And your grandfather, God rest his soul, was one of the most respected preachers our church has ever known. So you have to protect yourself. Because people may pretend to be your friend, but it doesn't mean that they truly are. Before God sent you to me, and all my babies kept dying before they got born, you should have heard the things women whispered behind my back. Said things about how there was something wrong with me. Of course they never said anything to my face. In my face they were oh so nice."

Miriam, silent and unblinking, would stare up at her mother and draw a picture in her mind of the world as an enemy force.

"You see, we own our house, Miriam. Everybody else on this block, except the Johnstons, rents. I know you may not understand this now, but you will. Plus, your father has met and knows *very* important people. People who have power and make a difference in the world. Like people you will know one day."

Miriam thought about her father during these conversations—he in his beautiful uniform with the gold braids on each shoulder, how handsome he looked standing there. She'd seen him once at the hotel, gracefully lifting all those bags. Lifting them as though they weighed a single pound. Her father, working and working, and never breaking a sweat, always smiling. There were other daddies on the block. Not like what her mother said. They were there. There was Lucille up the block, her daddy was always around. But, Miriam admitted in the quiet of her own head, no daddy was like her daddy. None as handsome. None as clean.

Thus, as it was, so it would remain. While Miriam's childhood was not bursting with silly or exciting or fun or secret or any kind of memories beyond her mother's warnings and admonitions, it was a cared-for childhood. It was a childhood where Miriam got all the food and clothes she needed, the push toward education, a solid foundation in the church. This good upbringing, her mother would say, this home training that everyone used to notice and comment on when they met the quiet and polite little girl, guaranteed her a future filled with more than what her parents had had. "If you do things *just so,*" Maud Rivers would explain, "you will meet the right young man and have more than I even dreamed of having. That's a promise," Miriam's mother would state emphatically, while leaving her daughter to intuit exactly what *just so* meant.

Still, as much as Miriam wanted the good life her mother worked tooth and nail to prepare her for, and as much as the girl studied and did her chores and went to Sunday school—for all of her ability to recite what she'd been told to learn—Miriam, when she was brave enough to admit the truth to herself, knew she felt empty inside. None of what she learned or lived moved her. The promise of tomorrow her mother made to her somehow did not translate into a comfort and warmth inside of Miriam's heart, her soul. Miriam was a bored girl, a lonely one. She felt that every day, although she did not admit to it every day, because when she did tell the truth to her soul, she felt guilty. Guilty because she was lonely even as her mother tried so hard to fill her.

There were all these many times when Miriam would look over at the other young people she knew from class or from church. These were kids her mother had warned her away from for one reason or another. They became to Miriam what the world was to her: virtually faceless. They could, in her mind, be tossed up and exchanged. Mary could be Katherine. William could be Samuel. And Miriam could be any of the above, or none of the above. In short, Miriam Rivers was a recluse from her own life.

She was, unfortunately, smart enough to know this, which is what really hurt. It was something she whispered when she felt no one would hear. Something whispered so softly, eventually she stopped hearing it herself. The other young people, the ones at school, the ones at church, eventually they tired of reaching out to the girl who was a ghost. They may have known she was around, but no one ever really saw her.

By the time she was a teenager, Miriam Rivers had vanished almost completely into the details of her life.

Rise at six.
Straighten up the bed.

Take today's clothes out of the closet.
Turn on the iron.
Wash your face.
Brush your teeth.
Iron the clothes.
Eat your breakfast while it's still hot.
Wash up again.
Read a verse.
Get dressed. Always look your best.
Go to school.

As Miriam lived like that, in the margins of herself, and as no one noticed or at least no one said they noticed, her parents rested, content. While neighborhood girls were getting pregnant, or joining gangs, or loving boys who were in gangs, Miriam came home right after school, did her homework, helped with the housework, and shrunk more and more into modesty. And the Rivers would look at their daughter, their beautiful and obedient daughter, who stood as testimony to their own goodness. They would look at her and feel renewed. Miriam was major currency in their world of struggling families, missing fathers, and angry, often alcoholic mothers.

But by the time Miriam turned sixteen years old, there was no containing her—at least not physically. The girls' hips were completely rounded and full, like her breasts, like her behind. And no matter how much the Rivers may have wanted Miriam to keep peeking out at the world from behind her mother's apron, no matter how much they may have wanted to continue watching over and directing Miriam, walking her hand in hand to church and Bible study, no matter how strict the curfews, and no matter how long and thorough the lectures on bad girls and nasty boys who only wanted one thing, no matter how strict the dress code (no skirts above the knee or that cupped her backside, no fitted sweaters, no blouse that revealed a hint of cleavage, stockings worn even in the summer, no heels over half an inch, jewelry discreet, and no, absolutely, no makeup) the girl came of age, as finally girls do. Willingly or unwillingly.

Miriam's body began to demand that the rest of her be allowed to run and catch up with it. And it did—that is, she did. She caught up with herself, and began to mature, and people began to notice. All of that grace and fluidity, that softness, and that smile—without meaning to or trying, Miriam turned the heads of men and women alike. In a word, Miriam Rivers was stunning.

And she knew it, even though it made her uneasy, she knew it. Everybody knew it. When she came back to school after the summer she turned sixteen, the boys in her class, the boys who had seen and not seen her for all those years, tripped over themselves, over their words, over chairs and stairs, trying to get a good look at her. The girls cut their eyes and whispered, *Who does she think she is?*

Who she was, was the same, really. But her looks now defined her more than her silence. The sweet and smooth of her deep bronze skin, the watery brown of her eyes that pulled up at the corners like a cat's. The tiny nose that was not particularly special, but neither was it intrusive, which left men able to focus on her mouth, which was clearly soft, perfectly shaped, and thick. But if nothing else convinced the men, then what her mother referred to as her prize always did it.

Miriam had a head overflowing with so much hair that when her mother straightened it, as she did every Saturday morning, it fell more than halfway down her back. Of course her hair was worn pulled back and tight in a ballerina's bun, but it was not hard to see that there was length and thickness to it. Miriam did not have one of those little barely there poofs in the back of her head. She had a big, winding bun and to look at it was to know you could run your fingers through it all night and never touch it all.

And those girls who were never taught to love much about themselves, especially their own beautiful, short, tight hair—hair that invariably looked worse when it was straightened (but everybody did it anyway)—both despised and admired Miriam. But mostly, they stayed away from her.

It was for this reason, along with the continually overly watchful eye of her mother, that Miriam Rivers, in spite of her looks and in spite of the way the boys held their breath as she walked by them, still did not have many friends. Even now that she was so desperate to. Truth was, she didn't really know how to make friends. How do you begin a conversation after years of silence? Miriam would think and think, when she saw someone whose face she liked, whose spirit seemed to be one she wanted to connect with. Miriam would think and stare at the person, trying to figure out how to begin. But inevitably the person just determined that Miriam, despite her looks, was more strange than anything else. All that staring, all that silence. It was annoying.

So as it had been when she was a child, Miriam found it easier to be alone. She had had so much practice at this, that even though she was lonely, even though she had other desires that flowed from every part of her, desires that flowed every way in her, Miriam decided, perhaps not consciously, that it was easier to crouch inside herself.

She would come out only long enough not to appear completely crazy:

*Hey. Hey, Miss. How you doing?*
*Fine.*
*Nice dress.*
*Thank you.*

*What's your name?*

*I need to get home. Please excuse me.*

If she revealed herself, Miriam wondered, what would people think, what would they say? If she talked about the emptiness that defined her, no one would have believed it. Beyond her looks, they would have seen the two parents, the nice clothes and home, and they would not have understood. They would hate her more, they would think she was ungrateful, they really would think she was crazy. Miriam's mother continued to warn her,

"Listen to your mama, child. People are very jealous. Very. You have a lot. Compared to most, you have more. So don't be letting people get too close or they're going to want to take what you have. Believe me when I tell you. You don't think all these women running around here with no husband don't look at mine? Listen to me when I tell you these things."

Which Miriam did. And so mostly alone in the world, alone with herself then, Miriam tried very hard to become her own best friend. When the night came down and Miriam could escape the constant counsel of her mother, she would climb into the bed, and curl into the stillness, and draw herself into herself and talk to God. About how she could be a better person, how she could be more pleasing to Him, more perfect.

And then once, there, in that mystical space of night, Miriam spoke to God in a new voice. But before she did, she pulled in real close and checked to make sure no one was watching, and in that secret state, in that guarded position, Miriam asked her God if there could be just one person, just one, who would come to her and allow her to whisper herself to. One person to do that with the way she did it with God. Did that person exist?

No answer came that first night of dialogue. But in the days and nights that followed, when Miriam accepted that this process, this becoming of a woman, was one from which she could not turn back, the desire to whisper herself into someone's ear became stronger. It became stronger in size and also in sound. And then it was everywhere. It was a wanting in the whole of her, and it was loud. It was a clanging that eventually raged inside, beside, outside, everywhere around her. It was an inescapable and incessant thing, this clanging, but it was not a dishonest thing. It was not a liar.

The clanging, disharmonious as it was, was the truth that finally rushes out from all of our dreaming. For Miriam, the truth was that there was a new and even overwhelming desire to be seen, and to be wanted, to be touched, and to be heard— most of all, to be heard and accepted in the fullness of who she was. And not only that. Miriam wanted acceptance also for the fullness of whoever she might one day become. She was not supposed to feel this way, she thought, but she could not help it. It was bigger than the rules she had been taught to live by, this wanting.

And because it was bigger, despite her fear and despite her guilt that she was betraying her parents, Miriam did not fight it when she felt herself being drawn into this frightening yet magnetic place where she would come undone, limb by limb. And in that disembodied state, that state without armor or artifice, that state where only honesty and her spirit could determine the next move, Miriam Rivers, sixteen, not quite seventeen, began to pray for love. Not only in the night, but in the center of the day, at dawn, at dusk. Miriam prayed.

She prayed for a love she had never before known. Until that point in her life, the only love she had known had been the love that had been placed around her neck like expensive gold chains that were much too thick to be either attractive or comfortable. It was the miracle child love. The love that came from people who never thought she would get here, and secretly worried that she would, at any moment, leave. It was the love that never relaxed. It was the love Miriam no longer needed.

What she needed was the sort of love she overheard girls in the lunchroom whispering about. It was the sort of love she read about in books, or saw on the big movie screens. It was the sort of love that men sang about in the songs you danced slowly to, or else you cried.

It was grown up, weak in the knees, tell all your secrets, carry it in your pockets, pull it out for your friends to peek at, pull it out at night for one last glance before curling up with and sleeping with it love. It was twist it in your hair, rub it on your lips, wrap it around you twice, dance and grind with it, sing to it, cry on it, beg for it, worry about it, run down the street after it, knit it into a sweater, wear it with anything love.

And in that season when she was sixteen almost seventeen facing the wind of becoming a woman, secretly needing and wanting a love that all the rules and verses suggested strongly against, there was a boy, already a man, who was named for his father, and his father's father.

This boy, already a man, was born and baptized Albert William Joseph Jefferson the Third. He saw Miriam exactly. Not just the curve of her hips, or thick of her hair, but the search of her eyes. And her eyes, looking out from behind themselves for something more. Something saving. And in the season when she was sixteen almost seventeen, not only did Albert William Joseph Jefferson see Miriam exactly, but she saw him.

# 7.

Albert William Joseph Jefferson the Third was known by everyone as Bird. This was how he introduced himself to Miriam. It was late in the afternoon because Miriam had been studying in the school library for the weekly math quiz her teacher had promised the students on the first day of class. Bird saw her there, walking alone out of the school at the same time he was walking alone out of the school, and he felt he had to take a chance. Forget all that stuff they said about pretty girls and their stuck-up attitudes. He would just have to risk rejection since he might not get another moment completely alone with her like this.

Besides, despite the extraordinary quality of her beauty, the perfect symmetry of her eyes, nose, and mouth, the sway of her hair and hips, the melody that was her skin, there was something very humble about this girl's beauty; she made no attempt to slap people in the face with it.

Which is why Bird could not ignore his impulse. He could not set aside the opportunity to reach out. And so standing there after a day's work, dressed in neatly pressed black slacks and a simple tan sweater, he approached Miriam. Delicately. He said, "Excuse me. Excuse me, sister. I don't mean to bother you, but my name is Bird. Do you have a minute? Can I please have a word with you?"

Miriam was struck by both the gentle beauty of the man's face and the turn of his voice, which was somehow confident but not arrogant. Bird had a voice that came down like water running slow. And his voice, both malleable and firm at the same time, held her, however lightly, even as she knew her parents would say this was the sort of man she should avoid. He was older than she, and there was a sense he carried a world behind his eyes. A world her parents denied existed. But Miriam could not avoid him, she did not know why, but she just could not do it, and so Bird began to speak.

"Listen. I'm not some crazy man or anything like that. I just took a job here at the school. And I've noticed you the last couple of days. I mean since school started. And I know we're not supposed to talk or anything. You being a student. Me working here. But I saw you, and you have to forgive me if I'm out of line, but you're just so beautiful."

Bird paused, almost waiting for Miriam to turn away from him. She could not turn away from him. She looked down slightly, but completely away. So he continued.

"And I just thought you should know that. I mean . . . probably people tell you all the time. But I wanted to tell you. For me." Bird paused again and then, "That's all. Thanks. Thanks for letting me tell you."

Miriam looked at Bird, and for a terrifically long thirty seconds, she heard her mother's voice like a shrieking in her head. The admonitions about how most men only wanted one thing. How you can't trust a man. How men will use you and then talk about you, ruining you for one of the few decent ones who might be out there. Black men, her mother had warned her, don't know how to stay home and take care of their families. But what about Daddy, Miriam would counter quietly. I worked with him, Mama would say. "Believe me. He didn't come like you see him."

Still, Miriam looked at this man who called himself Bird, and he didn't feel wrong. He didn't feel like someone to avoid. When he spoke, the timbre of his voice, the welcome of his eyes, they moved something inside the girl. It was a noticeable shift. It was a comfortable one. And because it was comfortable, comfortable and comforting, Miriam said slowly, "People don't do that. They don't come up to me and tell me I'm beautiful. My mother's said it. And my father. But no one else." Miriam waited before she continued speaking, and then, "So thank you. It was very nice to hear. Really." Miriam said this and then did one other thing. She stood there, willing to speak more.

When Bird realized this, he smiled a smile that was fast as the sun, bright and wide. And that smile was the final thing to convince Miriam that her mother was not right on this question of men. At least not about this man. A man with a smile like that. Whatever defenses Miriam had been trained to maintain were suspended then, in that moment. Miriam and Bird—there in front of the school, there and never having spoken before—fell into a full-blown, no turning back, first of many conversations.

"I work here. At the school. I just started."

"Oh. I haven't seen you. What do you do?"

Bird hesitated. "You know. Cleaning up. That type of thing."

Miriam, sensing that Bird felt a measure of shame about the sort of job he had, said quickly, "My mother always said there was nothing wrong with an honest day's work. And it's good, you know, really nice to come to a place that's all neat and put together. I think it helps people learn better. You know what I mean?"

"Yeah. But it's not the kind of work I want to do forever. It's just that it's what I could get and I have to take care of my grandmother, and jobs are hard to find right now. So sometimes you have to take what you can get until something better comes along."

"What would be something better?"

"College. And law school. One day. I'm getting ready to apply to colleges soon. The City University is free, so I'm going to put my application in there. I have my high school diploma. So I figure if I can work here and go to school at night, it might take me a little longer, but I can get there."

"I'm thinking about the City University, too," Miriam said. "My parents want me to stay in New York, and I know there are other schools, but I don't want them to worry about college bills so much. It's so expensive," Miriam continued and then switched the subject back to Bird. "Why the law?" she asked.

"Because you know though things have changed for Black people, or are starting to change, it's not enough."

"Yeah," Miriam said, though she wasn't sure why. What laws still needed to be changed? Things were better than they had been, weren't they? Her parents lectured her on that almost daily.

Bird, seeing the questioning in Miriam's eyes, began to explain. "Like for example, I still get stopped by the same police on my block a couple of times a week. You know what they do. Want to know where am I going, where have I been, etcetera, etcetera. And what can I do about it? I get patrol cars following me down my street. It makes me so mad!"

"I understand," Miriam said softly. Miriam, who'd never been stopped or harassed by the police herself, but the stories of what cops did to Black men were in the papers every day. Her mother always said that most of them deserved it. Most of the guys who got stopped were out in the street up to no good anyway. Selling drugs, drinking, bothering women—they were doing something they had no business doing, Mrs. Rivers had commented over and over. But Miriam looked at this man and knew there was another story to tell.

"And you know what makes it so bad?" Bird's voice began to rise, but he caught himself and brought it down. "I'm a veteran! You would think I'd get some respect since I risked my life for this country. You know what I mean?"

"You were in Vietnam?"

"Yup. Just came home four months ago."

"Wow," said Miriam, stunned, because someone who had just been in a war should have looked different, she figured. He should have had that crazy look in his eyes, or be in a nod like the men in her neighborhood who went to Vietnam and came home addicts. Her father pointed them out all the time and said those men had really died in Southeast Asia and the government just sent the bodies back. Looking at Bird, Miriam thought he should have been in a wheelchair or walk with a limp or have an arm that didn't work or speak in sentences that didn't make sense. He should have been splintered somehow, some way, but was not. At least not in a way that she could notice. Not in an easily identifiable way. Bird, a man just home from war, appeared to be like any other strong, handsome brother Miriam might see. In church, at the store, on the stoop, anywhere. And Miriam marveled at this, at him, but not knowing how to put those feelings into words, too shy to put those feelings into words, she said simply and sincerely, "I'm glad you made it home."

"Yeah, me too. Listen. You think we could walk over to the park and talk a little more?"

"No, I can't. I have to get home. I'm already late."

"Sure. Sure," Bird said. And the two looked at each other again, long enough for both of them to blush. "See you around," Bird said.

Miriam smiled, said good-bye, and rushed home feeling

guilty, feeling as though, by this conversation, she had somehow disobeyed her parents. By the time she arrived at her front door, guilt had completely overwhelmed her. She began apologizing immediately to her mother, saying sorry she was a little late, saying she'd gotten caught up at school.

Her mother, who hadn't noticed that her daughter had come home twenty minutes later than usual, paid her little mind. "When you finish your homework, come in here and help me with dinner."

"Okay, Mama."

Miriam retreated to her room to finish the last of her assignments, and then went downstairs and began setting the table. She was completely distracted by the young man she'd met earlier, so much so that her mother said, "Where are you tonight?"

"Huh?"

"You here, but you not here. Something happen at school?"

"No," Miriam said at little too quickly. "Just tired. All this studying."

"Hmmph. This the easy part of life. What you gonna do when you got real troubles?"

Miriam nodded and folded the napkins at each place as her father walked in, grunted hello, and headed for the bathroom. Fifteen minutes later, the three were sitting down to a quiet meal of salmon, string beans, and potatoes. Miriam poured water for everyone as her mother broke the silence with a story about some wayward girl from the church who got pregnant.

"By some man who up and left her. Some man she barely even knew. Don't know where her parents were. She's fifteen. *Fifteen.* You know her, Fred. Mrs. Williamson's girl. Not that that woman sets much of an example, but *fifteen!*"

Fred Rivers nodded his head and continued to eat, so Mrs. Rivers focused her attention on Miriam. "See what I mean about *real* problems, Miriam?"

"Uh-huh."

"A baby and no man is *not* the way to go. But it's all over everywhere these days. I see girls who ain't no bigger than a minute pregnant wherever I go these days. Even to my doctor. They sitting right up there in the office, just as big as they want to be and proud! No man, no wedding ring, big as a house and *proud*! Not one of them gonna turn out to be anything. You mark my words."

Mrs. Rivers continued on and on as her daughter and husband tried to lose themselves in their dinners. Tried to chew so loudly it would drown her out.

But that night after the dishes were cleared and washed and the house was locked up and quiet, Miriam, lying still but wide awake, could have sworn she heard something that sounded like her mother crying. Not possible, she thought, and turned over and fell asleep.

≈

The next day at school Miriam saw Bird as she moved through the hallway from English to history class. He smiled at her and she looked at him and then quickly looked away. He waited for her after school, watched as she went into the library and then sat outside until she came out. "Hi!" His grin was wide and welcoming.

Miriam smiled at him, "Hi!" she called out over her shoulder, and then, "Got to get home. Bye!"

"Bye," Bird said softly long after Miriam was out of earshot. But he was not deterred! He waited again the next day, and then the next day after that, and even the next day after that. Miriam was nowhere to be seen. Bird got the message. This girl was not interested in some man who cleaned gum off the bottom of desks for a living. It didn't matter what he was going to be one day. It mattered what he was now. "Fuck that stuck-up bitch," Bird actually said aloud one afternoon as he changed out of his uniform. He stormed out of the staff locker room and started walking out of school. Miriam saw him as she headed toward the library. "Hi!" she called out from the other end of the hallway. Bird looked at her and kept on going. Fuck her, he said to himself.

Maybe he didn't hear me, Miriam thought as she entered the library. But he must have. He looked at me. And why wasn't he outside when I came out? Miriam couldn't concentrate on her studies. She tried, but her mind alternated back and forth between her conversation with Bird, and the hundreds of conversations she'd had with her mother—or, rather, that her mother had had with her—about men.

After dinner that night, Miriam decided to call Joan, a girl from church her mother approved of since Joan's daddy was the minister. Joan who led the youth choir, and who was quiet and studious, attractive but hardly beautiful—if only Miriam's mother knew the girl had been messing with boys since she was twelve years old, maybe even younger if you could believe some of the nastier rumors. As of late, Joan was trying to get Miriam to finally shed her parents' yoke and get out and have some fun.

"Girl," she had said a few weeks ago when no one was around and they were making chicken for a church picnic, "you better get out there and enjoy your life. If our parents had their way, we'd spend the rest of our lives sitting in some damn church messing with all this chicken and grease, ushering people to their seats, and wiping sweat from our foreheads. And if they let us talk to any boy, it'd be some loser with buck teeth and Coca-Cola glasses. Well that ain't gonna be *me*. And it shouldn't be you. Look at you, Miriam . . . if I looked like you . . . Listen, you need to just get out there and meet some damn body."

Miriam, shocked and embarrassed, just smiled and said,

"When the time is right, Joan. I need to make good grades in school right now. I just want to concentrate on that." And then she walked away, Miriam did.

Joan caught up with her later and said, "Listen to me. You got to find the way to give your parents what they want but still get what you want. I'm telling you." Miriam nodded but refused to discuss the matter anymore. And Joan went away feeling sorry for Miriam, and Miriam went away thinking she might always be alone.

But on the night after the day when Bird ignored her, Miriam read through her parents' phone book until she found Joan's number. She slipped into the den and called Joan. At first she hesitated, and then finally she blurted out, "I need to ask you about men."

Joan was in it, right from the start. "Wh*aaat*???" she began, as surprised by the phone call as she was by the news. "You met somebody? Tell me about him," she continued. "And do *not* hold back. Where'd you meet him, what's he look like?"

"No. It's not that. I mean . . . it's a little bit that. But I mean . . . I just want to ask. What if you meet a man and first he's nice to you and then suddenly he's not?"

"After you did it, you mean?"

"Did what?"

Joan hesitated. "You know. Listen, you can be honest with me. It's happened to me." Joan's voice was suddenly edged with pain, and Miriam was totally baffled.

"What's happened to you?"

"You know, after you do it with a guy, then they act like they don't know you."

"Oh God! No! *That's* not what I mean."

"Oh." Joan sounded embarrassed. Miriam changed her tone.

"I mean . . . I know that can happen, but I just met this man.

We had a nice conversation. But you know, I'm trying to focus on school. I'm not really allowed to date anyway. But I like him. I mean we had a really nice talk."

"So why was he mean to you?"

"I don't know. I haven't said anything to him. Just haven't had a chance to talk to him again since the first time."

"Forget about him. If he's mean now, he'll always be mean."

That wasn't what Miriam wanted to hear. But maybe Joan was right. Maybe her mother was right. "Yeah," Miriam agreed. They got off the phone and Miriam admonished herself: All this foolishness and wasted time over some idiot she didn't even know.

The next day as she left the library Bird was standing outside the school. "Sorry I didn't speak yesterday. This is for you." He handed her a flower. Miriam didn't know what kind but it was yellow and beautiful. "I know you have to go. See you around." This time he walked away first, and this time it was Miriam who stood there and watched him go.

≈

The dance between them continued for two weeks. They would alternate between offending each other and making each other smile until at last Bird caught Miriam one afternoon and said, "Listen, isn't there some way we can spend a little time together?"

And she wanted to. Miriam wanted to so badly. But she just shook her head, and said, "I really don't see how. I have a lot of responsibilities. I have a curfew. There's a big history test coming up."

Bird pursed his lips and nodded. "Well, fine. Just know that I tried. I really did. I really wanted to get to know you. I mean . . . I was sincere about that. Not trying to play any games. I really wanted to get to know you."

Miriam nodded and walked away, but she thought about

him all weekend long. All through chores and church. She thought how there was someone out there who really wanted to know *her*. It actually brought tears to her eyes, and it made her mother complain that she was acting funny, and it compelled her, after conspiring with Joan to concoct a lie about going to the movies, to find Bird on Monday, to seek him out and say, "What about Saturday? Can you meet me at the Brooklyn Library?"

～

The school week dragged on and Bird could barely focus on his work and Miriam could barely focus on her studies, but finally it was Saturday and they saw each other walking toward each other. Each one, Miriam and Bird, were both trying to look so cool, so distracted. Both failed miserably, but so what? The excitement between them was tangible, the air between them a rapid breath. Everything, even the sidewalks, the streetlights, and the trees gone slack in the changing season, all seemed in some way radiant and new. Everything grinned.

Yet only an hour ago Bird and Miriam had both been in their respective homes changing clothes over and over. Each one had been fretting in front of the mirror, fretting and frowning. Miriam tried on no less than four skirts, two dresses, and one pair of shorts, three blouses, and one halter top. The halter had been a gift she'd received, unbelievably, at the church Christmas party last year. One of Joan's cousins, a young woman who was visiting from Oakland for the holidays, had gotten it for her.

Mrs. Rivers, who had been there when Miriam opened it, barely contained her shock. "This is disgusting," she said sharply as soon as the party was over and she was alone with her daughter. "I cannot believe that girl's taste! Maybe that's fine for California. There's so much strange stuff out there. But here?" She'd let out a deep breath, and then instructed Miriam to promptly get rid of "the thing." Miriam had said yes. She'd said she would do it the next day. But the next day came and went, and Miriam forgot about the halter.

Later, when she was going through her drawers and she discovered the tiny white top at the bottom, for whatever reason she could not do it; she could not throw it away. That's why today, on this late September afternoon that felt more like June, it suddenly seemed like an option, wearing the halter. And Miriam took it. She finally settled on a long and flowing blue skirt to go with it. She also pulled out a white oxford and tied it around her waist, so that when she headed home later, she could put it on and not risk her mother seeing the halter.

Dressed and nervous, Miriam wrote a note to her mother saying she was going to the movies with Joan, and that she might stop by the library before coming home in time for dinner. Then Miriam quietly slipped out of her house, nearly running toward the bus stop.

Alone in the small apartment he shared with his grandmother, Bird kept switching between a black T-shirt and black slacks, and jeans and a dashiki. He felt so free in the dashiki; he liked how loose and cool it felt. But finally he decided it was better to wear all black. He looked more serious, more like a man, in his black on black. Plus Miriam would be able to see how defined his chest was, his arms, and even his back. Standing at the bathroom mirror, Bird trimmed, combed, and patted his mustache and beard for more than twenty minutes before he left to go meet Miriam.

Now finally here they were, hair and clothing troubles aside. Here they were glowing, together, looking at one another, trying to think of what to say besides hello, trying desperately not to betray the desire each one felt for the other. Bird was the first to speak.

"So. Umm. It's good to see you. You feeling all right?"

"Uh-huh. Yeah," Miriam said, nodding her head. "You?"

"Yeah. You know," Bird replied, and then there was a long pause. "So I guess we can go into the park right here." The mouth of Prospect Park was less than a minute's walk from the library. Bird led Miriam, just slightly, by the arm.

"Okay," she said, moving with him.

And the two walked toward the park silent and awkward, until at last Miriam broke it with a laugh.

"What you laughing at?" Bird asked, and Miriam could not tell if the question was good-natured or not. She assumed it was.

"Us. We ran our mouths so much the first time we talked, it made us want to talk more. Finally we have the chance and nobody's saying a word. It's crazy."

"I still got things to say," Bird responded, quickly though not defensively.

"Like what?" Miriam teased.

He looked at her for an endless minute, and then Bird said in a voice barely above a whisper, "Like how it feels like I'm finally back from the war, being here with you."

≈

They did not make it through much of the park that day. They did not walk even half a mile. Miriam and Bird made it only as far as the second set of benches, the ones that were a little off to the side and tucked under a tree just beginning to turn colors. There, beneath the easy spray of green and gold and orange and red, they spent hours talking, holding hands, and daydreaming.

"When I first saw you and said you were beautiful," Bird said, looking directly in Miriam's face, "I meant beautiful in a way that's bigger than what you look like on the outside. Although you are. You really, really are. But what I meant was more than that. You're like one of those people everyone always wants to stop and ask directions from because you seem like you'd be willing to help. That's the kind of beautiful I meant."

"You can see that in *me*?" asked Miriam, who only saw the shy, the reserve and fear, when she looked in the mirror. She wanted to know how he saw that. And could it possibly have been true? That there was something illuminating from her, something people could see?

"Oh yeah. It's obvious. It's part of what made me stop you in the first place. I mean, like I said. You're beautiful in a physical way and I noticed that. But I wouldn't just stop a girl because she was beautiful. Beautiful women can be the worst to approach because they're either too stuck on themselves or else they've been bothered so much for so long that they're defensive. But you don't have any of that. You look . . . I don't know. Open to things I guess. That's what I saw. An opening."

Bird paused for a long time. Miriam didn't know what to say to this man. She wanted him to keep talking, to keep saying things she had never heard before. Things that made her feel new, that made her feel as though she belonged somewhere. But Bird was silent for a while. The look on his face told Miriam he was losing himself in his thoughts, and she would have felt it rude, like she was interrupting a conversation, if she said anything. So as much as she wanted him to go on and on, speaking and speaking, Miriam didn't say a word, and neither did Bird. For a few minutes the two were quiet together, but at the same time, they were unfolding with one another. Finally Bird said, without even trying to disguise the nervousness he felt in asking the question, "Why did you stop? That first time, I mean. Why did you talk to me?"

"Well," Miriam began slowly, because she knew that she could not hold back with this man. She knew she could not minimize or deny these unfamiliar but wonderful feelings. She had no practice. All Miriam could do then was pace herself and hope that she didn't sound immature or stupid.

"Well. It was your voice." Then she stopped, started again. "No. Wait." Miriam looked down and then over at Bird. "The first thing I noticed was you. Was that you are"—Miriam interrupted herself with a broad and embarrassed smile—"handsome." She said this in a hush.

"And then your voice is a good voice." Miriam could not believe she was talking to a man in this way. She could not believe she was speaking to *anyone* in this way. But the words were in her, the emotions, as they had always been. Miriam blinked long and let her heart overtake the warnings in her head, her blood. "You sound like you know what you're talking about but you don't sound so . . . so aggressive. You know how some people are like that? How they say what they say as though they want to be in a conversation with you, a dialogue, but really, they just want to *tell* you something?" Miriam was thinking of her mother, thinking about all their "sit downs." All the times they were having mother-daughter talks that were really lectures. "I think I'm just more used to being talked at . . . that's what I'm trying to say. Because God forbid if you ask a question or worse, disagree with them. Then they get so mad at you. But the way you said things, the other day, I felt like even though you believed in what you were saying, I could still ask questions."

"No one ever told me anything like that about myself."

"No one ever said to me what you did. So we're even."

They grinned widely at each other, these two young people hungry for connection and warmth and safety. They leaned close together, close, as though they knew each other intimately. They talked about their plans to go to college. "I'd be the first in my family," Miriam proclaimed with something close to pride in her voice, as their conversation flowed from the inside out, from dreams to the war, to the so-called Watergate scandal. "Nixon's crooked as I don't know what," Bird exclaimed.

"My father says the same thing. Never liked him at all," Miriam offered. She had no opinion of her own.

Bird looked out across the park, out at the children playing softball in the near field, out at the runners and dog walkers and then back at this beautiful girl sitting beside him. All those images of death he carried with him from the jungle—the shredded limbs, the blown-up children, how you stepped over pieces of them; the mothers frozen in death with their mouths wide as if to scream, but they never did scream—they were faded, suddenly, those images from his head. Faded of their own volition, here, with her, and without him having to do his usual begging and pleading, to please, just please . . .

Then and there, unencumbered by the details of death, the details of life, the two felt they could be completely open— about everything or nothing. There were places Bird wanted to see in the world, he exclaimed, but he couldn't deny it: He loved it here in Prospect Park, in Brooklyn. Miriam nodded, seeing her city for the first time through this man's eyes, and he continued that it wasn't just that Brooklyn had its own museum, and park and zoo and gardens. Bird said there was this energy, this swagger that made you feel proud, made you feel like you came from someplace that was clearly defined, a place with borders and history, like France or Italy.

"Yeah," Miriam said.

Manhattan wasn't like that, Bird continued as Miriam thought about how rarely she'd ever even been there. "No clear feeling in Manhattan except money and noise and everybody rushing. People will stop to talk to you in Brooklyn, maybe try to help you out." Miriam nodded. "Brooklyn was its own city once, did you know that?" Bird asked with a great measure of pride.

"I didn't know that," Miriam said and thought Bird was the smartest man she had ever met. How did he know all these things, especially being so young!

"Yeah, it was. Downtown where all the courts are used to be our City Hall. No other borough is like that." Miriam nodded her head in agreement, and Bird leaned back against a park bench, surveyed the landscape and almost under his breath, but not without feeling, proclaimed once again, "I love Brooklyn."

"Me too," said Miriam, who before today had never given much thought to the place she'd spent her entire life in. "I love it here, too," she said again and took in the rush of colors all around her and smiled. Neither of them spoke about all the streets in their neighborhood that had caved in five years ago now, imploded some of them, others virtually air-raided— that's how they appeared. The wooden boards on apartment houses where windows used to be; the potholes in the streets you could drive a van into; buildings and shops burned into shells that looked like the hollow eyes of ghosts. And these positioned asymmetrically beside tiny neat homes, or else brownstones that architects came from all over to admire, to study; storefront churches and also grand ones; corner liquor stores and family-owned markets. This was Brooklyn. Everything Bird said and everything he left out. Brooklyn: disorganized but decipherable. Fragmented, but familial.

"Still, much as I love it here, I want to see a place in the world that's completely at peace. It has to exist. A place where there's no war, and nothing that even feels like war is about to start up. You know what I mean?" Bird asked.

"I do," Miriam responded, nodding. "I do." But did she really understand? She wasn't sure she did, and then again, she wasn't sure she didn't.

Bird saw Miriam's confusion, and offered, "I mean like here, even though there's no war going on per se, it's like there's an undercover one. When you see the police can just kill us, just *Bam!* shoot us up like that. It's insanity. Look at that little boy,

Clifford Glover. What was he? Ten years old? Remember him?" Bird's face changed slightly, reflecting anger.

Miriam noticed the change, the look of anger, but it did not cause her to pull back from Bird. She remembered that terrible shooting. "Yeah, I do."

"Remember how that arrogant cop just said, point blank, he didn't see size or age or nothin'. Just color. Can you believe that? He just came right out and said it and they let his ass off anyway. But you know what's really sick, Miriam?"

"What?"

"How this country could send me halfway around the world to kill people who are half my size. People I ain't got no struggle with. People who didn't enslave my ancestors yesterday, or patrol and endanger my community today. Those Vietnamese never threatened my life and it was okay for me to kill them, but it's not okay for me to even talk about defending myself against these pigs over here who are pointing guns at me. You understand what I'm trying to say?"

"You sound like all those protesters."

Bird's face tightened. "Well, it's the truth," he snapped. Miriam looked at him, both surprised and hurt. She began to shut down. She'd said the wrong thing, she thought. Bird noticed, regretted that he snapped, and quickly softened, "Well, that's how I see it," he said and then paused. "I hope you don't look at me like I went off to war and now I'm just some crazy, angry soldier."

Miriam shook her head vigorously. She didn't see him in that way, not at all! Bird continued, desperate to be understood.

"I mean, I am angry, that's true. I'm angry about a lot of things. But more than being angry I'm just trying to live. Just want to get a decent education—"

"Me too," Miriam agreed, but without the passion. Not because she didn't want to be passionate, but because this was the first time she ever had a conversation like this and it was all so much to absorb. Here was a man with a vision about life that seemed so different and yet so much the same as her parents'.

"I want a family," Bird said and it nearly sounded as though he was begging, but he was not a man to beg. "I always did. And I want to live long enough to have a past that I can feel proud of."

"What do you mean?" Miriam asked.

"I mean I hate violence. And right now, what do I have to look back on except violence?"

Miriam nodded, but she still didn't really understand. True, he had been to war, but what about his childhood, his mother, his father, the friends he must have had growing up. She wondered all this, but did not ask. She just let Bird continue to speak in his sad but resolute voice.

"But I will say this. What I learned from Vietnam—shit, I learned it before I went to Vietnam—is that I'm down with protecting my people. That's one thing I am proud of when I think about that time. How brothers really looked out for each other. So if I don't wind up ever being about nothing else, I'm gonna always be about that." Bird said the last sentence looking directly at Miriam. And without him saying it—because it was too soon for him to say it—Miriam felt that she was his people.

Which is why she took Bird's hand in hers and they walked in peace against the spill of autumn.

# 8.

Both Miriam and Bird had been raised with armor. With armor and walls meant to shield them against a world that could, without warning, send you people and experiences meant to break you down to the core and heartbeat of yourself. Down into where there was no flesh, no bone to protect you. There were so many people who demanded to know the place of your beginnings, the place where you stored your dreaming. They were dangerous, those people, the ones who did not earn their keep with you. They were potential killers or thieves. That's how Miriam and Bird had been raised to encounter the world, and they lived like that and they kept their souls out of the street, secreted away, secluded. But it wasn't nice.

After that first date, Miriam and Bird went home, both feeling elated. But that night, laying in their separate beds and worlds, differences emerged. Bird began to feel as though he should set down his armor. He thought about how good it would be to have his legs, arms, and back all relaxed, loose, unstrained. He was so tired, wanted so much to just be held and loved. So did Miriam, but she couldn't imagine how she would be able to travel this path to that joy. She knew she couldn't keep lying and sneaking around. She also knew she couldn't bring home a young man who was almost twenty years old, someone who'd been to war, someone who was a janitor at her school. Her parents would never allow it. When she saw Bird at school on Monday, she would tell him that they were just going to be friends, just see each other around the school. This was her last thought before she drifted off to sleep, and when she woke up in the morning, it was her first thought: Bird. She thought about him at church, through dinner, and later when she was supposed to be studying, she doodled his name instead of copying down notes. Nevertheless, she woke up Monday morning resolved. She went to school ready to confront Bird, and saw him almost as soon as she walked through the door, which caught her off-guard; she'd expected to see him at the end of the day, not at the beginning.

Before she could get out a word, Bird, looking to see that no one was watching, slipped her a card and then quickly said he had to get down to the music room, get things in order, bye! In English class Miriam opened up the card while Mrs. Graves discussed *Ethan Frome*. On the front of the card was a little boy with an exaggerated toothy grin. On the inside the message read simply, *Thank you*. But Bird had written in his own words (Miriam had never seen that done). He wrote:

> *For listening to me*
> *For making me feel smart*
> *For walking with me and sharing Brooklyn with me*
> *For being curious and open*
> *And so beautiful*
> *Thank you*
> *Love,*
> *Bird*

The rest of the day was a blur. As soon as classes ended, Miriam did not go to the library. Instead she hung around the locker room until Bird came out. She motioned for him to follow her. He did. Out of the school, down five blocks to Tom's, a small family-run diner that had been a neighborhood meeting place since the 1930s. No one from the school went there though, because it was a little bit of a walk. But Miriam had stumbled upon it last year when she walked an alternate route home. She liked it there; everyone was so friendly. And it was her own thing, a place even her parents didn't know about. It wasn't much of a secret to keep—a place she went to perhaps once a month for fifteen minutes. But it was hers and now she was sharing it with Bird who was asking her, "No library today?"

"No," Miriam said, shaking her head. "Wanted to see you." She paused. "The card was beautiful."

"You're beautiful."

"Thank you. I mean, for both things. The card and the compliment."

The waiter came over and they ordered chocolate egg creams. Miriam continued, "Bird, I had a great time on Saturday . . ."

"But?"

"But . . . Bird, my parents don't let me date. Especially someone who's not in the church. And I lied to them about where I was on Saturday. I can't keep doing that."

Bird looked sullen. He nodded. "I understand." He looked at Miriam, hurt, not knowing what to say, wanting to scream, Fuck your parents, what about what you feel!

"Listen," he began, reaching into his pocket, "I have something I have to do for my grandmother, so I really can't stay."

"But—"

"You kind of rushed me here or I would have told you that before. That's why I gave you the card in the morning. Didn't expect to see you this afternoon. Anyway, I gotta run." He put enough money on the table to cover the bill, and almost sped out of Tom's. Miriam sat there with her mouth open. When the waiter came over, she made an excuse to him, paid the bill, and walked home, the whole while getting angrier and angrier, but not at Bird and his sudden departure. She was angry at her parents, their restrictiveness, their boring life, the way they wanted to possess her.

Miriam had no life. None! She wasn't normal, never felt normal, never laughed, never looked forward to the day. How could this be life, she wondered as she stormed past the vacant lots, the old women sweeping brownstone steps, the kids playing ball in the middle of the street, the music that was always blaring out of the storefront churches—the life. Of this neighborhood, these people, even these buildings. Life.

The only invisible thing, the only inconsequential thing was her. Miriam was sure of this. Tears that seemed ancient as the sky began to collect in the corners of her eyes, and then suddenly they pushed for real. Miriam started walking faster and faster until the walk became a run and then she was home. And at home, she stopped. She walked, slowly, through the front door without saying a word. She did her chores, her homework, ate her dinner, without saying a word beyond the usual pleasantries or pass the salt. No one said a word to her either. Everyone went to bed that night. Everything was fine.

# 9.

It began as simply as this. Miriam found Bird and said to him what he had wanted to say to her: It's about what I feel, Bird. And I would like to get to know you. Okay? I would like us to be friends. Okay? Bird said okay. He laughed and said okay and that day and every day after school Miriam would study for an hour in the library. This was two hours less than before, but enough to keep her grades decent and her parents quiet. Bird finished work at 3:30 and they would meet halfway down the block at the candy store where Bird would buy some small gift for Miriam: a chocolate bar, a soda, something, and the two would walk and talk for the next hour and a half. At six o'clock Miriam needed to rush home in time for dinner.

"They think I'm leading a small tutorial group at the library, so I can get away with staying late every day after school, but if I start missing dinner they're going to lose their minds. That's 'family time' my mother always says." Miriam was explaining this to Bird one afternoon. "And you know what's really stupid about the whole dinner thing?"

"What?"

"We don't really talk. The radio is always on or my mother's telling the latest church gossip, so we all wind up eating silently, chewing silently, not banging silverware. It's *so* stupid! You know what I mean?"

Bird nodded and then told Miriam about a brother he met in Vietnam who talked about how slavery still impacted Black people. "In slavery you just had to keep it moving, even when they snatched or killed your children. Had to do it to stay alive, to keep your other children alive," Bird whispered, though he hadn't meant his voice to fall into a whisper right then, or after, when he continued, "What's different when they come for your children now? They get one, you still got to look out for the others or they'll get them, too. That's why we don't *really* talk. We always got to keep it moving because if we ever stop to think about what's really going on, what we're really up against, we think it would kill us. Just might."

What Bird said made Miriam realize something else. She didn't know her parents, what they had faced in life, what struggles, what challenges. There must have been some; her mother was forever implying a memory bordered by hard times overcome. But who were they, her parents? Who was she? The words that came out of Bird's mouth felt like bullets, each one of them, but moving in slow motion, moving so you see where each one was going to hit. The girl, sixteen, almost seventeen, looked up at the boy too soon a man, blinked twice, and held his arm tighter. She thought of her family, she thought but did not say: He's right. This is how it is—even if your spirit cracks by what you've seen, what you've come to know, you just have to keep it moving. Pray the cracks don't spread.

≈

"Did you really have to kill people there?" Miriam asked this one day when she and Bird were walking slowly toward her house.

"Kill people? What do you mean?" Bird genuinely looked perplexed.

"I mean in Vietnam," Miriam clarified.

"I don't know how to answer that kind of question, Miriam,

you know? I mean it's hard. It's hard to think of it like that," Bird said this with his voice low down and sad. "I was at war and I did what I had to do *not* to be killed. That's what I did. And I didn't do no more than that. And believe me. There were plenty who did. That time in the jungle turned cats, I don't know. Cats over there . . . they acted different than they act over here. Even the most mild ones. But I swear to you. That place didn't take me all out of myself, all out of the way my grandmother raised me. I could say honestly, I only did what I had to do to survive. But I saw things—" Bird cut himself off.

And now the space between the two was dense and strange, unknowable and unclear. Still, Miriam felt she had no choice but to push. She wanted to know this man and so there was no other option but to ask, and then ask some more.

"What do you mean by that? That you saw things?" she ventured.

"Miriam," Bird said with a measure of frustration in his voice, "it's complicated, okay? And it's not pleasant."

"Were you scared all the time?"

"Yeah. I mean, I guess so. I guess. It's hard to remember what I felt there. Just surviving in that kind of way doesn't give you time to feel much of anything. Mostly I just remember thinking how it may be true that we ain't gonna get out of this life alive, but I didn't want to die so far away from home, so far away from my grandmother. So I wasn't really afraid. Well, I wasn't afraid of dying. If I was afraid, I was afraid of dying there. Dying alone, unnoticed."

Bird took a deep breath and looked at Miriam, who was rapt in his words. He continued, "One time this brother got shot," Bird said and then paused. "You want to hear this?"

"Yes. It's fine. Yes."

"Well, one time this brother got shot all in the neck and the medevac came and I helped get him on to the copter and there was blood coming from everywhere and it was going onto everything and I was telling the brother it was fine, he was going to be all right and I kept saying it so much that I think I convinced myself, because I really did feel shocked, and for a minute I couldn't even breathe when the brother died.

"I was holding him and talking to him, a living man in one second, and then he was dead and there was blood everywhere. And I couldn't find his tags. And the medics said, Okay, okay. You need to go back to your company soldier. The guy who died wasn't in my company. There were two companies in that area at that time. So I didn't know this brother's name, and I couldn't get to his tags. I just happened to be there when the bullets got him. And when he died he was just a body that had to be gotten off the field. A body to get sent home." Bird was shaking his head now, trying to deny the tears desperate to flow. He was lost, completely, awash in a sea of memories he could not escape, no matter what.

"The United States likes to act as though it honors their dead. But if it did, there'd be a whole lot more people alive. And that brother was young, so young."

"Like you," Miriam offered softly.

"Like me. And he died without a name."

"He had a name."

"But what was it? Even if they found it out later—I mean, I'm sure they did—what was it then, when he needed me to say it? Needed me to say, *Michael or John or Richard, or Paul. You got to fight.*" Bird looked away from Miriam, took a deep breath, and then looked back at her.

"That's why I didn't want to be away from my grandmother, away from home when I died. I didn't want to die without a name."

≈

*The rain is furious and everywhere, but he can only feel it. He cannot see it. He cannot see anything, but he knows he is not alone, because in this jungle you are never alone. A leaf the size of a towel flies out from nowhere and slaps against his face. He is startled, but stifles a gasp.*

*He just wants them to come out. Whoever they are. Come the fuck out and fight like a muthafuckin man, goddamnit. This is what he's thinking. He wants a fair fight. A fair chance to live. A fair chance to die.*

*He cannot stay still. Staying still feels like they will just encircle and kill him. If he is a target, let him be a moving target, right? He thinks this and then begins to move, but wait! Where's my company, he wonders? Paul? Junior? Big C? Where y'all at? Y'all leaving me out here with Charlie like this? Come on. Y'all my muthafuckas. Where y'all—oh my God. What the fuck is this? Mama!*

*In an instant there is light, but it is not the light of a clearing. It is the light of gunfire. Gunfire that has suddenly taken the heads off three of his closest friends who he is now tripping over in the dark wet unknown. He knows there is no time to mourn but at least their tags, he thinks, and reaches down toward the blood and hanging flesh that had once been Junior's head. He removes the tag and crawls over to Big C who no longer seems huge, or even average-sized. And this is when he feels it, the unforgiving press of metal against the side of his head. He does not look up, only straight ahead, and so he does not see the tiny, thirteen-year-old hand holding the automatic pistol. It is so quiet he can actually hear the trigger being squeezed into his right ear. He hears that, but not the brutal explosion.*

Bird wakes up from his dream and for several seconds he cannot figure out where he is. He can smell his own sweat, the terrible length of his own fear, but this is not the jungle, is it? Is it?

Bird switches on the light next to his bed, and his eye catches a T-shirt laying on the floor. It's the blue one with the white peace sign on the back. The way it's laying on the floor, sort of folded over, he can see only half of the symbol. Miriam had given this shirt to him. She gave it to him one day when something spilled on his shirt just as he was leaving work. "Hold on!" she'd said and run back to her locker. She had a big T-shirt in there that she was going to use for gym class the next day. "But you take it, baby," she'd insisted, shoving it into his hands.

Bird went into the men's room and changed into it. He had to admit, the shirt fit him nicely, left little to the imagination. Plus it worked well with his blue jeans. When Miriam saw him in it, she smiled, and later, for the first time, she asked him to kiss her. It was their first real kiss, sweet and messy and full.

And all at once as he lay there in his bed still wet with the memory of his recurrent nightmare, it came back to him: the gift and the kiss and of course his beautiful Miriam. She was there. He closed his eyes and could feel her there, with him, wiping his brow, making him believe that the coming day was going to be a good day. Bird's pulse slowed and his shoulders relaxed and eventually he allowed himself to lie back down. He was in a new place. He said this to himself. He said it and said it until he got tired of trying to convince himself. He closed his eyes and breathed in as deeply as he could, and tried as hard to quiet the chatter in his head. Some of it receded, but not all of it. Even in the best moments, that never happened. Would it ever happen?

# 10.

They spent every moment together that they could, Miriam and Bird, and now weeks and weeks had passed and the late October air broke against their backs. It was only 5:15 but already the day had lowered into dusk. The young couple was walking along the outside of the park, and Miriam pushed closer into Bird, holding on to his arm tight. Tight as though if she let go she would fall, or he would.

"You know what I love about you?" she half asked, half stated. "How you just say what you feel. How you just let it come out. Most of the time anyway. You just say what you want, what you dislike, what you love. You don't expect that from a man. You don't expect that, period."

Bird looked at Miriam and just smiled, just let her speak.

"I want to be like that, too," she said and meant it.

"Why aren't you?"

"I don't know. We're not like that. My parents, they don't encourage that kind of talking. It's almost like disrespectful, you know? I think if you say how you feel it's either considered complaining, not being grateful for your blessings, or else not being in control of your emotions. You know what I mean?"

"Yeah. I do."

"What about your parents?" Miriam asked. Bird had met her after class one day. "You only ever mention your grandmother.

But what about your mother and father?" It was two months now since they had met and he was walking her to the library when she suddenly brought the subject up, seemingly out of nowhere. When she did, Miriam sensed an extraordinary discomfort fall over them like some heavy tarpaulin.

Finally Bird said, "Well . . . it may seem strange for me to say this . . . to say it after what you just said about me. But my parents . . . that's one of those things that's hard for me to talk about. I mean, it's not a secret, but, you know, I wasn't raised by them. They're both dead. And you know. I just don't like to talk about it. But I will. Just not right now, okay?"

"Okay. Okay. That's fine. That's fine, baby," Miriam said, trying to use her voice as a comfort, a security blanket, a pair of open arms. Because between them, it was always about the talk. It was always about the way Bird shattered even the idea of silence, the notion that it was golden, godlike, some sort of virtue. So that in this singular moment when language either escaped or betrayed him, Miriam found it easy to understand, because she trusted completely this man of voice and reach and touch and reason. What else was there for her to do but what she did? Miriam smiled gently at Bird, and she took his hand in hers, and whispered, "Yes, baby. Another time."

The two held each other, there in the presence of whoever was walking past. They held each other as though they were alone in a world they had created together, a safe place. And that holding, that long and clear and definite embrace, it was unmistakable, more pronounced and lucid than any speaking could possibly have been.

# 11.

Bird never wanted to go to war. He didn't even want to join the service. What he wanted was a way out of the fire, and at sixteen, when he first began thinking about the army, he thought that the only way out of the fire was through the fire. There were men, men and boys he'd met, who had seemed so excited to carry big guns and troop through a country they had only just heard of a few years ago and kill people they didn't know. Even in the antiwar climate that had overtaken the country, Bird heard men say they were ready to go, the benefits they'd get later would be great. They were ready to do what they needed to do.

He never imagined, when he enlisted at seventeen, what it would be like after. Bird thought about training and he had thought about fighting. But he never thought much about the time after. Not once did he go beyond the vision that he could go to war and come back, sort of in the way you go and come back from the store, or down South. He actually thought that, because what other context did he have?

So finally he became comfortable with the idea of going to war, he accepted it. He told himself, if I go, and if I survive (and he was sure he would survive because that's all he'd ever done, survive), I can send my little money home to Mama, and I can go to college after and I can get a better job. He wanted to do, he had to do, better than his father did. He had to be nothing like his father. Bird wanted to make a difference, if not in the wide world then at least in his immediate world. A difference that brought joy to people's lives, a difference that brought calm.

But despite all of his desires, all of his wants and dreams, Bird was not greedy in his pursuit. He was a man who wanted simple things. A home that was safe. A home that had enough room inside of it for a whole family. And a yard with a willow tree right outside. A home where he could rest quietly with his family, and barbecue with his neighbors. Bird wanted a home he could call his own. He wanted that, and also the knowledge that neither he nor anyone in his family would ever feel the mean, dizzying spell of hunger, or the disquieting sense that everything might come apart in the very next second. He needed only those two things, and of course a wife and children who knew love more than they knew rage.

Bird believed that the army would help him achieve these things. He thought the army would help with school, help to position him. Never once did he imagine how he would come home to the nightmares, come home having seen things that twisted his brain and crashed against his soul. Bird did not know he would come home, but only halfway. And that no one would notice.

On the block they saw the boy now a man who survived a war, and old friends and neighbors would laugh and say, "What's happening, soldier?" They said it not knowing that, to Bird, the word *soldier* felt like a curse. But the people who didn't know him, the people who only saw his army ID, they did not see the man who survived a physical and spiritual firestorm. They saw a killer and rejected him. On job searches, Bird was met with near or blatant hostility. At department stores, in restaurants. He went to OTB, he went to grocery stores. No one was hiring and no one was helpful. Sometimes he wondered just what secrets they knew about him, what he carried in his eyes. He wondered how they could know if he never told, if even he could barely put together the days, the nights, the blood and violence, the begging and the screaming, the ripping and more. Things he could not think about.

But as soon as he wondered why he was being rejected, he let it go. He had to in order to focus on the problem at hand: Without a job, college was out. Even with the money he received as a vet, and even though the City University was tuition-free, the rising cost of living demanded that he be out there trying to bring something into the house. So Bird was, by some measure, grateful for the job at the school. At least it was something. But it wasn't enough, and he didn't want Mama out there working anymore. He had told her when he came home that as soon as he got a job, for the rest of her life, she'd never have to pay another bill. He meant it, with everything in him, he meant it. He meant to do right.

Before bed each night, Bird would pray and pray to God to help him do right. There had been so much wrong. From his father to the war, Bird wanted, he felt he needed, to make up for it all, not only for the wrongs he'd done, but for the wrongs he'd seen, the wrongs he'd turned away from. The wrongs that would come back when he closed his eyes each night.

They came like stalkers who could not be deterred. Some-times it was dead friends, but more often it was the screaming women and girls who called to Bird, the ones he saw all that year in Vietnam with their legs yanked, stretched brutally apart. Bird never touched any woman, any child, but he saw the attacks and did nothing. Even as the children and women called to him, to anyone. Even in a language he did not know, he understood a mother's cry. *Please. This is my child. She is only eleven years old. Please. We are people just like you.*

Bird walked with those voices. They called out to him, they

begged him, they demanded from him. When he was with Miriam, the voices generally backed away, let him have some of his own space. It was the way she trusted and looked up to him. It was her belief in him, in his future, in their future. Her faith backed down the voices when they made their advance.

In an effort to keep them from tracking him, from sobbing and wailing behind him, Bird responded with exercise and work. He worked hard at his job while also keeping constant watch out for a better-paying one, and every morning he would go for a long, hard run through the park. During that hour he would bargain with the voices. He would tell them what he wanted to do with his life, the good he would bring to people, the family man he would be, the worker. *Just give me a chance,* he would tell the voices, *and I will prove myself. I will get into school. I will become a lawyer. I will take care of my family. I will fight on the right side of a war next time. Just give me the chance.*

He made this request during each of those runs, and then he went home and cleaned himself up and made lists of what had to be done to move him and his grandmother into another reality.

≈

"I'm not going to work at that school forever, Miriam." Bird declared this as he walked Miriam toward her home.

"I know that."

"It's just that I have to do something to take care of my grandmother, and no one else was hiring. I mean, I went everywhere, Miriam. But I won't be there forever. I swear to God I won't."

"Bird, I know. I know, baby."

"I just want to say that," Bird paused, "because even though you don't say anything, this is what's going on: You're a top student. When you graduate, you're going to go to college and get a job and do something really incredible, and I don't want you to feel like you're stuck with some janitor."

Miriam smiled and tried to lighten the mood. "Planning on staying with me, huh?"

"Oh, ain't no doubt about that, girl. But listen, I'm serious. I want to tell you what I did this morning, why I came into work late today. I applied to the post office for a job because it pays so much more, plus it gives me good benefits. They weren't taking applications when I first came home, but I saw in the paper that now they are. So I applied. But that's not really the thing I want to tell you. I want to tell you what else I did."

"What?"

"I filled out my application for the City University. I'm going to go over it tonight when I get home, and then I'm going to mail it out."

"Really?" Miriam threw her arms around Bird. "My college man. I'm so proud of you, baby."

"Well, I haven't done anything yet."

"Yes, you have. You got started. A whole bunch of people never even do that. So let me be proud."

"Miriam," Bird began slowly, "Miriam, I love you. I really do. I love you."

They were two blocks from Miriam's house. Usually Bird didn't walk her this close to her home; the risk was too high of running into her parents. But with all that promise and possibility and the scent of a brilliant tomorrow informing both of their senses, neither one noticed exactly where they were. They only noticed the love that encircled and then lifted them, as though they were in the world but not of it—not of the hard times, not of doing without, not of the loneliness and persistent confusion. They were not of any of that. They were, right then, from a world of real security, clear paths, fast laughter, touching that is welcomed, encouraged even. Miriam pulled Bird aside, leaned up against a building and asked him to kiss her, which he did, and they traveled.

What brought them back was Miriam's mother's voice, a shocked and high-pitched call. She almost screamed,

"Miriam!"

And then her father, "Get your hands off my daughter!" Mr. Rivers yanked Bird away from Miriam. He grabbed his daughter, saying, "Get over here."

The Rivers had left a church meeting late and had been hurrying home to get food on the table before Miriam got home. They were stunned to see their good and innocent baby girl pressed up with some man who looked so much bigger and older than she. For sixty seconds that seemed like sixty minutes, all of them just stood there, not knowing what to say next. It was Bird who broke the miserable silence.

"Mr. Rivers, Mrs. Rivers," he began cautiously. "This is my fault—"

"I don't want to hear nothing from you!" Mr. Rivers was uncharacteristically bellowing. "I don't know who you are or how you got my child into a position like this, but I would advise you to be on your way. Or there *will* be consequences!"

"Yes, there will be!" Mrs. Rivers added angrily.

"Mama, Daddy, listen to me—" Miriam pleaded this, though she knew it was futile. When had they ever listened to her? Listening was not a parental requirement, they felt. Actions speak louder than words. Don't talk, just do. That's the life and way this family knew. Not a world of discussion and dialogue. Discussion and dialogue wasted time better spent just getting things done.

"Not a word, Miriam," said Mr. Rivers, in a tone that demanded obedience. "Come on." He pulled his daughter's arm and turned in the direction of their block. Miriam tried to look back at Bird, but her father yanked her away. Mr. Rivers walked quickly, forcing Miriam, whose hand he held, to nearly jog to keep up with him. Mrs. Rivers followed a few steps behind, like some last line of defense.

≈

At home, Miriam was told to wait in her room, which she did. She sat on her bed and tried to sort out what she felt. Guilt, fear, embarrassment—perhaps a combination of all of these lay in some crevice of her. But what she felt more than anything else was longing. That and love. It wasn't so different a feeling from the one she had every time she had to leave Bird and come into this house of no attachment or affinity. Whatever her parents intended on doing, whatever it was that they intended on saying, it could not overwhelm, it could not dismantle what existed between her and Bird. They were not stronger, her parents, not more compelling, and never could be. Miriam was resolute.

When they called her, told her to come down to dinner, Miriam smoothed her skirt and calmly descended the stairs, and as though nothing had happened, she sat down in her chair at the dining room table. She placed her napkin in her lap, and said softly, typically,

"Dinner smells good, Mama."

This normalcy, this regular tone in her daughter's voice, and those everyday words, infuriated Mrs. Rivers. It did not occur to her that Miriam was behaving exactly as she had been raised to behave. Mrs. Rivers opened her mouth to ask Miriam, How dare she?! Where did she learn this insolence?! But Mr. Rivers held up his hand to stop his wife, and turned to address his daughter.

"Young lady, do not sit there and behave as though things are normal. Everything has changed."

"Yes, Daddy." Miriam looked down and thought about how

things had indeed changed, how things were at this time last year. She thought then about all that was missing: a tomorrow she could look forward to, and be excited about. She thought about how she used to know days only in terms of their details. There was Bible study and meditation. Garbage out on Tuesdays and Fridays. Laundry on Saturdays. Ironing, grocery shopping, helping Mama prepare Sunday dinner. Nothing was wrong, but nothing was right. Nothing was bursting, bubbling. Nothing was a life that just *had* to happen.

Until now, until Bird. And Bird, who found and made magic with a simple walk through a park Miriam had looked at for years but had never seen. Bird, who sang to Miriam and laughed too loudly at his own terrible jokes. Bird, who would suddenly pick Miriam up and exclaim how good it was to be here in this place, with her. And where were they? Walking down the ramshackle streets that bordered the school. Waiting for a train to come amid the dirt and exhausted people and rats scurrying along the tracks. He was happy, excited because, he said, it wasn't the jungle and living was what he could see right there, in the reachable distance. Not death. That was all you could see ahead of you in the jungle—ahead of you, alongside you, behind you. Your death or someone else's. Despite all that made life back here in Brooklyn a struggle, despite days that sagged at their center, here Bird could always call himself back to hope, back to vision. He told Miriam so.

"Are you listening to me?!" Mr. Rivers's raised voice startled Miriam, who had cocooned herself in thoughts of Bird.

"I *am* listening, Daddy," Miriam responded with rare frustration.

"Do *not,* I repeat, *do not* take that tone with me. What is happening with you? How long have you known this character? I mean, my God. Your mother and I see you necking *in the street* with some . . . some animal—"

"He's not an animal, Daddy." Miriam barely got those words out, but when she did, her conviction was unshakable. And her parents knew it, her father knew it. Which is why, out of shock and fear and not having any idea of what else to do, Mr. Rivers slapped Miriam. He slapped her so hard that the imprint of his hand could be seen on her face, and her right ear was ringing. Mr. Rivers had never once, neither had Mrs. Rivers, slapped the girl. For several minutes all of them froze. Miriam didn't even cry out. She just looked straight ahead, and did not see her mother staring at her, trying to understand where her beautiful miracle child had gone.

Who was this new person sitting in her place? This rude and defiant person. This person who would kiss some man out in the street and speak back to her father. Mrs. Rivers was hurt, surprised, and confused, and her eyes were pleading with her child to *Come back. Come back, baby. The devil has you, but you're stronger than him. You can fight him, you can win. Come back. Come back to your mama and daddy and be who we raised you to be. Be perfect and respectful and polite. Come back.*

But Miriam did not see her mother's eyes. In truth, had she looked directly at her mother right then, she still would not have seen. All around her was Bird. Bird laughing and singing and thinking, out loud. Bird wondering and planning and dreaming and hoping, out loud.

Mr. Rivers finally broke the silence and said quietly, resolutely, "You may not live under this roof and carry on in any manner you choose. Do you understand that, Miriam?"

"I do." Then a pause. "May I be excused?"

Her father, who could not look at his child, whispered, "Yes. Yes. Go to your room."

Miriam rose—rose as if she was lifted and carried away, carried up to the room she had slept in all of her life. She knew what she wanted to do, and did not hear her mother saying,

"The devil got her, but he won't get her forever. You'll see. This gonna pass. You'll see."

≈

The night was divided, split at its center, as if in that one house there existed somehow two lands, two nations distant and different, populated with peoples of opposing cultures, languages, mores, gods. The moon, for example, its light fell wide and graceful through Miriam's curtains, while next door, in her parent's room, it nearly bristled, hesitated before slipping in.

Mr. and Mrs. Rivers lay stiff and awkward, each at opposite edges of their bed. What was there to say, to do about a child who was your miracle child, your good and perfect girl for seventeen years, a child who cooked and cleaned, who attended church, who obeyed her parents and did well in school, who did not involve herself in the messy and drug-crazed and gang-ruled so-called modern youth culture.

Where was their Miriam, where was *her* Miriam? Mrs. Rivers asked herself this, so did Mr. Rivers, though he was less concerned about that at the moment than he was still shocked by the slap. He had slapped his girl. How could he? Never once had he raised so much as a finger at that child. What evil, what huge otherworldly evil could have turned their lives around in a matter of hours? It was as incomprehensible to him as it was to his wife.

Slowly, mostly because they were more comfortable with not touching than touching, Mrs. Rivers slid over to her husband's side of the bed. Mr. Rivers felt the movement, but could not imagine that his wife was coming for him. She didn't do such things. He ignored it, tried to sleep, but there was no choice, finally, when Mrs. Rivers slipped her thick arm around his waist, and pressed into his back, but it was not sexual. It was desperate. Mr. Rivers understood this, and took her hand in his.

"Let's pray," he whispered, and they did. For God to send their daughter back to them.

*Come back, Miriam. Come back.*

But she was gone. Even as she lay there in her room next to their room, Miriam was gone. There was nothing to keep her there, really. That was the issue. There was nothing in this room to which she felt connected. This bed, those sheets, most of the clothes in her closet, that desk there in the corner, what of any of these items did she select? None. Her mother had done all the selecting. "You don't need to be worrying about these things, dear. You just do well in school, learn your scriptures, and manage your chores. I'll take care of the rest. It's what a mother's for."

Miriam knew her mother was well-intentioned, but here was the result. She had grown into a young woman who could not tell you what her favorite color was, what style of clothing she felt most comfortable wearing, if there were books beyond the Bible and academic texts she could get lost in. Miriam was a girl set aside from herself. She could see this now, this separation.

Really, she'd begun seeing it when Bird started seeing her, when he started reflecting her. He did it with his conversation and touch, with the openness of his ear and heart. Bird reflected her, and she could not lose that now that she knew how it felt to be seen. Seen as opposed to noticed only, a shadow in someone else's dreams. With Bird, Miriam had been seen fully and completely, and she had been heard. It was not a luxury so much as it was an absolute need. She could not lose Bird.

So there in that divided and split-down night, that night of no language or sound, Miriam was able to find a way to swell with imagination, with visualizations. She thought about how she could leave this place that had never been her place. About how she and Bird *could* really make it together, as a team. It would be hard, but Bird had been through war and survived. And as for her, she had been raised with her face down, low and on the ground. Raised, but without sky or length or width or light. And she had survived.

Surely they could make a life together. Miriam felt convinced of this. As difficult as it might be, they could build a clean, safe place, plant themselves in their own garden, paint a broad and colored landscape, climb inside and be, just be.

# 12.

The morning was cold and sullen everywhere except behind the bright hope of Miriam's eyes. Things could almost have seemed normal: the sound of the alarms at 6:00 A.M.; Mrs. Rivers rustling in the kitchen to prepare her husband's breakfast; Miriam ironing her dress and double-checking her school bag for homework assignments and books. It was the absence of greetings, of early fussing and light conversation, that gave it all away.

Mrs. Rivers would have said something if she could have conjured the words needed to reach her daughter. She did not know that that language was one she had never learned, and it was probably too late for her to learn it now. To learn it now required a complete submission, a letting go of all that was familiar and comfortable. Comfortable only because it was familiar.

Miriam needed her mother to talk with her about what loving someone who loves you back means. How it expanded you, made you bigger than the sum of your parts. How it encouraged you to take risks, to see wide and intricate patterns against the plain and retreating. But her mother could not have that conversation with her daughter, because for Mrs. Rivers, love had always been contained in the world of strict functioning, of chores and getting the work done. Why let it go now? This way of thinking, this way of being, had proved useful for all her life. It had provided a husband, a twenty-five-year marriage, a home and food, a child when the world had supposed motherhood was beyond her reach.

If there was an emptiness in this way of life, Mrs. Rivers could cover it with God and family dinners on Sunday, with respect from her community, or else jealousy. Anyway, who had ever said that there should be more? When people all around, her people, were hungry and jobless, when they had families violently broken, left jagged and bleeding, how was she to know that this life, this three-bedroom, two-bathroom, daily-bread, quiet life wasn't in fact a miracle?

She could not know, and so she could not see, what her child was missing. She could not even see that her child felt something was missing. Even as Miriam moved through the house that morning, and made her cereal, and softly said good-bye as she walked out of the door, Mrs. Rivers could not fathom the hole in her daughter's soul. She certainly could not imagine that Miriam was headed out to fill that empty space at whatever cost.

This is what she told Bird when she saw him at school that day. That he filled in the missing place. After Miriam told him the details of the fight, she told him she really was not upset by it. It just made things clear for her: where she wanted, where she needed, to be.

"I'm going to ask you something," Miriam began, "and you can say no if you want, and I won't be angry, okay?"

"Okay. Just ask."

"Well," Miriam began nervously, "I'll never be able to see you if I stay there, with my parents. They're going to start monitoring me. I know they will. They didn't have to say I should be home immediately after school, because it's absolutely expected. I know them. They'll take me away from you."

"What are you getting at, Miriam?"

"The thing is this." Miriam stopped herself again. What if he said no?

"Just ask," Bird pushed, though gently.

"I was thinking maybe I could come stay with you." There. It was said. And then she added, "I'll get a job on weekends. I'll help with the bills and everything. I promise. I don't expect—"

"Just pack up and come on," Bird interrupted her. "My grandmother will love having another woman around. Just come on."

~

It was after dinner now and Miriam sat in her room. It could have been the first, rather than the last time she would sit here. It was not her place and never had been. Nothing here belonged to her, and here, she belonged to nothing. Not to the newly painted pale yellow walls, or the gold-colored cross hanging over her bed. Not the dresses there in her closet. All part of another person's life.

Miriam looked around and wondered what she should pack, what was worth taking. Her heart raced, and she broke into a smile. It surprised her, the smile, as did the tears that fell when she packed her school bag with underwear and four dresses, a pair of black slacks and two T-shirts. Her bag looked stuffed, but she could slip out tomorrow morning without her mother noticing.

Miriam got up from her bed and opened the drawer where she kept the shoe box filled with the savings she'd collected from years of baby-sitting. Three hundred and two dollars. Enough to get started. She shoved the money into the bottom of her bag and climbed into bed, and was nearly asleep when her mother knocked and then came into her room.

"Miriam, are you asleep yet?"

"No, Mama."

Mrs. Rivers turned on the light, and said, "Listen, I want to talk to you."

"Yes, Mama?"

"Look. None of us like what happened the other night. Your father feels very bad about slapping you, and I imagine you must feel bad about putting him in that position. But you have to understand who you are, Miriam." Mrs. Rivers paused, and her voice cracked.

"You are a child who they said would never get here. Everyone, even your father, had given up, except me. I always knew you would come. And when you did, I made a promise to God and to myself that I would protect you and keep you and raise you so you could get through this life, not only safe, but with some measure of comfort. I felt I had a greater responsibility to do this, because it felt like you were handed to me so . . . so delicately.

"And so if there are times when I've seemed strict it's because I know what's out there in this world to get a young girl in trouble. And I knew I had this duty to keep you from it. There's a lot of bad in this world, Miriam, and I've tried to shield you from it, so I know you don't understand. You don't understand the ways of men. What they'll take from you. I'm not blaming you for what happened with that boy the other day. But you listen to me, girl, you have to stay clear of him. He's no good. He'll just take from you, and trick you into thinking he's giving. That's how they do. And in the end you'll wind up becoming a woman no one wants. Who no one respects. Can you understand what I'm saying to you, Miriam?"

The girl looked at her mother, and took a deep breath. "I love him, Mama."

Frustrated, angry even, at this response, Mrs. Rivers said, "You only think you do! You better love God. You love God first. And when you do, you know how to behave, how to act. And it's not necking with some . . . some *nigger* out in the street like you're somebody's fast woman. I won't have it. You were raised by God-fearing people in a good and Christian home. This is not the way we behave. You hear me? You better love God first."

"I understand, Mama," Miriam whispered. Her mother sat there at the edge of the bed for long minutes and then stood up, admonished her daughter to think about what she had told her, and turned to leave. Then quite suddenly Mrs. Rivers did something she'd never once done before. She looked her daughter squarely in the face and said, "We love you, Miriam."

Miriam stared at her mother, not knowing what to say, so she just nodded and whispered, "Okay, Mama." After Mrs. Rivers left the room, Miriam did think about all her mother had said. She thought about what it meant to love God, to walk in God's light, to walk in accordance with God's will. She wondered what love meant to her mother, to her parents, what loving their child meant. And then she thought about the voices and truths she had uncovered with Bird. She thought about how her heart beat more clearly since knowing him, how she smiled more, and laughed more, and was more patient with people. How she saw life in every sidewalk crack now, even in the dull eyes of the dope fiends on the corner. She saw life in even them, and since knowing Bird, when she walked past them, she remembered to pray for their return. In the months of knowing and loving Bird, Miriam found that there was more of herself to give to herself, and to the world. She was just not willing to stifle that giving. Truly, she was not able to.

The next morning when she prepared to leave, Miriam felt no longing, no lament. Half of her felt numb, half felt excited. She wrote a two-line note that said simply:

*I chose not to stay under your roof. I love this man. I'm sorry that this is the way things worked out. Your daughter, Miriam.*

She left the note on her pillow, and quickly said good-bye to her mother. It occurred to her on the way to school that she had not exchanged a word with her father in two days. It saddened her for a moment but in no way stopped her. She did not, in fact, think about it again. Not as she sat through her suddenly boring classes, or at lunchtime, and certainly not after school when Bird met her at the corner, and said he'd spoken to his grandmother, who said that she was looking forward to meeting Miriam. Who and what she was leaving only came back to Miriam in the moment when Bird looked down at her backpack, puzzled, and asked, "Is that all you have?"

"Yeah. That's it. Come on. Let's go home." It was a Friday, and all Miriam wanted was to rush into her new life.

# 13.

Miriam was shaking as she and Bird entered the small apartment he shared with his grandmother. And his grandmother, whom he called Mama because when he was small he could remember his own mother calling her Mama, and because it was one of the only things he could still remember his mother saying.

So grandma was Mama to him because it comforted, because she comforted. Even against her thin and wiry frame, she comforted. Even across her serious countenance: comfort. The comfort that came from a woman committed to family and children; Mama had raised more babies than she'd ever given birth to. But she never thought of it in this way. She never thought of it in any particular way, except here were people in need and here was her hand. It's what you are supposed to do. That's what she said.

And that patience was a virtue, and love a requirement. Mama, who loved and who welcomed and who questioned little, who accepted a lot, who at times laughed too loud, who usually drank gin and soda on Saturday with Mrs. Roberts, and who went to church every Sunday, "whether rain or sleet or aching feet." Mama, who quoted the Bible, Moms Mabley, and Bessie Smith. Who, after her husband left, kept a man friend until last year when "that no good cullud man up and died on me. All I did for him. Just up and died on me. If he had took care of hisself the way I tried to tell him, he'd be here right now. Probably getting on my nerves. But here."

Yes, Mama, with her hair still long enough to be braided down to the middle of her back, though she never let it hang that way. (She braided it, and then twisted the braids together into a bun that sat like a big wildflower on the back of her head.) Mama, with her fast eyes, and teeth all her own. This was the woman who looked at scared little Miriam and nearly commanded her to "Come on in here, girl. Let me have a look at the child my Bird has got hisself all turned around for."

Miriam stepped into the small railroad flat apartment. She could see from one end of it all the way to the other since Mama had been cleaning and all the doors were left open. In one instant the apartment smelled like just-baked bread, in another it smelled like ammonia. But all around, it felt like home.

Mama looked at Bird and said, "Well, she certainly pretty."

"Thank you, ma'am," Miriam said shyly, looking at the floor.

"Look up, girl. Go through life looking down you gonna wind up walking into a whole bunch of unseen trouble." Mama laughed as she said this, but Miriam followed the instruction, and Mama continued softly, "Listen, don't look so scared. You're welcome here, so it's no need to be shy. You're welcome here."

"Thank you," said Miriam, still trying to find her space in this home.

"I'm gonna go put Miriam's things in my room," said Bird, picking up the one bag, which Mama looked at and furrowed her brow, wondering why the girl hadn't brought more things. But she didn't say a word and Bird headed through the narrow living and dining room space, through Mama's bedroom, and into the back room where he, and now Miriam, would sleep.

Mama, still sensing Miriam's nervousness, guided the frozen young woman by the hand over to the sofa. "Sit down, baby. Let me tell you something. And I'm old, so you got to let me preach a little bit. It's what people do when they get my age, okay?"

"Okay," agreed Miriam, nodding her head and smiling lightly.

"What I want you to know is that I learned a long time ago that family isn't always who you're born to. It would be nice, but it's just not the way things often turn out. It turns out that family is who you take into your heart. Sometimes it ain't got nothing to do with blood. Sometimes blood less of family than a person you meet for the first time. You understand what I'm saying?"

"I do," said Miriam, really understanding. Mama continued, "Bird tells me he loves you. He tells me you love him. So to me, that makes us some kind of family. I don't know if that's right or wrong. I only know it works for me thinking like that. So what I would like is just for you to get comfortable, and get settled. If you're uncomfortable and unsettled, this whole house is gonna be that way. And this apartment is too small for that."

"I understand. I do," Miriam said in a voice just above a whisper.

"All right." Mama paused, and then, "I made some dinner. When we sit down to eat, we can talk about how we all can make things work around here."

"Thank you, ma'am."

"Mama. You not gonna live here and address me like I'm a stranger."

"Mama," Miriam said, correcting herself. Bird, who had come back in the room, smiled and told Miriam to come, to see the apartment, to see the room they would share. Rising, Miriam glanced around the living room. The walls were once-upon-a-time-white walls that had, over the years, slid down into a color with no name. The sofa was fading and brown, but nevertheless dressed up with a beautiful orange caftan thrown across its back. But the winding deep green ivies hanging in each of the two front-room windows—they sang color and life into what could have been a dying space. The hi-fi system and television set sitting in the center of the living room notwithstanding, everything here was old, but everything here seemed to have meaning, a story and time attached to it.

Here, Miriam determined, would be home. She felt sure of that, especially when she entered Bird's room, which was virtually empty. There was a bed, a desk, a lamp, and a dresser. Just the basics. It was as though he was waiting for her to come in, to insert herself into corners, attach herself to walls. Yes, this would be home. Miriam ran her hand over her bag, touched the bed, turned to Bird, and kissed him gently on the cheek.

"Thank you, Bird. Thank you so much. I love you," she murmured.

"I love you, too." Bird took Miriam by the hand and the two headed back out to have dinner with Mama.

≈

Miriam was a virgin, and she told Bird so as soon as they had changed and gotten into bed. She wore one of his black T-shirts, curled herself into his arms, and said matter-of-factly, "I'm a virgin, Bird."

"What are you telling me that for?" Bird asked, surprised more at the timing than at the admission.

"Well, I mean . . . obviously. Look. Here we are in your bed. I asked to be here. You didn't drag me. So I know that it has to have sent some kind of message."

"And what message is that?"

Miriam sucked her teeth at Bird, and exasperated, she declared, "You know! That I want to have sex."

"That's the message you think you sent me?"

"Of course it is!"

"Well, I thought that the message was that you wanted to get away from your parents. But since you brought it up, let me go ahead and ask. Do you want to have sex?"

Bird smiled and nuzzled closer into Miriam, who didn't say anything in response to his question. She just let him hold her and tried to vanish into the embrace. Bird did the same. As much as he wanted to touch her everywhere, every way, no part of him, not his mind or his hands, would have allowed him to pressure that girl. He loved her. And in the face of that love, he was so grateful for whatever she gave, that to ask for more would have been greedy. It would have been something close to sinful. He would not do it. He just smiled, an honest, from the inside out smile, and held his Miriam, and they lay like that for so, so long, an hour at least, until Bird started drifting off to sleep, and as he did Miriam whispered,

"Yes."

≈

They move slowly into making love, almost gingerly. He begins by licking her lips, by sucking them. She pushes against him. She kisses him back. She uses her fingers and tongue to play with his mouth. She loves him and says it. Then she says it again. I love you, too, he says. I love you, too. He says it slower the second time.

Her hands slip behind his neck. She is holding his face to hers. Their eyes are open. They want to see each other. He slips the T-shirt up over her head. He pulls her on top of him, and this is when he suddenly feels it.

With their skin touching like this, touching without encumbrance, he feels the mean accumulation of his memory begin to shrink to a manageable size, a size he can at last ignore, and now he is coming back to the man he was always supposed to be.

The man before the losses, before the violence, before the guns and the grenades, before the explosions and the burials, before all the things that could never be explained or understood, only lived with. Against her, he is home. The home that only ever existed in the deep night of his dreams. The home of his prayers and tears. He is there, with her, and free.

She is, too. And no, she did not have the violence. She did not know bones scattered across the years. Scattered and making it impossible to walk casually. She did not have that the way he did. But what she had were wide craters. Holes where imagination should have been. Holes where a filled-out childhood should have been. A childhood bigger than a single square block, a church pew, gold-starred quizzes, and very proper manners.

Even at her young age she could sense that there was something she had left behind. Something lost or forgotten in a rush to get done all the things that the day required. She knew her own life should have felt more relevant.

Never before did she feel who she was, that the truth, the center of her, was vital, was the pulse and breath of a thing.

Until now. There was no one else who could be here and bring him what she was bringing him. As scared and unsteady and clumsy as she was this first time making love, she knew this. She knew it. And the same was true for him. No one else could touch her and make it matter. Touch her and make it whole. These two who were young, hungry, scared, secretly hopeful, tentatively passionate, and indisputably in love—they were there in each other's arms, and they rocked themselves into freedom, momentary as it was. And somewhere far away both of them suspected this—that complete freedom was always momentary, but what else could they, what else could anyone do?

Without hesitation, they took the gift that was there before them, and stretched it out far as they could. They savored it, rolled it beneath their tongues, held it between their teeth. And the taste of it, the taste of them, lasted for such a very long time.

≈

In the wake of their love, their come home together, eat, share a bathroom and bed together, accept bad moods and revel in silly ones, in the wake of this all day, and everyday love, the other parts of Miriam's life became minimally important. She still attended school, and she still did well, but it wasn't exciting anymore. Her grades, which had been slipping, slipped even further. The onetime honor student was now a steady C student. Teachers pulled her aside, asked if everything was all right, Miriam assured them it was. She assured them she'd get her grades back up. No one asked again after that.

What was exciting to Miriam was the talk of one day marrying Bird and having children with him. It felt bigger than school, than college, than a career, than anything. Miriam wanted to create, and she told Bird so, a home like the home she had never had. She wanted a warm and welcoming place. A place of good smells and running conversations. Miriam would tell Bird about this, about the life she wanted them to live, and he would agree but argue that she still ought to go to college. "Just so you can know things," he would say, and Miriam would give him a halfhearted nod. She'd say, "I know. And I'm not telling you I won't go. I'm just asking if there's something wrong with making a career out of family?"

"No, baby. There's nothing wrong with that."

Their conversations went like that, a sort of back and forth, but not really arguing. Miriam hated arguing. More often than not they'd just delve further, deeper into the details of how they would make their dreams come true.

Then there were times when Miriam missed her parents, when she even picked up the phone to call her mother. Several times she thought she saw her mother across the street from school, but whoever it was disappeared so quickly, Miriam could not be sure. But at the end of each day, Miriam was too afraid of losing this good and close feeling she had with Bird, this good and close feeling she had with herself. A relationship with her parents, she was certain, would ruin it all, would separate her from all that had come to bring her joy. She never did call.

Neither did they. Not that the Rivers had a phone number for Miriam or even knew where she was living. But they didn't go to the school each day and demand their daughter come back home. They did not want her home if it meant she was not going to be the person they had raised her to be. When people asked, as they eventually did, Miriam's parents lied. They told people that Miriam had moved in with a sick relative across town. "She's needed more there than here," they lied. Everybody commented on what a wonderful girl Miriam was. "Yes," her mother said, and pretended to smile.

Later, when rumors of Miriam living in sin with some man began to creep through the congregation—thanks to Joan, Miriam's one confidante who did not keep secrets well—no one had the courage to confront the Rivers. No one wanted to deal with the fallout of such a confrontation. It was easier to believe the lie. So they all did, even the Rivers. They lied so often about where their daughter was that after a time they started to believe it.

Joan told Miriam what her parents were saying about her whereabouts. Miriam shook her head, and said simply, "If that works for them, fine. I'm trying to make my life work for me."

"What's it like living with a man?" Joan wanted to know. "I mean, it's like being married. But you're not."

"Well, we want to get married—" Miriam began.

"He asked you!" Joan exclaimed.

"Well, no, not formally. But we talk about it all the time."

Embarrassed by Joan's question and her own anticlimactic response, Miriam started explaining the details of their every-day reality—the money struggles, the need to find a place that was big enough for all of them. "This place is okay, but it's a little tight, and we want to get a house." Miriam continued on and on, until Joan, bored by a conversation that was no longer sexy or edgy, said she had to go. "I just wanted to let you know what your parents were saying."

"Thanks."

Joan laughed and added, "You and Bird ought to come to church Sunday and shake everyone up."

Miriam laughed, too, at the ridiculousness of the suggestion, but suddenly was overcome by sadness. "How is everybody? At church? Everyone's okay?"

Joan sensed the sadness in Miriam's voice. "Everyone's okay," she responded with unusual pathos. Then, she thought to lie, and added, "Your parents *do* seem to miss you, Miriam."

Miriam didn't respond to that statement. She didn't know how. Did she miss her parents? She didn't know what she felt about them. She couldn't find those feelings, even now as she wanted to. What came to mind was that they were gone and her mother always told her that you can't go forward trying to look back. "I'll talk to you some other time, Joan. Bye."

# 14.

One month to the day after Miriam moved in with Bird, things began to shift. Miriam noticed it immediately, a reversal in energy had taken place, but, she thought, this is just a bad night, just a few bad days, just a bad week. She was not worried, and she did not say a word. She continued to go to school, help Mama with dinner, straighten up the apartment, tell Bird she loved him.

But Bird had begun spending hours and hours searching the want ads for jobs he could not get; increasingly they were asking for college degrees. He would lose whole evenings trying to stretch money, adding up the same few dollars. His frustration turned to silence. More and more he retreated into himself, not answering Miriam when she said she loved him, not making dinner conversation, not smiling. Miriam understood his mood, and thought, *Just be patient. We'll get past this.*

Then one evening Miriam heard Bird slip into the apartment. It was late, after dinner. In the time she'd lived with him, Bird hadn't ever come home after dinner. But on this night, Bird slipped wordlessly into the apartment; indeed, had it not been such a tiny space, he might have gone unheard. As it was, he was seen only from the sofa where Miriam sat reading—in an effort to be supportive—the want ads in the newspaper. She looked up at Bird and saw his face slick with anger. Again.

Miriam's inclination was to say nothing to Bird; people, she knew, were easy to temper when they looked like this. But she just could not stand to ignore this man anymore, this man whom she loved so deeply, this man who had seemed so different, so vexed, for the last several days now. She said softly, simply, "Hey."

"Hey," Bird responded, and rolled hot and tight toward the back of the house. Mama looked out from the kitchen where she had been preparing dinner: brisket, rolls, string beans, and salad. "Bird come in?" she asked Miriam.

"Uh-huh," Miriam nodded, glancing at the old woman. "Didn't look too happy though."

"That's his way these days. Don't pay him no mind."

"Why do you think so, Mama? He doesn't talk to me." Miriam hesitated and then found the courage to ask the next question, "You think it's me? That he doesn't want me here anymore?" Miriam was terrified of what her answer might be.

"Oh no, baby. No. He been like this before. You just haven't known him like that. He was like that when he first came home and couldn't find no job. So that's probably what it is now. Something about a job." Mama held her eyes on Miriam. "Go talk to him. You'll see."

"I don't want to talk to him when he's like this. He doesn't want to talk and I don't want to make him madder."

"Don't pay that sour face no mind. Go talk to him. That boy loves you. May take him a minute, but he'll talk."

Miriam considered Mama's words. She knew that somebody was going to have to speak to Bird. Somebody was going to have to find out what was happening with him and figure out a way to change his mood. And that somebody was Miriam. It was her job now to help sort that man out. This is what you do when you're part of a couple, Miriam thought. She nodded at

Mama, took a deep breath, and slowly headed toward the bedroom, where Bird was lying on their bed with his eyes closed.

"Baby . . . ?" she ventured.

"Not now, Miriam," Bird growled low after an awkward pause. "Not now," he repeated.

"Baby, please. What's going on? I can't stand to see you like this."

"Guess what, Miriam? This isn't about you. Can you get past yourself for a moment?"

Miriam ignored the dig, and moved cautiously closer to Bird.

"If something bothers you, it bothers me. If you tell me, maybe we can fix it together."

"Listen, that's not possible," Bird barked, and then continued, softer, "I know you're trying to help, but it's not the kind of problem you can help with."

"But don't keep it from me, Bird. We're a couple. Don't pull away because things are rough. That's when it's most important for us to work together." Miriam pleaded through her eyes at Bird to, please, baby, open up, come to me, baby, please.

Bird leaned his head back against the wall behind their bed. He began to speak in a voice that was at once both sapped of emotion and sagging from the weight of it. "The post office had stopped taking applications. Because I had worked late that day at the school . . . for *no real damn money* . . . I went the day after I told you to turn in my application. But the cut-off date was the day before. I didn't realize that. Not even then. I had just dropped my application off in this place they had set up for it and left out. So when I went back today to find out when they would be calling people, they looked up my application and told me that it was handed in too late, and mine was being sent back to me."

"But, Bird, if they were hiring before, then they'll be hiring—"

"Miriam! We need money now. I want to move us out of this apartment. I want to start saving money so I can go to school, so you can go to school."

"I told you I was going to get a job, too. Soon as I graduate. College can wait."

"No. No. I don't want to hear that! You didn't leave your parents' house so you could live worse. You left so you could be free. You think you're going to feel free cleaning toilets some damn place like I do?" Bird paused, but before Miriam could respond, he started talking again.

"You won't. So don't try to act like you will. Your parents may have held you back in a lot of ways, but they provided for you in ways most Black folk only dream about. I'm not going to do worse by you. And I want my grandmother to live out the rest of her life in peace. I can't do that cleaning toilets or pulling gum off of desks."

Miriam thought she saw tears forming in the corners of Bird's eyes, and then she thought she was wrong.

"You know, I don't want to be the damn king or something. I just want my fair share. I just want a chance to take care of my family."

"I understand. But, baby, even if we have to sacrifice a lot now, it doesn't mean it's going to be forever. And believe me when I tell you what a family needs is about more than material things," Miriam said, struggling to make each word she spoke relevant. "Like you said, look at my family. We had material things, but I would have traded it all for someone to talk to me. You and I are further along than a whole lot of other people. I'd be here for the rest of my life before I ever went back to my parents' house."

Bird, lost in his own anger, continued, ignoring Miriam's earnest proclamation.

"I went in the damn jungle for this damn country. I'm saying—how much more sacrifice am I supposed to make? But you know what else? On top of all this shit with work and money, you know what else I have to deal with?"

"What?"

"The fucking police. I got stopped by these pigs when I was coming home today."

"What?" Miriam was taken aback.

"Yeah. Again! I *told* you they do it all the time to brothers. And I'm not saying they should harass anybody, but I know I do my best not to be looking like I'm just standing on the corner slinging, you know?" Miriam stared at Bird as he paused thoughtfully. He went on, "I ever tell you why I stopped with the jeans and T-shirts, and started carrying that stupid briefcase and trying to look nice when I'm just going to clean toilets?"

"No."

"So I don't have to *feel* like a nigger who don't do shit but clean toilets. I mean, I'm not above doing what I have to do to take care of my people. That's why I took that job. But I didn't want to . . . like . . . become that. You know how some people become their jobs, even though their jobs are shit? They always look like they about to a clean a car or scrub a toilet. No matter where they're at—they could be at a damn wedding looking like a janitor.

"And I didn't want to feel that or be that. So I decided to try to dress and walk the way I feel inside. And inside I feel like someone who's going to be a professional, an attorney, a person who changes the laws and people's lives."

"I do understand that, baby. I do. But what happened with the police?"

Bird began to shake his head. "They rolled up on me as I was walking from the train station. I saw them, but for some reason it didn't really occur to me that I was the one they were about to hassle. I don't know why I didn't realize it. They've bothered me so many times before. But I was surprised this time." Bird stopped for a moment. No matter how many times he'd been stopped and frisked by the police, it never got easy, never felt routine. He began speaking again in a tone that shook from the center of his being to the top and back all the way down.

"So they told me to get on the wall. And I tried to ask what was up. I even told them I was a vet, what was the problem? Before when they've stopped me, they've just asked for ID, where I lived, that type of thing. I thought if I tried to reason with them, tried to say who I was, that I wasn't out here slinging no drugs, just a vet trying to work, they'd back off. But they told me to shut the fuck up and get on the motherfucking wall.

"And one of them had his hand on his pistol. He told me to hand over my briefcase. I did. I couldn't see but I heard them open it, go through it. There wasn't anything in there but a few old newspapers. They threw the briefcase down, and said, 'All right. This time.' And then they got back in their car and drove away."

Anger creased Bird's face, and Miriam's as well. Small tears of rage fell down her cheeks.

"Miriam, please. Don't start crying now. It's about the last thing I can deal with."

"I'm . . . just . . . so . . . mad," she sputtered, wishing she could order the tears back into her eyes, back down into her gut.

Ignoring her, Bird continued, "You know what was the worst thing of all?"

"What?"

"All them kids on the block seeing this whole thing happen. They always see it when it happens. It is *so* humiliating,

Miriam. I mean I *know* these people here. I grew up here. Some of them boys who saw what happened tonight, I knew their mamas when their mamas were damn near babies."

Miriam furrowed her brow, wondering how she could make things better. Bird, lost in his anger, succumbing to his hurt, railed on.

"I'm supposed to set some kind of example," he said, and then his own tears pushed for real, but he did not care. "You know what I mean? It's so many of the brothers who died in the jungle. They got babies back here left behind. Like the brothers who are locked down, or dope fiends. They got babies left behind. So I'm trying so hard to be something different. An example to a whole bunch—"

Bird's voice failed him, and for two or three minutes the young couple sat there, the reality of their lives a dark and heavy shroud over their shoulders, over the muscles in their arms, the curve of strength in their backs.

They just sat there until Bird hissed, "Let me tell you something. That's why I admire the Black Liberation Army. I know people say they're just a gang, that they're crazy. But if you ask me, the damn police are a gang. And who's going to back them down? Why do they get to do whatever the hell they want with no penalty? Brothers get penalized for walking down the damn street, but they never have to feel *nothing?* It's not right. And even though I'm not supposed to feel this way, and even though I don't like to think of myself, Vietnam aside, as a violent man, I swear every time I hear the BLA took one of those pigs out, I don't feel bad. I don't feel bad at all."

"Listen," Miriam said softly. "You're angry now. And you have a right to be. But, Bird, don't make the police change you into sounding like some kind of criminal, like some kind of bitter, crazy person."

"You really think that's how I sound?" The tone in Bird's

voice was almost menacing. His face folded into a deep frown.

"No, no. I'm not saying that," Miriam stuttered. "I didn't mean it like that. I'm just saying—"

"What, Miriam? What are you saying?"

"I'm saying that I agree that the police don't treat you right, and they're allowed to get away with it a lot. But we don't win by becoming like them. By becoming killers. That's all."

"We *don't* win? Are you really, *really* sure about that? I just came back from war. Wasn't nobody talking then about not killing people. Wasn't nobody in the jungle talking about peace. Far as I'm concerned, this is the damn jungle, too. It's just that there's no trees here, and here, niggers are the enemy."

"That may be true, Bird, but you also said that the war was wrong."

"Because I didn't agree with the principles of it. But don't misunderstand me, Miriam. I believe in fighting for what's right. And I believe I have a right to walk down my damn street without being harassed. Without feeling like if I turned around, if I said anything, that pig would have did me right there. Smoked me in front of those little boys across the street. And if it's the only thing that's gonna make them understand that I deserve respect, then I'm glad there's a BLA."

"Bird . . ." Miriam touched his hand. She knew there really wasn't anything she could say with him feeling as enraged as he did, so she just tried to listen.

"Let them keep fucking with me, and I'll be a Black Liberation Army by my goddamn self. And believe me, they'll be humble then."

"Dinner!" Mama called out from the front of the apartment. "Come on, y'all." Miriam looked squarely into Bird' eyes. She wanted to see what he saw, and exactly the way he saw it. More than that, though, she wanted to see her beautiful and gentle Black man again.

No matter how hard she stared at Bird, in the hours after he returned from the post office, in the hours after the police, his face was blurred. And the radiant colors she once saw as the two of them were slipping off the canvas, melting into an amorphous dark in the cold December night.

≈

The wish was simply for consistency. For days and times that could be predicted, anticipated, and planned. There were moments when Miriam thought she would be happier even if the struggle to survive and be content was made somehow more complex; complexity would be fine as long as it was consistent, as long as she could expect what was coming around the corner. But the life she was living, the life she and Bird and Mama were living, was characterized by resounding hope one day and near absolute despair the next.

It was Bird, really. He was unhappy and unsettled. He could not make sense of the challenges, the obstacles he faced on a daily basis. There were times, and he would say as much, that he practically wished he was back in the jungle. "At least there I knew I was supposed to be looking out for an enemy. Here, the enemy looks like a friend. Smiles and tells me he's so sorry, no jobs available. Then behind my back he whispers, 'Not for that nigger.'"

"Maybe there really isn't anything open, Bird."

"Miriam, please. I see the signs in the window, read the ads in the papers. I call. Something's always available until I walk through the door. You have to stop being blind to the kind of world we live in."

"I'm not being blind," she protested. "It's just hard for me to believe that they can't see what I see in you. You're so brilliant. Such a hard worker. And it shows, baby."

Bird sat quietly, frowning, his eyes closed.

"I know there's racism," Miriam offered, trying to let him

know she was on his side. "And I know it's hard right now. But if it takes a long time, then it just takes a long time. I'm not going anywhere. I believe in you and us."

"Right," Bird responded, sounding emptied out.

Not knowing what else to say, what else to do, Miriam kissed Bird on his forehead. "I love you," she murmured as she kissed all down his face, then down his neck. Miriam looked at Bird squarely in the face and smiled, though slightly.

Bird did, too.

He pulled Miriam to him, pulled her onto his chest, wet her face with his mouth, and whispered over and over, "Yeah. Yeah."

They rose then, in those instants, they ascended. The two left the Earth entirely, left behind the memories, the pain, the losses. They needed, in these moments, nothing. Not food or water or a new job or social change or anything. Or anyone. But each other: the touch and vision and belief and absolute grace of each other. If only they could live there. Both Miriam and Bird thought this as they began making love, while they made love, after they made love. If only they could live in the place above the harsh and dirt; the place beyond cold and disregard. If only they could live in the place of equity and embrace, and divination and forever.

But it did not happen, it could not happen, that sort of permanent escape, and so they went ahead and along, hobbling and hoping. They went along loving each other, but struggling. Dreaming but also afraid to dream.

# 15.

Even before she went to the clinic for the test, Miriam knew she was pregnant. For years she'd heard in detail from her mother about the symptoms, and so when her period didn't come, plus she was devastatingly tired, plus she felt unusually cranky, plus she was continually nauseous, there was no question in her mind about what was going on.

Had there been any questions, Mama set them aside one morning as Miriam sat across from her at the breakfast table. Bird had left very early that morning to go for his usual long run around the park. It was just Miriam there with Mama—two women suddenly a family, but each still largely unknown to the other.

There were big pockets of awkward silence between them as each woman tried to think of something to say. Finally it was Mama who was watching as Miriam's eggs and toast got cold. Mama was thinking about how funny Miriam's mood had been the last two weeks, how sleepy she'd been, how different her diet had been. Mama was remembering her own daughter once sitting across this very same table when she was pregnant with Bird, moody and unable to eat.

"What's happening with you, girl? Seem different this morning. You all right?"

"I'm all right, Mama. Maybe just a little under the weather."

Mama stared at Miriam until the girl looked away, and then she said it, Mama did, "When your cycle due?"

"What?" Miriam was shocked. Her voice shook.

"You heard me."

"I . . . I think . . . umm . . ." Miriam was nearly stuttering.

"Girl, don't stutter. When your cycle due?"

"It was due. Before."

"Before when, girl? Don't play with me."

"About ten days ago, Mama." Tears began to roll down Miriam's face. She was trembling in her seat. Mama got up from her chair and walked over to the one next to Miriam. She turned Miriam's face toward her own, held her hand, and over and over murmured, It's okay. It's okay. When Miriam calmed down, Mama led her over to the couch and began to talk.

"Listen to me," she began softly. "I had a child in my life, I lost a child in my life, and I raised other people's children. I spent my whole life around women who did nothing but have them some babies, including my mother. I'm her oldest. Helped almost all of my brothers and sisters come into this world. If it's one thing I know, it's when a woman is ready to have her a baby. At least in the physical sense."

"Mama," Miriam sobbed, "Christmas is coming. We have no real money. Bird's been so uptight about that. How am I supposed to tell him this?"

"You just tell him."

"He's going to be so mad."

"Maybe. But then you know what? He's going to figure it out. We going to figure it out."

"How? How's he supposed to handle this?"

"Because that's what we do. We figure things out. We handle them."

"I don't know how."

"Nobody does before they do it. And then they do it, and then they know."

Miriam nodded, agreeing with Mama about something she had no way of really understanding yet. Mama continued:

"Listen. You just tell my grandson soon as possible, Miriam. It's going to be all right. Just get it over with, get the fears over with, and then do what you supposed to do. Which is take care of that baby. Not starting in nine months. Starting now."

"Yes," mumbled Miriam, calling her tears back, trying to steady herself. Mama passed Miriam a tissue.

"Wipe your nose. Go clean your face. And when the boy gets back, just tell him, Miriam. We're going be all right. One way or another." Miriam stood up, began to move like an object that was on remote control. She went into the bathroom, washed her face, gagged, rinsed out her mouth, and came back to sit beside Mama, and tried to look composed. She did not succeed, and Mama could see this. The old woman took pity on the girl.

"Listen to me," Mama said, her voice tender, "I understand the worry. You're not married. Money ain't acting right. Things funny between you and your people. But believe me when I tell you the good you get from a child is worth the hard part. So you have to relax knowing that. Okay? We gonna make do. We just are. Your job right now is just to claim that baby. Love that baby. That's how the baby gonna get here and be fine. If you claim it and love it with everything in you.

"Make that baby your own, Miriam. Be all the way proud. Otherwise that child won't never belong nowhere to nobody. And people are made to belong to people. That's just how we are. You do that—that's your part. Other folks, and I mean Bird, gonna do his part. I'll do mine. And we *will* be fine. We will make it. We always have."

~

Not long after Mama and Miriam finished talking, Bird came in from his run, apparently trying to make as much noise as possible. Running was the one thing that always lifted his mood, and now he was making his usual grunting sound, jumping up and down at the door, shaking out his legs, bellowing, "I'm back!"

"My God, you have to come in here so loud," Miriam asked through giggles that surprised her.

"What do you mean?" Bird asked, feigning shock at Miriam's question. "I'm quiet as a mouse. It's my army training." He came over, sweat and all, and kissed Miriam who pretended that this messy, stinky Bird was unappealing to her. Of course Bird, in any state, appealed to her. "Yuck! Go take a shower. Please. *Please!*" Miriam laughed and kissed Bird back, and for a moment she forgot that the two of them had a very serious issue to discuss. Bird walked down the hall to the bathroom, and Miriam said, low as possible, to Mama, "I'm going to go talk with him."

"Good," Mama agreed, shaking her head, and then added, for encouragement, "It's going to be fine. You'll see."

Miriam knocked on the bathroom door, and asked Bird if she could come in. In his most lustful voice, Bird said, "Absolutely." And even more lustfully he added, "Come get in the shower with me."

Miriam undressed and joined Bird in the shower, where he began to moisten her face with kisses and water. Miriam slowed him down and murmured, "Do I look different to you, baby?"

"More beautiful. Every time I look at you, you look more beautiful than you did the last time I looked at you."

"I mean seriously."

"I am being serious."

"Bird, I think I should look different in some way because—" Miriam stopped herself.

"Because why?"

Miriam didn't say anything. She stared at Bird, trying to gauge what his reaction would be. Would he be happy, overwhelmed? Would he be angry with her? These questions raced through her head, knocking down her language, her ability to speak the words she needed to.

Finally Bird said, "Miriam, whatever you have to tell me, baby, it's fine. Just say it. I can take it."

"Okay. Okay." Miriam looked down and said in a voice so soft, Bird almost didn't hear her, but then again when she spoke, he heard nothing else. Not the water hitting against the tiles, not the sound of his lover's slightly labored breath, nothing. "I'm pregnant," Miriam said, and closed her eyes.

Two words and the whole world turns over. Skin goes inside out. Two words and not one thing in life can be viewed as it had been before. Bird had to be sure he'd heard what he thought he heard.

"Could you say that again?"

"I'm pregnant," Miriam stated, more bluntly this time, and more worried.

"You're pregnant?"

"Yes," Miriam said, her voice shaking now, scared. Was he angry, disappointed? Why didn't he hug her, why didn't he say everything was going to be all right? She pleaded with Bird through eyes that were willing back tears. *Hold me, baby, make it feel fine. Make me know we can face anything, handle anything, succeed at anything. Bird. Bird.*

But he did not see Miriam in this moment; he did not see her need. He saw only what they did not have: enough space, enough money. And then there came terrible and sudden flashes of his own father, followed by flashes of himself: Bird, a small boy screaming, groping, pleading, and lost. Bird, a small boy severed and splintered, calling out, calling out, but no answers, no soothing, no nothing at all.

"Listen," Bird said in a low, but not soft tone, "give me a minute, okay? Let me finish my shower. Could you give me a minute?"

Miriam did not want to give him a minute; she did not want to leave. Even more so than in any of the other recent moments when Bird was filled with bitterness or despair, something unfamiliar had descended between them. It frightened her. Miriam went back to what she had been raised on. She did not question Bird, or circle him with her own needs, with the wild puzzle of her own fears.

"Okay," she whispered. "Okay." And with that, Miriam got out of the shower, wrapped a towel around herself, and went into their room, which for the first time did not seem like their room. It seemed like a foreign space, a mean and unusable one. A warehouse for the forgotten.

Miriam dried herself off and crawled beneath the sheets and blankets of the bed they had made their baby in. She wanted to cry. She could feel it everywhere in her, the tears. But they would not come. They backed up inside of her, an ocean some-how drowning in its own waters.

Fifteen minutes later Bird walked in the room, his green towel around his waist. Miriam did not turn to look at him, but he looked at her. He looked at this young girl, barely a woman, who made more of a man out of him than any war ever did. He slid into the bed next to her. Miriam did not pull away, but nei-ther did she ease herself into him. She just lay there, and let Bird run his fingers through her hair, and kiss her neck and tell her again and again, "I love you, girl. I love you." Miriam did not respond, however, and finally Bird broke. He said, "Listen, baby, I'm scared. It's not that I'm not happy. It's not that I don't want you and only you to have my child. I mean, baby, you know how things are with money, how it's been so tight. And so I'm worried about that. I'm worried. I don't have money for Christmas presents, you know? Where am I going to get the money for a baby? It's a lot to figure out, Miriam."

She didn't say a word.

"But we will figure it out," Bird said, though without the confidence with which Mama had said it an hour earlier. Bird continued:

"And plus, there are things you don't know. You don't know about my family entirely. About my father." Miriam turned now toward Bird. What did he mean, what was he saying? Bird did not explain. Not then, and not right after, when he got out of the bed, pulled on his undershirt and shorts and mumbled something about needing to get something to drink.

All the rest of the morning, all the rest of the afternoon, the apartment, the life in it, went still. Even as Mama blasted her gospel and sang, or later when Bird changed the record player and put on Marvin Gaye, stillness was everywhere. Through the dinner that only Mama really ate, through the washing of the dishes, the brushing of teeth, the requisite exchanges of good nights and sleep wells—stillness.

In bed, alone, Miriam lay immobile, except for her hand, which massaged her stomach. An hour later, she heard Bird turn the television off, and head back toward their room. For the first time since she'd moved in with him, she wished he would stay away and sleep on the couch. That did not happen. Instead, Bird climbed into the bed, and held his woman, and finally began to speak. "When a man gets told he's going to be a father, the first thing he thinks of is, can you really do this?

That's what I thought about. All day since you told me." What Bird was saying was of no comfort to Miriam. And he could sense this, so he tried harder to make her understand.

"Baby, imagine being told that you had to drive an ambulance to save someone's life, but you'd never been behind the wheel of a car. Try to understand what I'm saying, Miriam. I never really had a father. I never had a role model for a father. So you tell me I'm going to be a father, and I think, how can I do it?

"I know you don't understand about having no role models, because they may not have been perfect, but your parents, your father, was nothing like mine. There's just no comparison." Bird was speaking deliberately, painfully. His voice began to drift, to disconnect from his body.

"Everybody says like father, like son. I'm going to pray like I never prayed before that I'm the exception to that rule. I swear to God I am. Miriam," Bird said, his voice cracking, "Miriam, I've tried all my life not to be anything like him. But this is the real test, I guess. We're going to have a baby. I'm going to be a father." He paused, and then, "What happens if I can't do it?"

Miriam turned toward Bird, and said with a very small measure of anger in her voice that she tried to cover up with real sympathy,

"I may not feel everything you do. I mean, I did have a father. That's true. But I'm scared, too, Bird. It's *my* body. I feel very, *very* scared. People are going to judge me, not you. But besides all that, how can you say I've had role models? You know I don't want to be anything like my parents. You know how lonely it was growing up how I did. Meeting you was the first time I ever got past that loneliness, and I had to leave my parents' house to do it. So we're both scared, Bird." Miriam softened her tone, and now she fully turned toward her lover. "All I want to know is that you're going to work with me.

Because I think we can do it *if* we work together. I think we can make ourselves bigger than everything we're afraid of. I mean, don't you?"

Miriam searched Bird's face for that strength, that fearlessness she'd seen in him the first time they'd met. That look in his eyes that said he'd never back down from anyone, anything, anytime. Why was he backing down from himself and backing down now? Now when she needed him so badly.

"You don't understand, Miriam. There are things I haven't told you."

Frustrated, Miriam snapped, "Well, maybe it's time then. Because if I ever needed an understanding, it's now. Okay?"

There was silence for so long after she spoke, and in that unknowable frame of time, their universe shrunk down, shriveled, as Bird, now trembling visibly, began to say the ugly words, the ones he had never before uttered. Bird looked at Miriam, this woman, this girl whom he had not known for even four entire months yet, and he said,

"She's dead. My mother. Like I told you once. Remember, I told you that my parents were both dead?" Miriam nodded. "Well, that's not all the way true. My father's not dead. That wasn't true. I lied. I'm sorry. I lied to you. My father's in prison." And then, with a mixture of pain and deliberation, he added, "My father's in prison for killing her. For killing my mother."

Miriam looked at Bird. She didn't know what to say. How could she know what to say? How could anyone? She let her body react for her. Miriam reached over, and put her hand on Bird's face. "No," she murmured. She pulled Bird close to her, "No, no, no, no." Miriam's arms circled around Bird, her body rocked against his. "Oh, baby," she said.

And Bird let himself go in her arms. He had held the terror in a thick knot at the base of himself, now it was unraveling, suddenly, wildly. Where was the fear he'd known so intimately going? How was Miriam able to make it go away? It was such an odd sensation, what he felt in his blood and his brain, in his heart, behind his teeth, at the bottom of his feet, but he did not question it. So Bird let himself be rocked and comforted in Miriam's arms, and it occurred to him that he could not remember anyone ever holding him, ever rocking him like this. Not Mommy or after, Mama.

It just wasn't their way. The way of his people was to cook, and joke, and drink, and keep the house clean, and pray. No one anywhere tried to really soothe the six-year-old instantly parentless child. That's how old he was when Daddy burst into the apartment screaming and drunk and pulled out a pistol and shot Mommy while Bird was crunched in a corner of the bedroom, hearing everything, everything. *Bitch!! You dirty fucking no good ass fucking whore. I will kill you. I will kill your nasty fucking ass dead.*

Then the gun. Three times and Mommy fell. Bird heard her. Mommy fell, and then silence, and then the running footsteps and silence again. Bird, tiny and alone, crawled over to his mother and touched her and his hand came back bloody. White foam and bright red blood bubbled out of her mouth and he screamed and then tried to wipe it away. Bird looked at his mother and began to bang and bang on the floor next to her. He banged and his tiny hands became bruised, but he just kept banging, until finally Mrs. Hendricks from next door came and found the boy banging, and she tried to pull him away from the lifeless body, but he said, *No, no I have to. To wake up my mommy.*

Mrs. Hendricks allowed the small boy to continue banging on the floor, banging and calling out to his mother, until the other neighbors came and the police came, and then finally his grandmother came. She walked in slowly and looked at the sheet that covered up what they said was her daughter, and she stared at everything and everyone in that room, looking to see some piece of normal, but she did not find it. Mama took a long breath, hung her head briefly and said a prayer, and then picked her grandson up off the floor, and said, "Come on now. Come on. We all right. We all right." But Mama had a tear in her eye as she said this and Bird, six years old and small for his age, knew things were not all right.

They were not all right then, and they were not all right five days later when there was the funeral and all that crying (though not from Bird). Things were not all right when there were prayers and songs. Not when there was the cleanup and then the move to Mama's house. Not when there was a trial and when Daddy went to prison. Things were not all right. But everyone seemed to learn how to act as though they were, and that's how it was. Straightened up somewhat, but terribly dusty if you checked underneath.

Fourteen, almost fifteen years, and not a single day of real peace for Bird, not a single day that felt right, from the top to the bottom of it and all around the sides, until just now when he could lose himself in Miriam's strong, young arms. When he could climb inside her voice as it said, "No. No no no no no no." Bird cried between the pauses in Miriam's words. Not a full-out wail, not even a sob, but after all these long years, tears, and so a beginning, a cleansing, a clearing, a release.

≈

There were nights after this when Bird would stretch out beside Miriam. He propped pillows up under her knees, asked her continuously if she was doing okay, and then he rubbed her feet with cocoa butter. He rubbed her feet as though she'd been walking twenty years barefoot. He massaged her hands and head, and Miriam would pretend to fall asleep, but she was never asleep. This time with Bird was such treasured time.

Besides, how could she sleep with such insistent beauty

beside and within her? She did not want to miss a second of it. Not the touching, and certainly not the singing. Bird resting his head near her stomach and singing "Ain't No Mountain High Enough." Miriam would join him when he sang that song, and together they said, "To keep me from you."

In the middle of that singing, in the middle of their voices coming together, their mouths met, hungry and wet, and they went into each other again and again, and every way they could. And they talked about what it meant to create a life in this time, in this place.

They talked about all they had going against them, but also all they had going for them. They talked about how this baby was going to be safe, how this baby was never going to go to war. Never going to scrape its knuckles to the ground digging for love and acceptance. This baby would know peace.

# 16.

Although he worked as much overtime as the school allowed, which was consistently five to ten extra hours a week, Bird still worried about how tight money was. His mood, which for about two weeks had been good, began to sour again. When Miriam would bring up getting married, Bird would huff, "We *are* going to get married, Miriam. But there are other financial concerns that have to come first." She'd try to debate him, to say that they could just go to City Hall, but he dismissed her with, "That's not how we're doing it, okay?" Mama and Miriam learned to live with Bird's unpredictable emotions by being quieter and quieter, at first whenever he was around, but after a while, the quiet just stayed.

Miriam did some small baby-sitting jobs around the neighborhood to try to help out; she understood Bird's worries and fears, which were getting bigger and more unmanageable as the pregnancy progressed. But she tried to do whatever she could to ease any burdens, to bring light into the narrow tunnel where it seemed their life was caught. Miriam asked for nothing, and accepted everything: Bird's moodiness, the discomfort pregnancy and raging hormones brought about, she swallowed it all. Now, instead of Bird rubbing her feet, Miriam took to saying, "Baby, come here. Let me rub your head." She told herself that this was the hard work of becoming a woman her mother used to talk about. And accepting this reality, Miriam ignored her needs and desires almost right out of existence.

The holiday season came and went without fanfare. Miriam told Bird she thought that no gifts should be exchanged this year. "We have to save for the baby, and besides, it's a greedy holiday. Why don't you just come to church with Mama and me. That'll be my gift."

Bird agreed but inside he felt he was less than—less than the provider he should be, less than the man he should be. Still, with a forced smile, he escorted his two women to church that Christmas morning, and in the afternoon they came home together and as Bird relaxed in front of the television with a drink, Mama and Miriam finished making the feast they'd begun the night before: turkey with chestnut stuffing, roast beef, potato salad, homemade cranberry sauce, cornbread, candied yams, collard greens, macaroni and cheese, with apple cobbler and sugar cookies the shape of Christmas trees for dessert.

They set the huge meal down on a twenty-five-year-old Queen Anne lace tablecloth Mama had been given by one of the families she'd worked for so many years ago. The cloth and also the china, though some pieces were slightly chipped, which is why they had been handed down to her from that family, were still beautiful. Lenox plates with gold borders. Only the utensils were common, everyday steel knives, forks, and spoons. But on that Christmas, Miriam surveyed the table of abundant and good food, the lace and china, and she thought it was the most beautiful setting she'd ever seen.

"Now this is a table for kings and queens," Miriam said.

"We *are* kings and queens," Bird countered.

"Well, come sit down, Mr. King, so this queen can eat," grumbled Mama through a smile.

They did, and as Miriam ate, she thought about all those

Christmases in her parents' house, with all the fancy gifts that were devoid of love; they were gifts given so that later you could say, I got this, I got that. She now knew that this was just where she was supposed to be, living just as she was supposed to live. This was a good place. Even with the ups and downs, the worries, the fears.

Because—and Miriam was comforted by this—more often than not, Bird's preoccupations would subside, and he would attend to her dutifully. There were even times when, laying there in bed, he would take her through a gorgeous fantasy of what life was going to be like when things fell into place. He would talk about the home in the country he was going to buy her one day soon, the backyard their child would play in, the willow tree that would stand in front. In those moments of optimism, Bird could even joke, "All right, all right, we may be a ways off from that now, but it's gonna happen, baby. I'm telling you. It is."

Miriam never doubted her beloved, not for a second. She believed in Bird and his dreams for them, and she lined her soul with his dreams. She did it the way the faithful do with ritual and verse, because it was those beliefs, that faith, coupled with the fervent desire to avoid any conflict, that kept Miriam held in and silent in the times when Bird would withdraw; belief and faith that kept her from letting any disappointment show, or hurt. Belief and faith later, after the new year arrived and no leads had turned up in his job search, and Bird began leaving the house in the evenings, mumbling something about how he needed to go have a beer. "Okay," Miriam would say meekly, or else nothing at all.

Sometimes Miriam would remember those first weeks and months when they met—did Bird ever have a drink back then? She didn't believe so. This had all started, when? Around the holidays? It seemed innocent at first. A beer or two in the house was very different from this new habit of stepping out. Miriam hated it, but she didn't want to fight with Bird about it. She told herself that as soon as the pressure let up, he wouldn't need to go to bars, that it really wasn't his personality. She fell asleep many nights with that idea as her wrapping, her blanket, her warmth. She fell asleep alone with it.

When Bird would slip in late on those out-at-the-bar nights, Miriam would turn toward him after he climbed into their bed. She would nuzzle her face against his, rub his head the way she knew he loved his head to be rubbed. She'd ask, "You doing okay?"

Bird would hold her, though tentatively, out of a sense of his own guilt, and he would mumble that, yes, he was okay, was she? Miriam would tell a lie that she could not recognize was a lie. She would say she was fine, and alone, together, they would fall into a sleep.

Most of January was like that, and now February, which was nearly over, had been the same: In the mornings Bird would be gone, out for a run before the sun came up, back to the house, back out to work, home long afterward only long enough to eat and change and go for a drink. Miriam wondered if March would also be Bird disappearing for three or four hours, two or three nights a week? Would he do that as Mama and Miriam acted as though everything was as it had been? The women would wash dishes and talk about baby names and pretend they did not notice Bird was not there. Mama liked biblical names: Sarah, Mary, or Rachel if it was a girl, Isaac, Elijah, or Michael if it was a boy. Miriam would nod, but in secret, she'd read the book of African names Bird had surprised her with one afternoon right after they found out she was pregnant.

She would read that book and tell herself when the baby came things would change. Once, and once only, it occurred to Miriam that perhaps she'd made a mistake. Had her parents been right? Should she have left Bird alone and stayed with them? But she pushed that thought away quickly. Going back to them was impossible now anyway. Miriam just prayed for things to get better, for things to get better and stay better. And it seemed as soon as she'd given herself over to that prayer, saying it over and over, it was heard. There was the evening when Bird came rushing back into the house about an hour and a half after he'd left. Miriam and Mama, who had been sitting on the sofa watching the evening news, were both startled by his noisy entrance.

"Guess what? Guess what?" Bird roared, the broad smile on his face easing the women's initial concern.

"What is it, baby?" asked Miriam, feeding off of Bird's excitement.

"Whatever it is, say it a little quieter for goodness sake," grumbled Mama, pretending to be annoyed.

"I . . . got . . . a . . . *job*!"

Miriam jumped up and ran toward Bird. "What do you mean? When? Where? Tell me everything!"

"Hold on, hold on. Let me get myself together." Bird let out a breath and continued. "Okay. Here it is. You know I been going over to the Lounge these last couple of months. You know, trying to just, like, relax. Take some time out. I know you haven't been happy with that, but it's what I kind of felt I needed to do."

"Never mind all that," said Mama. "Get to the job part."

"Right. Okay. So there's this man I talk to in there when I go, an older brother. He was always polite, once or twice he bought me a beer. Mostly we talked about sports, but once he said I reminded him of his son, the way I looked, even the way I carried myself."

"Get to the point, Bird."

"I am, Mama. I am. Well, last time I was in there I saw the

brother. His name is Mr. Hicks. And he was very drunk. I ain't never seen him drunk. I guess that's why we used to talk. Because everybody else in there used to really get pretty messed up, but me and him, we'd nurse our beers and then go home."

"Bird!" Mama yelled, pushing him to go on with the story.

"Just hold on. Okay, anyway, he was drunk, so I was a little worried about him. I said, Mr. Hicks, let me take you home. At first he resisted, but I said the streets were slippery and so were the people, and it's no shame in letting a brother help you out. I told him I learned that in the war.

"And he looked at me, drunk as he was, and said, 'You was in the war?' And I said I was. And tears came into his eyes. He didn't say another word, except to tell me, when I asked him, where he lived at. It was only about four blocks away, so I took him home.

"When I went back to the bar tonight, Mr. Hicks was there. He asked me to come talk to him. So we moved from the bar to the table, and first he thanked me, and then he told me about his son, John. He had a son who was killed in the war. The last time I saw him, it was the anniversary of his son's death. That's why he was so upset. He started saying all the dreams he had for his son, how he had built this business, this men's clothing store, and he wanted to pass it on to his son. Figured his son would do his tour and come home, and have a business, get a wife, have kids.

"But that's not what happened. And he says on some level he feels he failed as a father. Shouldn't have let the boy go to war, should have sent him to Canada until the whole mess was over like the way white kids do. So I was trying to make him feel better. I said I wished I'd had a father who thought about me even a little like he thought about his son. So one thing led to another, and I wound up telling him that I had a baby coming, and he wound up telling me that he needed an assistant manager for his store!"

Miriam hugged Bird hard. "Are you serious?"

"I'm dead serious, baby. And you know what? I'll make more money on that job in three days than I make working overtime at the school. Plus, even though I'll be assistant manager, if I make sales I'm going to get some kind of commission. And you know what else?"

"What?"

"I have to be at the store at twelve o'clock. That means I can take classes in the morning when I get into college."

"See, baby," Miriam squealed. "I told you things were going to work out. I told you."

"You need to have a little bit more faith, like *I* told you," Mama chimed in, grinning from ear to ear.

Bird told them that the job would probably start in two weeks. Mr. Hicks just needed to deal with a couple of the employees he had right now, ones he said weren't doing the job right. They would talk tomorrow, Mr. Hicks had said. "Let's meet here at the same time and finalize things."

Bird told Mama and Miriam that he was going to make sure he could start school in September, and, he added, Miriam better do the same. "Well, not in September. I'll have just had the baby then," Miriam reminded Bird. "But the following semester."

"Okay, right," agreed Bird, and the two began to fade into their own world, into the promise of their tomorrow, until Mama scuttled them off to bed, where they went, happily. Where they held each other and kissed for a long time until Miriam, overcome by exhaustion, fell asleep, Bird's mouth still on hers.

≈

Bird woke up the next morning, as he often did, feeling nervous inside. Despite the good news he'd received the night before, despite all the hope he'd felt a few short hours ago, Bird always seemed to wake up with the sense that there was danger just on the horizon. He told Miriam this once, and they'd determined it was a leftover of the war; this idea that no matter how still things were, no matter how peaceful, one wrong step and you're on a land mine. But Bird knew he had felt this way long before the war, and this morning his heart pounded hard and fast and he began to sweat. He pulled Miriam, who was still very much asleep, close to him, and tried to relax his breathing, tried to make it conform to hers. It did not happen. It never really happened. Not all the way.

Bird taught himself to live with it, to let the feeling pass, as it eventually did. The day would take its course and he would usually find something else, something good he could focus his thoughts upon. Sometimes that good was just watching his beautiful Miriam walking around the house, doing her thing: studying, straightening up, reading the Bible.

This day, Bird felt, would be no different. He rolled out of bed, waking Miriam as he did, headed into the shower, and let the hot water calm him. He thought about his new job, the baby, Miriam, the apartment they would move into as soon as he saved enough money. He wanted a three-bedroom place. A room for him and Miriam, one for the baby, and one for Mama.

Maybe they could get one of those two-floor garden apartments in a large brownstone. Bird ran down a list in his mind of what needed to be bought right away: a crib, baby blankets, clothes and diapers. They could use this old furniture for now, and then get some new furniture, maybe on credit, later. It was a lot, but at least he was in a position to make it happen, he figured, and felt good.

Bird wanted so much to believe that life would work out

right. Maybe now, at last. He did have real and tangible reasons to believe that things were looking up, were shifting onto a road that could be navigated, didn't he? Bird didn't want to be the pessimist, the prophet of doom. No. That wasn't his calling.

His calling was to be Miriam's husband, the father of her children, the caretaker, the bringer of love, and a lasting peace. He was here to be a lawyer, ethical, erudite, enlightened. He was here to be the Black man who dodged stray bullets and bleak statistics, who went back and back to escape others off the plantation. He was here to be a brother—an everyday brother, a *reliable* brother, the brother you could believe in. The one the boys on the block looked up to and told stories about. He was here to be those things, and just one other: a son who quietly and consistently made his mothers, the one who birthed him and the one who raised him, proud.

Bird trimmed his goatee neatly, and brushed his hair. A towel around his waist, he stepped out of the bathroom and into his room, where he dressed methodically, then picked up his briefcase with its old newspapers and magazines inside. He kissed Miriam, who was eating a huge breakfast with Mama, on the top of her head, and stepped out into the very definite winter. *Forgot to tell them I love them,* he thought, as he rushed toward the school, excited to announce that these would be his last two weeks.

# 17.

*He is wandering now, angry and erratic, a storm looking for its center, or else lightning seeking a place to strike. Deep in the middle of himself he feels the measure of every unfairness he has ever known, and it is growing. It is growing as though it is a tumor, swelling and malignant, a certain killer.*

*I don't want to feel sorry for myself, I don't want to live in anger. He says this and says this. He tells himself, I've tried, I've tried: to let things go, to not be overwhelmed, to not come undone. But all that he has ever seen is now terribly stacked up. From his feet to his head, it's all stacked up and heavy and taking up space where his heart should be, free and beating. He is crowded, on the inside. And all that makes him who he is, all that makes him beautiful and righteous and hopeful and forward-thinking, all of this is shoved small and tight into a corner, down a hole that he cannot pull out from, reach for, liberate, shake the dust off of.*

*How could his father have shot his mother?*

*Why did he grow up so poor that war felt like freedom?*

*How could he be treated so badly by a country he nearly gave his life for?*

*How long will the nightmares come and warp the possibility of sleep, of a simple good night's rest?*

*How long will Miriam stay with him if his life is a roadblock? She loves him now, but what about later? Now she's young, now she is filled with romance and hope. But no one lives forever on romance and hope.*

*People live on regular paychecks, decent wages. They live on dreams that are not dreams but realistic goals. She will leave him, abandon him, it's only a matter of time. Maybe not even much time. And whenever she leaves—he is sure now she will leave—certainly she will take the baby with her. She will tell the baby, your father was no good. I am good he thinks, but no one is noticing.*

*No one can be trusted, relied upon, believed in.*

*Goddammit, why, why did the school have to fire him now? Just because he accepted another job someplace else? He gave them proper notice, they tell him he needs to leave today. He goes to meet Hicks, and for the first time in how long, the nigger ain't there. Was the nigger for real? Is he going to get the fucking job or is Hicks going to leave him hanging? That nigger gonna leave me hanging. What should I have expected from a motherfucker I met in a bar. A damn drunk.*

*Bird continued to trample through the streets. Why had he believed that man, why had he even hung out at that bar? How had it seemed like a refuge, a place where visions could take shape over bourbon and beer? Why only now did he see it for what it really was: a gutted-out space where people just as gutted-out come to feel normal, to feel in the company of something less than strangers, not quite friends? A place where human beings could judge the broken-down appearance of the bar—the paint chipped past its lead base, down to the concrete wall, the lights gone out, the bathroom overrun with filth. The people could judge this place instead of themselves or each other, and feel good.*

*Angry, and getting angrier, erratic and getting more erratic, questions wrap around fears that wrap around Bird's mind like razor wire. He feels as though blood is spilling from every opening on his body. He feels as though he is losing his mind, suddenly extrapolated from the world he's always known. Of it but not in it. He doesn't even feel part of the body that is his own. He's watching himself rumble through the streets. He's watching himself as he's leaving himself. Fuck everything. Fuck it all. I'ma get up outta this place.*

The walls shake when Bird enters the small apartment,

slamming the door. Miriam looks up from the book she is reading. She wants to say "What's wrong with you" but she restrains herself, and anyway Mama says it for her. "What's wrong with you?" she yells at her grandson from the dining room table she is trying to clear. Bird doesn't even look over at his grandmother and Miriam. He continues, a billowing gray cloud, through the living room, through Mama's room, into the room he shares with Miriam. The women look at each other. It is the end of the day and both of them are tired. Let him get himself together, both of them think but do not say.

"Help me finish clearing this table, Miriam," Mama directs.

Miriam hoists herself off the sinking old sofa, and begins removing dishes, glasses, knives, and forks. Let's just get it all cleaned up, make everything neat, she thinks.

Mama calls out to Bird, tells him there are leftovers in the kitchen, to come get something to eat before it gets too late. Bird doesn't respond. Instead he emerges from the bedroom dressed in his running clothes and sneakers. The women are confused. *Is he thinking about going running at this time of night?* they wonder, but do not ask. The look on Bird's face closes down the possibility of any questioning. Miriam is certain of this as she looks over at the man she still loves deeply, the one she knows is still in there, buried beneath the weight of the frustration and anger. If only she could dig him out. She thinks, *If I ask him to stay, it will surely push him out*. Finally Miriam manages, "Mama made your favorite, salmon cakes and rice."

Bird looks at Miriam and he looks at his grandmother. He doesn't see two women who love him. He sees people who will betray him, people who, if they could, would get up right now and leave him flat. So he leaves first.

# Part 2

Room 902 is getting smaller and smaller, shrinking and shrinking. People come in, go out. Who are they and why are they able to move when Aya is not? Get out, get out, get the hell out, Miriam thinks but does not say, as she buries her head into her daughter's chest, brushing aside wires, the useless IV line, the white, white sheet with the blue stripe down the center.

*Beloved can you hear me*
*You cannot leave me      you cannot do it*
*I am you      you are me      we can survive      we have to*
*There was never a choice*
*Isn't that what I taught you*
*Stand up*
*Take my blood baby girl*
*It's not mine, it's yours*
*Take my heart my bones my muscles my eyes my legs my hands*
*my breath are yours*
*Come back crawl back get back*
*Into me*
*My womb where I never should have let you leave*
*You were safe*
*Inside me*
*Come inside me*
*I'm your mama*
*You are still my baby*
*Still mine mine mine mine mine*
*Come back*

*Please*

≈

Miriam looks up from her prayers, from her demands to God, to her daughter, to the sky, to anyone, anything. She looks past the ramshackle maze of broken and breaking furniture, past the sick green chipped-paint walls. She looks out to where a collection of police officers are standing. She stares at them. They see her staring and avoid her eyes. They do not seem to move, Miriam observes, they do not seem movable. They seem impregnable. They seem a morbid blue boundary. Miriam thinks: *On one side of that boundary is life, on the other, we don't ask.*

A nurse approaches Miriam and says gently, "Ma'am?" Miriam does not acknowledge the woman; she cannot stop staring at the cops. *Was it one of you who did it?* her eyes ask. *Which one? WHICH ONE OF YOU DID IT?*

The nurse says again, "Mrs. Rivers?" She touches Miriam's back gently. "Please, come with me."

Miriam does not move. The nurse waits a moment and bends down toward her and now both arms rest around Miriam's shoulders. "Mrs. Rivers," she hesitates, "I'm so sorry. But there's nothing more . . ." The woman's soft Jamaican lilt fades.

Miriam, her face swollen and wet with pain and rage, turns toward the kind voice, but she does not speak. She can only think, *Who did this to us?* The nurse begins again,

"Mrs. Rivers . . . I just can't imagine . . . and if there was something more . . . please . . . I'm sorry. There are some papers. Let me help you with them. Please. Come with me. We'll do them, and you can go home," the nurse offers, which is when the reality sets in for real.

Miriam shakes her head, no. Not so much to be defiant but more because she cannot understand what is being asked of her. Is she supposed to leave Aya here? And also: What is this thing this woman says is home?

# 18.

The dreams that color and expand the space of life are born in a place beyond knowing or touch. They are born in place of an unspoken faith. A faith that carries along sight even in the dense and obscure of dark. Miriam had not been raised to know that sort of faith, although in those once-upon-a-time months of loving Bird, it had begun to take on a cautious shape in the corners of her soul. But with Bird gone, with Mama gone, and with even her parents disappeared, Miriam returned to the arena of belief she had been suckled on. But it was not what she needed. Neither was it what little Aya had needed.

Far more complex, far more thorough than hers or any religion, Miriam needed to know a way of believing that would have propelled her and her daughter past survival and on into celebration. And that need was too complicated to be codified by scripture or preaching; too broad to be contained by commandment or psalm. Yes, Miriam needed a faith never uttered, felt only, along the edges of her own smile—or else her own child's bouncing step and infectious giggle. But no one had ever explained that to her, and so she could not know, nor have raised her daughter to know.

What Miriam did know, and Aya would come to know, were bottles warmed just so, and diapers changed precisely. Aya knew naps at one, and bed by eight-thirty. She knew Saturday afternoons at the playground, or the children's museum when it rained. Aya knew that she would never be hungry, and that she would never be cold.

What Aya would never know was being washed in a mother's warm kisses. She did not know long walks to nowhere. Or ice cream before dinner just because it was Saturday and very hot outside. Aya did not know impractical but fun birthday or Christmas presents, or singing loudly with her mother walking down a Brooklyn street. And because she did not know these things, it was strange that this little girl who was taught to walk at exactly twelve months, who was potty trained at exactly two years, who was in nursery school the moment she turned four—this little girl somehow knew to look for what she never was told had been hidden away.

If Miriam baked chicken, Aya asked for it fried with bananas on top. When Miriam ran clear, warm water for Aya's nighttime bath, the girl asked why there were no bubbles in her tub. When Miriam told only one story before bed, she would leave the room and hear her child whispering to herself her own made-up tale. When Miriam told Aya not to run through the house, the girl would stop there in her tracks and begin to dance to a song no one else could hear.

And when Miriam admonished Aya that she needed to listen to her mother, that it was just the two of them and they needed to respect one another, they needed to get along, four-year-old Aya looked up into her mama's brown eyes, and asked, "But what about my daddy? When is he coming home?"

≈

In the hospital room where her daughter lay dead, Miriam remembered these questions. Not only questions about Bird, but about grandparents, aunties, uncles, and cousins. Why was it just the two of them, Aya had always wanted to know. Other families were so big. "No two families are alike," Miriam would explain and explain. "Ours was always small. In ours, people died. They went away. In our family," Miriam would explain, "we're what we have and that has to be enough." When Aya would get really angry, feel really isolated, she'd shout at her mother, "Well, it's not!" To this, Miriam never responded. Now, briefly, in the room, she wished she could answer her daughter's questions—questions that still pierced the air. In this moment, in this room, they pierced Miriam, too, and they were all she could hear, feel, taste, see. Unanswered questions. Unanswerable questions.

They drowned out the sound of the doctors, the administrators, the police officers who spoke to Miriam when she was finally led out of the room. She could not tell you how she signed the papers, got on the elevator, rode down and down and down until she was out of that place. Out and walking on streets that could have belonged to any city. San Francisco, Decatur, Chicago, Akron. Nothing was familiar or known. She could have been anyplace because she was no place. She walked.

She had ignored the efforts of sympathetic members of the hospital staff, the people who offered to get her a cab, and even one who said she would drive her home or wherever it was she needed to go. Where could she need to go now? Miriam walked and walked—against lights, in front of cars, and she did not flinch when they blared their horns, and asked, Was she crazy? Did she want to die that night? Too late, she thought. Way too late.

She continued to pace the coarse dark following no clear path, having no clear end to this particular and mean journey. And when the night broke, and the light banged into her eyes forcing her to see, Miriam was standing at the front steps of the building where she and Aya had lived for nearly twenty years.

Ten minutes, fifteen minutes, an hour, maybe two. There

was no calculation for the amount of time Miriam stood at the foot of the steps, but at some point, Althea emerged. She was heading out to do some walking and then some grocery shopping before the store got crowded.

"Ms. Rivers?" Althea said, approaching her upstairs neighbor curiously. Miriam was always so neat and proper, so buttoned up and presentable. Why was she here in front of the building like this, disheveled, her face swollen, her makeup smeared? Althea descended the steps carefully—she was not a young woman anymore and could not afford a spill. "Ms. Rivers?" she asked again. Nothing.

"Miriam? It's me. Ms. Stone. Althea from downstairs. What's happened? What's wrong?"

Miriam stared at her neighbor but made no sign that she was capable of understanding her or capable of making herself understood.

"Let me help you. Let me help you get inside the apartment." Althea took Miriam by the elbow and began to guide her up the stairs. "Come on, dear. Let's get you inside," and as she had done for the last ten hours, Miriam allowed herself to be led. She offered no resistance, but neither did she offer any assistance.

As the women approached Miriam's second-story apartment, Althea asked, "Where's your daughter? Is Aya home?"

Those words gusted ferocious like a sudden windstorm that leaves nothing standing, nothing as is. Nothing as was. Miriam's legs felt as though they would give way, and indeed they did start to buckle. She surely would have fallen had it not been for the strong arms of her neighbor, who was calling "Miriam? Miriam? Miriam?" Again and again and again, until finally this woman, this childless mother whispered from far inside herself, whispered from her gut, from a voice that had never before been hers, "They killed my baby," she wailed. "They killed her, they killed her, they killed, they killed—"

It wasn't that Althea didn't hear or else didn't understand the words Miriam had just spoken. It wasn't even that Althea did not imagine them to be possible; before moving to New York at twenty years old, she'd grown up with the daily terrorism and brutality of the Ku Klux Klan in Alabama. Later, she and her family, some of whom scattered to Philadelphia, others to Chicago, made regular and dark jokes about "up South." They would say, "Yeah, they just a little neater about it when they killing you dead up here."

But despite the violence and murders that had marked her sight, despite her cynicism, despite her pain, Althea, like all the members of her family, still clung to the idea that things would not always be this way. She, her family, her friends, members of her church, neighbors, when they talked, as they sometimes did, about being Black and being here, they talked with the guided vision of the faithful. With the hope of people who had no facts, no promises, only conviction—conviction that allowed them to rise each morning; that encouraged them to venture out into the streets, onto trains and buses, toward their jobs, toward another day that might be better than the day that had gone. And if not better, at least no worse—the prayer of the faithful and unassured.

This is why Althea reeled when Miriam said the terrible words. All the days and nights that woman had spent in worship, all the tithing. And yes, all those already dead. How could it happen again, Lord, and why? What message are you sending with the killing of a Black girl? "Oh God, oh God, oh God." Althea cried these words and shook her head, and the two women held each other there, in the frame of the wooden door.

When they did finally begin to dig through Miriam's bag and found her keys, Althea walked her neighbor into the apartment and sat her down on the couch. "You just stay here. You just sit." Miriam nodded. Althea went in the kitchen, made lemon tea for both of them, carried it over to Miriam, sitting close as she could to her neighbor, the stranger. "What happened?" she asked, shaking her head. "What happened?"

Miriam, in the voice that was not hers, began to tell . . . to tell it in pieces. It wasn't much; she really didn't know much. She only knew what the police had told her. She only knew Aya was dead. "I suppose I need to make preparations," Miriam mumbled suddenly, painfully, her eyes dry now and unblinking.

Althea, whose own face was now wet with her own tears, nodded. "Yes. I'll help you. We'll get through this together. Don't know how. Have to believe the Lord will provide a way. He just *will*. Have to believe it. Have to."

≈

Thanks to Althea, word of Aya's death spread throughout the Brooklyn neighborhood in the space of three hours. People, none of whom really knew Aya or Miriam, but who had seen them at the grocery store, the Laundromat, the train station, were gripped by sadness and shock. Because despite everything that existed to divide this neighborhood—the weight of two-job schedules, the lack of even one gathering area, the distrust that permeated the streets because there had been too many shootings, and too many robberies, and too many addicts turning playgrounds into outdoor crack houses—the memory of closeness that had followed these families whose childhood homes had been small southern towns, still lingered. And so Aya being dead—not dead but murdered, one young woman said—was devastating.

They had, the people who lived in and around Manchester Place, come to live with the fact that when their boys committed some crime, even when the crime was an unarmed robbery, the penalty might very well be death. No matter how much it hurt when that happened, no matter how unfair it felt, if you said anything, there was always someone to counter, *He shouldn't have been out there like that.* So mothers and fathers learned not to say a word about their boys who were "out there like that." And they learned to shrink their pain into a permanent scowl, ferment it until one sip and you passed out, worship it until it became a holy thing, ordained by the Creator.

But Aya's death defied what they had known before. She was a girl, a college student, and although there were some rumors that she'd gotten in trouble years before, the general sense was that she was a good girl. She was out jogging, for goodness sake. But why at night, others asked—admonished, really. Still, a virtual role model, some parents said. *Always polite,* others piped in, adding, *And her mother is always at services.* The girl never came in here trying to take anything, the man who owned the bodega on the corner offered to whoever would listen.

Althea, who served as the sudden authority on Aya, nodded, agreed with all the neighbors' assessments, adding how the girl used to help her with her grocery bags. "They quiet people, but they good people. Aya's mother stay in church. Work and church. Twenty years and I ain't never seen no men traipsing in and out the building. Pretty as that woman is, she's humble. Just about the business of God, and keeping her daughter fed and clothed. Nothing else. Believe me."

"But listen," Althea was telling Ms. Williams and Ms. Roberts from across the street, "she ain't got no people."

"What?" The women asked this in unison.

"I asked her who I could call, her mama, anyone. She said it wasn't no one to call except her job. And you know, strange as that sounded, I realized I ain't never seen no one coming around for her. The girl had friends come around, and a boy I been seeing lately, but other than that, no one." Althea took a deep breath. "Listen to me now. We can't pass no judgment on that. We don't know the whys. What I know is we got to help. I told Miss Rivers, Miriam, that I would get things done for her as she needed."

The women agreed without hesitation, and began to figure out who would cook for Miriam, who would call her job, who would reach out to the Garvey-Tubman Funeral Home, who would speak with the pastor, who would inform Aya's school, and so on and so on. The details of death wound around the women like a heavy and endless cord, but they worked, nevertheless. Thinking about meals and funeral arrangements was better than thinking about a teenager's body shot up full of holes.

*What kind of mother am I, leaving the hospital without my baby?*
*Was it the days I missed from church?*
*Was it the money I borrowed from petty cash at work?*
*(I paid it back, every cent, the very next week.)*

*Was it that man, that terrible man? It was only once and so many years ago. I was so lonely, Jesus. Aya away like that. It was the only time since, since . . . since . . .*

*And I washed and I washed and I never saw him again. Didn't answer his calls. Made him disappear. Didn't you forgive me? I thought you forgave me. Oh, God, didn't I pay with Bird? With Daddy and Mama?*

*Did I not work hard enough? Was I too lenient, too strict? Should I have demanded more, should I have demanded less? Should I have visited her while she was away? I was trying to teach her a lesson. Make it so she'd never go back.*

*Was it the foods I cooked, the clothes I wore, the way I spoke?*

*Should I have married, gone to church for Wednesday night services also, made Aya join the choir, come home from work earlier? Please, God, please.*

*Make sense of something for me. I have been faithful. Loved you with my whole heart. Tried to give you my whole heart.*

*Why did they send me here from the hospital tell me to go home but this is not my home. Whose furniture is this? Whose brown couch, whose orange crochet afghan? Whose wooden chair whose window whose spider plant whose window whose door?*

*I don't know this place. I don't belong here. Get rid of that damn landscape painting those dead dried flowers the lavender vase the television the stereo system the entertainment center the books*

*Get rid of this garbage this useless this junk and bring my baby back to me*

*Wait a minute.*

*Wait a minute.*

*I know that book that is my daughter's book her book of poems*

*Aya where are you Your book is here so where are you Aya? Aya?*

*I know you're here because now I remember*

*I told you not to be late for school I remember*

*And wait a minute wait a minute*

*Look at this in the refrigerator baked chicken string beans rice and gravy I made you dinner and left it for you to microwave I remember*

*Aya Baby?*

*You can't be gone if the food is here*

Miriam stumbled through the rooms, fingered and held the books, and figurines. She looked for her daughter in everything but could not find her. She touched all the things that made up the everyday of their life, but still was not their life. In the distance the phone was ringing and ringing. The answering machine picked it up, and without thinking, Miriam listened to the voice that spoke after the beep. She listened for Aya. Of course it was not Aya, but mothers do not lose hope so quickly. It was a man's voice. Was that the office calling? Miriam looked at the answering machine and then looked away.

Walking over toward the dining table where Aya had left her book of poems, Miriam picked it up and held it to her heart, and then tried to turn her heart away from itself. It did not work. It pounded and beat and refused to slow down. Miriam closed her eyes tight around the anxiety and allowed herself to come loose. She felt herself fall, there in the middle of the polyurethaned floor. Miriam crumbled and then she began to weep. Only this time, not just from the eyes. This time, waters poured from every part of her that could spill water.

Sweat and urine mixed with tears and Miriam sat there in the center of it, the center of the pain, of the absences, of the death. She sat there as the phone rang and rang. She sat through the knockings at her front door. She sat there until the sound of her weeping finally and slowly faded away. It faded far and it faded deep until it became part of all the secrets the walls held. The secrets of a woman gut-sprung, torn open, a casualty left and forgotten on an undeclared battlefield.

When the phone rang again it was her office calling again to say they heard the news; they were horrified, what could they do, Miriam, who had decided finally to answer, said softly, said simply, "Nothing."

Her boss continued, "You're going to need a lawyer, you know. Someone to protect your interests. I know this sounds terrible to talk about at a time like this, but it's the terrible reality of the world we live in. I can help you with that." He went on, but Miriam heard only snatches of sounds, not full sentences, completed thoughts, or even entire words. When he paused, she told her boss, "Really, I'm fine. I'll be fine. Thank you, and we'll let you know the funeral arrangements."

# 19.

Days later, when that morning came, that morning of no light in a city crouching low behind its shadows and there was nothing to see that a person would want to see, not on the outside nor there on the terrible inside, Miriam could not pretend to strength. Could not pretend to be fine. Not where the empty was uncompromising. There in the hollow and echo. There in the place of no Aya. No Aya walking, talking, singing, complaining. There where Miriam now stood, blank and motionless in front of her closet.

She stood there because at 7:30 that morning, Althea had taken the spare key and let herself into Miriam's apartment. She had gently helped her neighbor out of the bed where Miriam was not sleeping; indeed, she had not really slept in the ninety-six hours since she'd come home from the hospital. She'd dozed off a few times, but sleep, honest and true resting, that was for people who were not burdened by the sound of violence clanging on the inside of their heads. It was as though there was a person occupying the space where Miriam's mind used to be, and that person was a woman, and she was screaming. That's what Miriam heard. A woman who would not stop screaming and now Althea was here. Miriam wondered, but did not ask, could Althea hear the screaming, too?

Could she hear it as she raised Miriam from the bed and

walked her into the bathroom; as she stripped off Miriam's dirty clothes, and drew the tub, and tested the water? Could she hear it as she eased Miriam into that water, sitting her down carefully, so carefully, as though Miriam were herself a child, a baby unable to maintain its own weight? Althea supported the whole of Miriam's body with a single arm, and she began to wash her. She washed her back and she washed her face. She went all under Miriam's arms and washed. She washed all down her legs. Althea washed Miriam in every place she would have washed her own self, or else her own daughter. Althea washed.

And she thought again, Althea did, as she was helping Miriam out of the tub, and drying her off, that although she had lived downstairs from her for all these many years, about how they had never once, not one single time, ever sat down and had a conversation together. Of course there was the usual exchange of pleasantries, the occasional borrowing of a cup of milk or laundry detergent, but no discussions of family or men, no discourse on the state of current affairs, no sharing of dreams or dislikes. Miriam just was not the sort of woman for that. She was polite and quiet, even neighborly in a very practical kind of way (Althea had had keys to Miriam's apartment and Miriam had keys to Althea's for years and years. "It makes sense," Miriam had said then.)

But despite their courtesies and practicalities, Miriam had always been unwavering in her presence, which said clearly that there was no opening into her, no peephole, no crevice. Althea never felt she knew her neighbor. But in this hour and in this place, she knew that whatever distance had existed, whatever distance had been demanded, must right now fall away.

Althea knew because she was both a mother and a grandmother. She knew because she was a Black woman like Miriam.

And because she was, what she understood without ever a conversation between them, was the brutal reality of having to bury a child, while simultaneously having to sort out the vile accompaniment of injustice.

This was an old story, reaching as far back through time, as far down, as the African bones still lining the floor of the Atlantic Ocean. It was a common story. As common as any Black woman walking any given street: the one who does not smile, who is not light in her step or warm in her demeanor. Yes, Althea understood what needed to be done, which is why she washed and dried the woman she did not know, but then again did know. After, Althea stood Miriam in front of the closet and asked for her help in picking out a dress for the funeral. Miriam tried to help, she did. She reached into the closet and tried to lay her hand on something she could wear, but finally she could not do it. She could not command her hand to do that which made no sense in her mind. Picking out an outfit so that she would look appropriate burying her child? It made no sense. None. Miriam collapsed onto the floor.

Althea lifted her. She brought her to the bed and sat her on it and rocked her and whispered okay, baby, okay. She went into the closet herself and found a navy suit and matching shoes, and she dressed that woman. She got pantyhose and a bra on Miriam. She got the skirt and jacket on her. She brushed Miriam's hair all the way back, and twisted it and pulled it up and clipped it tight.

She put on Miriam's shoes and coat, and together those women who had never had a single, meaningful conversation, walked carefully down the stairs of 8 Manchester Place. They walked out the door, and they got into the sedan the funeral home had sent over, and slowly, deliberately, they went to do what Black women have done for centuries and centuries.

≈

It seemed as though the entire community came out to the funeral. Some knew Aya, but most didn't. They came to mourn in some part for her, but mostly they came to mourn for themselves, for the lives they did not live, the safety they did not feel, the joy they could not hold on to and view as a permanent fixture in the every moment of their days.

But dipped just below the sadness, mixing in with the hurt to form the shape of their tears, was a seething anger. Seething as it was, however, it was an anger with no home, no base, no focus, no intent. Waiting for the pastor to begin, some talked about protests, about how Aya's killing was a tiny story in the paper. Barely mentioned.

*That's because all them drug dealers keep killing police,* another mentioned.

*That's all I read about,* others observed.

*But you'd think, something.* Something.

*Well, she gotta do it. The mother. Get people together on it.*

*She ain't in no shape for that.*

*She sure not.*

*Anyway, you know how many niggers they shoot up. We protest them all, who gonna go to work and pay that rent?*

*I'm just saying I'm mad.*

*Me too. I ain't saying I ain't mad. I'm saying just watch out for your own.*

*Why she let her daughter run at night like that anyway? That makes me mad, too.*

*A lot of things going on to make us mad.*

*And sad.*

*Yeah.*

*All right y'all. Leave all that alone. The pastor coming.*

Even the pastor seemed to be angry. Even the pastor said he was going to have to sit a long time with God to understand this tragedy, and that the only possible good that would rise from these ashes would be if for once and for all their small community would speak with one voice, act with a single fist, allow the hurt in their hearts to transform, to become an action that ends forever this violence, this injustice. Everyone amened him, and in agreeing with him, they felt righteous.

The church, packed with deacons and nurses, with boys from the corner and the shopkeepers who were often annoyed by them, the around-the-way-girls, the mothers, the fathers, the grandparents and siblings, the students who knew Aya from class, and Bakar, who cried when he heard of Aya's death, remembering he was supposed to see her that day. He cried and then put it out of his mind, focused only on the anger he felt toward the police. Bakar had come with a few of Aya's classmates, but once at church, he'd seated himself alone, in the most remote pew. He had touched this girl and now she was gone and it had to be impossible. *I was supposed to see her that day,* he thought again, and then shook his head. Someone watching might have thought he was shaking it at the horror of the situation. But he was shaking away the piece of responsibility he felt but could not possibly own. Could not own and move on.

Dawn had heard about the shooting from her mother, who'd heard about it from a friend who knew Miriam from church. How long had it been since she and Aya had seen each other, Dawn wondered. Aya died without knowing that Dawn had never stopped loving her, and she'd never had a best friend and confidante since they'd been separated. She was a student now at New York University, there on full scholarship, and often when the pressure of studying and fitting in overwhelmed her, Dawn thought of Aya. She thought about Aya's energy and confidence and how she would be able to walk into any of those classes, any of those student clubs, and just take over. Then she'd look over her shoulder and say "Come on,

Dawn!" After the incident, after she'd so disappointed her mother, Dawn felt she had no choice but to follow her mother's advice, to leave that girl alone. She'd thought then, Dawn did, that perhaps her mother was right. Perhaps Aya was too wild. Perhaps she did push things too far. But sitting here, weeping, all she could think was that Aya was too filled with life in a world too small to accommodate her. The world preferred people more inclined to retreat. That's what Dawn was thinking as she sat there, holding herself in, noticing that Miriam was doing the very same thing.

Really, it was composure Miriam wanted. She wanted it desperately because in just moments she would have to stand up, walk over to the pulpit and eulogize her daughter. Althea had encouraged her to do it, mostly, she'd argued, because there was no one else who knew Aya the way Miriam did. No one else who could honor her memory properly.

"I'm not good at that," Miriam countered weakly. "I've never spoken before a group of people before. I would . . . I would . . . lose my words, my thoughts."

"No you won't. Write it down. Write down whatever is in your heart, and just read. Take your time. Ain't nobody going to be judging you."

Now had come the time for Miriam to do it. She rose and one of the deacons rose with her. He walked with her to the pulpit as the crowd, Black and ageless, tried with the collective force of their prayers, to will Miriam's one foot in front of the other. And it worked. Their spirits carried Miriam, who on her way to the front of the church kept having the sudden sensation that she would fall, but did not.

When she finally made it to the pulpit, Miriam felt her hands tremble as she reached into her jacket pocket, pulled out the paper she was to speak from, and began speaking, but her words were only audible because of the microphone. Even then, only barely so. Miriam began, "We wrestle not against flesh and blood . . ." Then it stopped, her voice, Miriam's, cut off by its own self. Now it was not her hand trembling, but the whole of her, the whole of this mother shaking. Miriam tried frantically to steady herself, but was unable to, completely unable. At last she said again, "We wrestle not against flesh . . ."

Then that was all for several minutes. The audience of mourners waited for her to gather herself. But it did not happen, and when they finally realized that it would not happen, two deacons and a nurse made their way to the front of the church to help Miriam down, and the pastor began to preach, but no one heard him. He didn't even hear himself. He was on automatic now. Everyone was. Everyone doing what they had been trained to do. The deacons and the nurse helped Miriam down, helped that mother, back over to the pew where Althea was sitting, waiting to draw her up. Which she did. Althea, in her sudden and stunning role of Miriam's mother-sister-cousin-best-friend-companion, stood and reached out her arms. She circled them around Miriam and eased her into the seat next to her. Miriam's head fell into Althea's chest, where it stayed as the choir sang a slow and painful rendition of "Order My Steps" and then "Amazing Grace." On the floor near the pulpit, lay the paper that Miriam had carried with her, the paper with Aya's eulogy on it. It was blank. But that was noticed later, and only briefly, by the pastor, who picked it up, looked at it, wondered where it came from, and then threw it away.

# 20.

Aya's coffin was carried out of the church by six neighborhood men who were organized by Althea. Really they were organized by Dante, who was haunted by an unreasonable sense of guilt over Aya's death. Should he have approached her differently that night? Would another approach have kept her there, talking to him, there and safe? Should he have offered to run with her? These questions came to him and would not leave in the moment his aunt had come to his apartment—something she never did and so he'd known her words would be bad. Aunt Althea had come into the apartment, offered no gentle lead-in to the discussion, and said plainly, "The girl upstairs. They killed her."

"What girl upstairs?" Dante had asked, unwilling to greet the truth.

"Aya."

The police did it, Althea explained after a time, after waiting for the words to fully register with Dante. Why would they kill her? What reason? How could she be thought of as dangerous, as someone who needed to die? Dante hung his head and told his aunt about seeing Aya just before the run. "Wasn't nothing you could do," she assured him, but the guilt lingered. Mixed in with it, mixed in with the profound sadness—and this was something Dante did not share with his aunt—was also a fear that stammered his breath. If the police could kill a girl like Aya, what could that mean for a man like him?

As his aunt sat quietly on his sofa, Dante walked over to the window, where incense burned in a wooden holder. He put it out and looked around his tiny space, and suddenly it seemed smaller, more dull. The couch woven in shades of black and gray seemed more worn. The white paint on the walls, more drab, like the old blue curtains, the ones his aunt had given him when he moved in here. Everything was older, so much older, right then, including him.

"Let me get you some juice," Dante said to his aunt, not because she asked for it, or even appeared to want anything. He said it so he could get out of that one room, into the kitchen, where he could, if only for seconds, feel the weight of his emotions. The weight of all the losses he'd known. And also the anger, and also the fear, and also the sadness. He poured Berry Berry juice into one of his four glasses, and brought it out to his aunt, who thanked him, but did not drink it.

"How's her mother doing?" Dante asked.

"It's hard to tell. But what I do know is she ain't got no people. So we helped her get it all together. Ms. Williams and them. They helping me. I'd like you to get together some of your friends to carry the coffin, all right?"

"Yeah?" Dante asked, surprised. But just as quickly, he recovered. "All right. It's no problem."

It really wasn't. The brothers Dante couldn't reach by phone or pager, he found around the way. He found them and told them about the girl almost a woman, the girl who lived over his aunt, the girl who was killed by the police. He explained about her and also about the mother who was left behind with no people and they needed to stand up for her. To a man, each one said fine. Without hesitation.

Students and drug dealers, one who had just come home off

a manslaughter conviction, one who cut hair for ten dollars a head at the barbershop on the corner of Manchester. They showed up in their very best clothes on the morning of the funeral; Ben, the one who cut hair, even bought a new shirt and tie. Before this happened, not one of them knew Aya or Miriam, and then again, they did.

≈

About twenty women gathered in Althea's tiny living room after Aya's burial. They were friends of Althea's, and some knew Miriam from church. As crowded as it was in that space, no one fussed or was bothered. It was good to sit close with people, people who were familiar, even if it was in the face of tragedy. Perhaps because it was in the face of tragedy. Dante was at the house, too. He'd wanted to go home, to be alone, but his aunt had asked him to stay with her, to help her get the food served, and later, clean up. He'd agreed, disguising his reluctance with a smile and nod of his head.

Dante poured tea, offered cake, and quickly removed any used plates and napkins that had been left on the coffee and end tables. He moved like a veteran waiter through the tight throng of women in the kitchen and living room, remembering to ask if anyone needed anything else. And when he became tired, not physically, but emotionally wiped out, but knew he could not yet leave, Dante excused himself and headed to the bathroom where he thought, Okay. Let me wash up, get a minute to myself.

Flipping on the bathroom light, Dante stepped inside, but almost tripped. There on the floor was Miriam, whom no one had seen as she slipped out of the living room and into the bathroom, and curled up on the cold black-and-white-tile floor, and pulled her knees into her chest, and wept.

It hadn't even occurred to her to just go upstairs, go into her own apartment. She'd felt simply that she needed a moment to get herself together. She'd known she could feel it, Aya's death rising in her, rendering her legs, her arms, the whole of her body, useless. *Just give me a moment,* she'd thought, *to pull it back together.* But the moment had come and gone, and then another, and then another. And now Dante was standing over her and the light was on.

"Ms. Rivers?" Dante paused. "Let me help you up," he said, gently offering his hand. And by this offering, the discomfort both of them felt—him discovering her, her being discovered—dissipated. Miriam took Dante's hand, and rose, somehow she rose. "Thank you," she whispered. "I . . . I was just overcome—"

"You don't have to explain—"

"I know I don't have to. I just wanted to tell you—" Miriam's voice broke as she stared into the wide, deep brown and young face of this man, this man who'd reached out his hand to her, this man who had helped her to stand. "Didn't you help? It was you, right, who helped carry Aya?"

"Yes, ma'am."

A glint of recognition sparked, and then Miriam realized, "You're Althea's nephew, right? You lived here once, right?"

"That's right. Yes."

"Tell me your name again. Please."

"Dante Jones."

"Thank you, Dante. Thank you so much. Your aunt has been, has been . . . I don't know how to say—"

"I understand, Ms. Rivers. We all do." Then, with slight trepidation, Dante ventured, "Your daughter . . . she was . . . ummm . . . she had . . . I mean. She had grown into a very beautiful young woman. I remember her as a child but she'd become a woman."

"Yes. She was." Wanting to move away from Aya before she was overcome again, Miriam shifted gears, "Where do you live now? Are you still in the neighborhood?"

"Yes. Right up the block. Number thirty-six."

"Oh, yes. I know the building. I pass it on the way to the subway." An awkward silence settled between them. Both Miriam and Dante took deep breaths, and finally Miriam said, "Listen, Dante. Thank you. Let me get out of your way. But thank you very much."

"It was no problem, Ms. Rivers. Really. You'll let me or my aunt know if there's anything—"

"I will," Miriam said, cutting into Dante's words. She wanted it all over with suddenly. This attention on her, this attention to pain that could not be eased. It could not be eased, could it? Miriam excused herself, took another deep breath, and went out into the living room and sat among the strangers who were oddly passing for friends and relations.

# 21.

Just like that, two days after Aya's burial, Miriam woke up from another fractious sleep, and decided she must move. Decided she *had* to move. Not so much from this bed, but from the entire of this space, this hell. Not move as in toward something, but move as in away from something. Hadn't her parents done that, and done it so well all those years ago. Just moved?

But then, they had had a place, and people. Who did Miriam have? No one. Not a one. She'd lived her life so completely at arm's distance from the world, now there was no one, no place. At first this realization made her sad, but sadness was an emotion Miriam had long ago learned to replace with determination and details.

To move required money and destination. She had savings, of course; thousands of dollars set aside for Aya's tuition and her own retirement. But that still didn't solve the problem of where to go. Which is how it came to her to instead redo the apartment. Make it new. Paint over, scrub over, change over the memories that spotted the walls, the carpets, the tiles in the bathroom. The fingerprints and footprints that belonged to a life now gone.

At 9:00 A.M. sharp, Miriam called her office and requested a month off. She had the vacation time stored up. She'd worked all those years for the mid-sized accounting firm, and although they were loath to do without her for so long, Miriam's supervisor had intervened on her behalf; the time was granted, however reluctantly.

And on the first day Miriam went shopping. Paints and brushes, curtains and new sheets, a new couch, new dishes, a new tablecloth. Everything white. I want cleanliness, she thought. Things without stains.

And on the second day Miriam began to pack. All the old things she was throwing or giving away. Bags and bags of sheets and towels preserved for years that still looked like new. But they were old and Miriam didn't want them anymore. She packed and packed all around Aya's room, and then there was nowhere else to go but into Aya's room. She entered it, cautiously. Entered it as if when she stepped inside the door, as in some predictable horror movie, it would slam shut behind her. Lock her in for good.

But the door sat open wide as she began going through Aya's closet, removing jeans and sweatpants, an occasional dress, the red sweater—hadn't Aya worn that just last week? She loved that sweater, Miriam was sure of it, and then suddenly she wasn't. She folded it neatly, placed it in a box for the Salvation Army with all of Aya's other clothing and shoes. She stripped the bed, got rid of the sheets. She cleaned off the dresser, threw away lotions, hair pomade, and the Burnt Raisin nail polish. She threw away cassettes, and packed Aya's radio and then alarm clock into the give-away box.

Miriam took the prints down off the wall, all four of them water and landscapes. She threw them away. Never once, in all of this cleaning, did she pause and wonder what was really useless, what was of value to her, the mother, the person left behind. She just kept moving. Underwear, bras, shorts, and T-shirts. Miriam removed it all. Finally she was in the last drawer, the one overrun with old nightgowns and pajamas. Miriam threw them away, and as she pulled the last nightie out from the back of the drawer, she saw a notebook, a journal, with a simple black cover. She opened it and saw her daughter's handwriting, and then and there, she froze. Where would this thing go, this thing that contained perhaps the full breadth of her daughter's feelings, the full breadth of her daughter? She held the book for a minute, and then placed it atop the now empty shelf in Aya's closet.

Miriam walked back over to one of the boxes in which Aya's books had been packed. She went through them meticulously, taking out the poetry books. These she placed in the closet near the journal, and then she exited the room and closed the door, walked out into the living room, and sat for hours without moving.

Until the third day, when it started all over again, this furious effort of cleaning, of change. Miriam began hauling the garbage outside early in the morning, before the trucks came. Nearly twenty years of life, twenty years of what she looked at, day in and day out, bagged and left on a street corner for a stranger to grab up, toss away.

Back inside the apartment, Miriam moved around whatever furniture she could, in her mind drawing a picture of where the new things would go. She switched around the entertainment center and the couch; the couch was going anyway. She wanted the new one there, underneath the window. Which meant moving the dining room table. Miriam moved it over, away from the window, away from beneath the spider plant where Aya used to sit and do her homework. Then Miriam took down the spider plant and threw it out.

On the fourth day she made calls. The first one by 7:00 in the morning to confirm with the painters, who'd assured her they could do her apartment all in white and all in a single day. It wasn't much. Two bedrooms, neither large, a small kitchen and bath, a combined living and dining room. They could handle it they'd told her, and so she was satisfied, and made the other calls as the painters, who showed up at 8:30, finished taping up windows and light fixtures. Miriam called the Salvation Army, and then the movers who would take her old things and dispose of them properly. Afterward she called the private delivery company she was using to pick up the new furniture the store could not promise an early and specific arrival date for. She scheduled them to come exactly three hours after the painters would be cleaned up and gone. They did it with precision. Took out the old, left the new.

Doing the entire job so quickly would cost Miriam so much extra money, but to her it was worth it. Didn't her boss sometimes do things like this to get something handled in the office more efficiently? *Time can be worth more than cash,* he'd admonished her as she had hunted for bargains once when they had needed to make some changes in the office decor because one of their biggest clients was flying in suddenly to take a meeting with the partners. She had thought then how white people throw away money. Now she felt differently. *Just get the work done,* she said to herself as painters moved into the kitchen.

On the fifth day, with an apartment painted a new eggshell white all the way through, Miriam gave out the rest of the orders to the delivery and moving men.

*Take this out first, put that over there.*

*Careful with the walls. I just had them painted.*

*Move it four inches down please, center it against that.*

*Yes I know that looks new, but I want to get rid of it.*

*Do whatever you want with it. Keep it, trash it, whatever works best.*

*Thank you for your help.*

On the sixth day Miriam rearranged. Not the living room, but the new dishes in the cabinets, the pots and the pans. She washed and then refolded all the new towels and sheets. She put them in different places in her linen closet. She moved her bed over to the opposite wall, put a new duvet cover on her comforter, reorganized her closet. And then Miriam got in the shower, and stood beneath the hot water for nearly thirty minutes. When she got out, she dried herself off in her old room made new where the window faced the west, and she watched the sky change colors and thought about how long it had been since she had noticed it doing that.

Just as Miriam sat down on her bed, just as she was trying to lose herself in the wash of oranges, reds, and yellows outside of her window, her doorbell rang. Annoyed at the interruption of the quiet, Miriam ignored it. "Go away," she whispered. But the bell rang twice more, and so Miriam pulled her beige terry-cloth robe on, and walked to the door. "Who is it?" she asked, her voice steady, betraying none of the frustration she felt at the moment.

"It's me, Miriam. It's Althea." Miriam sighed ever so softly, and opened the door for her neighbor. Why was she here? She never rang Miriam's bell *just because* before. Before. And now. Now Althea stood there, not sure whether or not she should feel comfortable or uncomfortable, said simply, "I just wanted to check on you, dear. I left you messages but haven't heard from you."

Sure enough, when Miriam glanced over at the answering machine on the end table, she saw the light that indicated there were new messages blinking on and off.

"Oh. Oh, Althea. I apologize. I've been so busy. You understand. Trying to reorganize. Trying to pack up."

"You're moving?"

"No. No. I mean Aya's—"

"Oh, yes. Yes." Althea peeked into the apartment. She knew

Miriam had gotten new furniture, had done things in the apartment. She'd seen the delivery men, the painters, the garbage bags out front.

"You changed things around."

"Yes. Mmmhmm. It's better."

"I understand. Probably would've done the same thing," agreed Althea, knowing she never had, not when she'd lost people through death or other departures. Maybe it was different, this sort of death. "Well, I wanted to know if you'd been watching the news. Also wanted to know if you needed anything. I made some chicken and rice. Thought you might be hungry."

"I'm not hungry," Miriam stammered, and then continued, "but thank you. What about the news?"

"Well nothing," Althea answered, "and that's the problem. It's been no news about Aya on the TV or in the papers. I only saw the stories about the police killed by drug dealers. You know the second one, the young one, died." Althea's voice displayed compassion as she told Miriam this news. Miriam looked at her impassively. Althea continued, "It's been all sort of coverage of that and how they ain't found his killer, but it ain't been nothing on Aya and we *do* know the killer."

Miriam nodded.

"You call a lawyer yet?"

"No."

"Talk to the district attorney's office yet?"

"No. Well, once. They said they were conducting an investigation. They were going to call back when they were done."

"They ain't called back?" Althea remembered the answering machine flashing messages. Miriam shook her head. "Not that I know of. I figured it would take a while."

Althea nodded and tried to think of something else to say. She could not do it. Finally Miriam stepped back and opened her front door wider. The whole of this conversation, and

Althea had not crossed the threshold into Miriam's apartment. "Would you like to have a cup of tea with me?" Miriam finally asked.

Althea shifted from one foot to the other. "Oh, I'd love to, but I'm so hungry. Want to get to my dinner." She smiled, told Miriam she was keeping her in her prayers, and then headed back downstairs wondering how they could have spent those days being so close, close like family, and now, right here, she felt nearly as a stranger.

"Good night, Althea," Miriam called after her. "Good night and thank you. Thank you so much." Miriam closed the door to her apartment and kept saying it, "Thank you, Althea. Thank you so much." Miriam went back to sitting on her bed, looking out the window, looking out at the sky, which was no longer flashing color, only dark. Miriam was used to it.

Dark was everywhere and Miriam did nothing to fight it. She did not turn on a light or pray for the sun to rise. She just laid there wrapped in her terry-cloth robe, on top of the covers, not moving. And she may have stayed like that, only eventually night passed and the sun did ascend and habit called Miriam up and out of her bed. On automatic she got off the bed and took a shower and made herself a breakfast of sorts: black tea and two slices of toast. She sat down on her couch to sip and eat, and then Miriam did something completely out of the ordinary for her. She turned on the television. She picked up the remote, the one she used to find in all kinds of odd places, compelling her to admonish Aya again and again to "Come on, honey. Put it back in the right place or you won't find it when you really want it."

Miriam flipped through the channels, stopping when she came to the local morning news. This is when she heard it. A newscaster saying the beleaguered police force, drained from the spate of injuries and deaths that were the result of the terrible epidemic of violence caused by increased drug activity, at least have received some good news: two of their own would not be indicted in the shooting death of a young woman in Brooklyn two and a half weeks ago.

No one had called Miriam, had they? She looked over at the answering machine still flashing the message light, and then looked back over at the television. Someone official was saying the ruling by internal affairs was sound and right, that it appreciated the fact that police officers had to go into harm's way every day, that this was a tragedy, yes, but now everyone just wanted to get back to their lives. Then came other words, a woman talking, a wife perhaps, tears in her eyes, her arms tightly holding on to her man. What was she saying? Miriam could not hear her. She could not hear anything except in slow speed, these words, these bizarre ridiculous nonsensical words, "get back to their lives."

The words repeated and repeated, they swung like a bat against her ribs, her stomach, her legs, and her head. They knocked her, those words, the weight and reality of them, that no one would be punished for killing Aya. It happened. It's over. Get back to our lives?

*What lives?*

*My life?*

*How do you get back to being a mother when your child has been killed?*

*Get back to where? To what?*

*What life do I get back to that doesn't include my child?*

*I work hard so she has a good home clothes tuition hot meals carfare her hair done soap lotion underwear books. I don't work for me. I never worked for me. I never—*

The television burst into Miriam's thoughts. The young wife of one of the officers, a woman Miriam noticed was quite pregnant, wiped the tears from her eyes and said to the camera:

*Yes. We just want to get back to our lives, especially now.* And the words, repeated one more terrible time, knocked Miriam again, only this time all the way down the wide and deep hole she had spent the last twenty years skirting the edges of. She knew she was at the bottom of it now, the hole she'd so desperately tried to avoid, even as she never heard or felt herself crash. She knew she was at the bottom and she could not get out.

Which is why on the seventh day Miriam Rivers remembered it all.

## 22.

*The news came in a sudden burst that left no room for compromise, denial, or escape. There was a pounding on Mama's front door, and at first Miriam thought it must be Bird, finally coming home. Perhaps after running he went to the bar. Maybe he had too many beers, perhaps he lost his keys. Miriam was laying on the couch resting, and so it was Mama who walked as quickly as possible to the door, the whole time calling, "Hold on. Hold on, now. I'm coming."*

*Finally unlocking the three locks, and unchaining the chain, Mama opened the door, but to her surprise, it was not a drunken grandson she saw standing there. It was the two little Mason boys from down the way. What were their names again?*

*"What y'all pounding on my door for like y'all lost y'all minds? Something happen with your parents? Why you out at this late anyway? Must be after nine-thirty."*

*"They shot him," the eight- and ten-year-old boys said in unison.*

*"What in God's name are y'all talking about?"*

*"Miss Davis," Jamal, the older boy said, calling Mama by a name she rarely ever heard, "they shot Bird." Miriam gasped, sat up, covered her mouth. What are they saying? What are they saying?*

*"What . . . what you mean? Bird's went out to the park or something like that."*

*"Miss Davis, we saw them do it. They did it right in front of us," Jamal continued.*

"Come inside, come inside," said Mama, ushering in the two boys who were shaking and small for their age. Miriam was standing now. "Sit down here," Mama instructed and then looked over at Miriam. "Everybody just sit down and calm down. Now, slowly, tell me what it is y'all are trying to explain."

Jamal took charge. "Miss Davis, we was standing on our stoop, me and Jalil." He pointed to his little brother. "We was waiting for our mother to come back from the store, and she had told us to stay outside and wait because she ain't trust us in the house. But she was taking a long time, and it was cold. So we went across the street to stand in the Spanish store because we could see from there when she came.

"So then we was standing there in the doorway of the Spanish place and then we saw Bird. He waved to us through the door. And then we saw the police roll up on him. And we ain't really pay attention 'cause they always doing that. But then they told him to get on the wall, and then he looked at us, and then he looked at them, and he said something. I couldn't hear exactly but now they arguing, and Bird turned all the way around kind of fast and that's when they shot him." Jalil started to cry.

Mama stared at the boys, stared right through them, right through the words. After a long time she said, "Where my boy at?"

"The ambulance got him and took him."

"He alive?"

Jamal shrugged his shoulders and looked down. "The ambulance took him. That's all I know."

Just then the telephone rang. Mama identified herself to whoever the caller was, listened without interjecting a word, and then hung up. She turned to Jamal and Jalil and said quietly, "Ahh . . . y'all need to get on home before your mother worries about y'all."

"She ain't gonna worry," Jalil piped in matter-of-factly.

Miriam was frozen in her seat. Didn't know what to say, to ask, to think or feel. Mama continued talking to the boys.

"Listen to me. Y'all need to go on home before she worries. Thank you for coming here. Thank you for telling me." She directed them out of *the apartment, and turned toward Miriam's unblinking eyes. Eyes that were losing their vision, their ability to see what was there, in front of her.*

*All Miriam could see was that door, the one Bird should have been coming through. Walking in, walking to the back, going to take a shower, singing in the shower, singing too loud thinking no one could hear him. Bird should have been coming out of the bathroom wearing his forest green terry-cloth robe. Should be headed toward the refrigerator looking for a snack. Should be opening the refrigerator, closing it, opening it again, closing it. Walking away. Coming back. Always coming back.*

*"Miriam," Mama called. "Miriam." The pregnant girl looked up at the woman, the woman she'd come to love, the woman who had already buried a child, who had pushed herself to live, willed an impossible strength and raised a boy, a man, a human being worthy of love. What would it do to Mama if that boy now a man was gone? What would that mean for the baby coming? What would that mean for me, Miriam wondered. She could not, of course, conceive of these answers. "He's all right, Mama. Shot doesn't mean killed. He's all right."*

*Mama nodded and simply said softly, "Bible say we wrestle not against flesh and blood but against spiritual wickedness in high places. Take unto you the whole armor of God that ye may be able to stand in the coming day."*

*The two women stood there for a moment, neither moving, neither speaking, until finally: "Get your shoes and coat, Miriam. We got to go."*

*When they arrived at the hospital, Mama told the shortest officer, the one closest to her own eye level, who she was.*

*I'm his grandmother, she'd said. Next of kin.*

*The officer scrutinized Mama. He scrutinized both women.*

*You have identification? he'd demanded. Nothing gentle in his voice.*

*Mama was shaking, she was stunned. She had not thought of this before she left the house.*

*Mama, your social security card, Miriam had reminded her.*

*The old woman began digging in her bag, she was digging and angry,*

*thinking if they ain't gonna be nice, I definitely ain't gonna be nice.*
*Mama grumbled under her breath. Here, she said, shoving the card*
*toward the officer. And then another cop, one who'd been watching,*
*waved his hand at Mama and said,*

*All right. All right.*

*As though he's doing her a favor. He pats the first officer, the short*
*one, a couple of times on the back. Pats him as though he needed relief*
*from stress. And then that second cop added with a frown,*

*Who's she?*

*My grandson's fiancée, the mother of his unborn child.*

*All right, all right, he'd said again, like he had to stretch the rules, or*
*instead, his own principles, to allow the two of them to walk into the*
*room.*

≈

Miriam, curled on her new couch, begs God. Please. Make it
stop. Make it go away. I don't want to relive this. Not again.
Please. I'm so tired. Twenty years trying to hold it together. I'm
so tired. There's no part of me that doesn't ache. No part that
hasn't ached for the last twenty years. Miriam is talking but in a
voice that can only be heard on the far inside. She opens her
eyes and she sees it. She closes them, she sees it:

*That long ago and horrific bed with the body in it.*

*The sheet up over its head.*

*The police officer who had followed in behind her and Mama, and*
*then moved ahead of them.*

*Moved over to the impossible form beneath the sheet, the one that was*
*now only a single foot away.*

*She sees him do it—the officer pulling back the sheet.*

*Can you identify this man?*

*Which is when Mama collapsed and Miriam was trying to help her,*
*trying to get her into that black fake leather chair. There's a rip across the*
*back. She wonders why she noticed it.*

"No," Miriam yells to God, herself. She yells twice and then twice more. "No, no, no, no." She says it now, she said it then. No.

*"Are you sure?" the officer who led them into the hospital room asked softly.*

"Please," Miriam remembers begging.

"Please, please, No." She remembers shaking her head and her hands, as if by this act, she could reverse reality.

*"Please," she begged, and begged again, nearly on her knees, a scream behind the whisper the officer heard from this girl, this girl so young. This girl, pregnant. This girl positioned to be a widow before she'd become a wife. This girl now down on her knees. Her voice was disappearing. She couldn't get her prayers out, couldn't sound out the pleading. But she was pleading.*

*Bird? Bird?*

*Don't make this the ending.*

*This doesn't have to be the ending.*

*We can make another ending     we have to make another ending.*

*We're having a baby. You have to come on get up let's get out of this place. Don't make me have this baby alone, Bird. I can't do it, I can't. Get up. Please baby please baby please baby please.*

Sitting there on her new couch, Miriam remembered how she had leaned over and rested her head on Bird's still and cold chest. And laying there with him, she had conjured the strength to finally be audible. "Live. Livelivelivelivelive. Live, baby. Livelivelivelivelive."

Mama had wept quietly alone, and rocked herself back and forth. Miriam remembered.

"I'll give you a minute." The officer had said and left the room. Miriam remembered everything.

How the world was an earthquake so violent it split every piece of the ground and also the waters and also the sky. It was a hurricane with no beginning no ending no let up no calm. Whatever had been known was suddenly unknown. There was no language no vision no sound no movement no color no taste no smell no star no night no day no breath no wind no tomorrow no today.

There had been weather the day they came to bury Bird. Miriam could feel it, even now, today, in her freshly painted apartment with its insistent steam heat. There, where Aya should have been but would never be again. She could feel the cutting of that long ago early March ice and snow. It had transformed the city landscape into a lonely ghost calling, and the wind was wild.

What had it been? About one hundred people who'd come to the service at Mama's small Bedford Stuyvesant church? They had crowded in together: the boys from around the neighborhood pushed up next to the elder members of the congregation whose long-held warm feelings toward Mama compelled them to brave the bite of the outside. They came, those elders, making apologies for the ones who did not. They came, shaking their heads and whispering Psalms and prayers, but not confusion. If only it had been incomprehensible, this shooting, this loss.

As though it were a scene from a movie playing on the television screen, Miriam could see Mama sitting self-possessed in the front pew. And now there's Junior, the seventy-eight-year-old janitor who had worked with Bird at the school, bending down as much as his thin, worn body could before Mama. Junior . . . why did they still call such an old man that, anyway? But Junior, shaking his head and wiping a tear from his eye. And Joan had come. She'd come to show support. But she had had no words for her friend. "I'm so sorry," she finally sputtered, her eyes, the whole of her face, uncharacteristically cloudy.

And Miriam could also see herself, a one-dimensional figure, a shadow sitting in that front pew holding her belly that was holding the baby that she and Bird had made. A baby growing, turning, stretching inside of her. Even then, on that day. Moving as it had never moved. Moving as though it wanted to get out, get away. A baby conceived from a love that was clean through and through, clean down even on the underside of it: clean.

Pastor Lovell took to the pulpit and began, "Let the church say Amen." And the people said, "Amen." And Pastor Lovell's voice, one of those thick, filling voices, a rich singing that nevertheless could not soothe her.

"This is a difficult day for us all here. I prayed and I prayed to know what to say." Miriam remembered how the preacher was preaching and the congregation nodding and crying. And she remembered herself. Disappearing. She was disappearing. Right there. Disappearing from the voices, from the sobs that soaked the air. She was disappearing, and now she couldn't see the casket and she couldn't see the stained-glass white Jesus trying to find her, stare her down. She was gone. Gone to find Bird so she could ask him,

*Bird?*

*Bird?*

*Where am I, where are you, what is happening?*

*Bird?*

*Is this some cruel joke?*

*Bird, they say you're going but you can't be going if the baby is coming.*

*And the baby is coming so you have to, too.*

*Come on, come back, Bird. Baby, please.*

*Show up, walk in, touch me, hold me, look at me here, desperate for you.*

*I waited all day yesterday and the day before that and the day before that.*

*I waited and you didn't show up and now I'm scared.*

*Bird, you said you would never let me be scared and I know you are a man of your word.*

*Listen, my stomach is growing and the baby is turning. We need to hear your voice. Okay?*

*You who sang to the baby. Bird.*

*Who massaged us with warm lotions. Bird.*

*Who said you would marry me and take care of us and I could finish school and you could finish school. Bird.*

*Where's our house with a yard and willow tree? Let's leave this place and go find it.*

*We were going to look at cribs next week. You promised me.*

*Bird. Baby, baby, babybabybaby. Please.*

*You promised me.*

*Bird—*

The Lord is my shepherd, I shall not want . . .

*. . . to be alone, to be in this place, to navigate and negotiate it all on my own. Not when I am part of a team. Like you said. How can I be a member of a team if the team is just me? I want you back. Need you back. Bird.*

He maketh me to lie down in green pastures, he leadeth me beside the still waters . . .

*. . . don't stay still. Waters change without warning. They change and they rush. So harsh and so deep. I am drowning. Pull me back, pull us back. Or don't. Don't and let me drown, too. Let me go to where you are, wherever you are. I'm coming, Bird. I'm coming.*

Miriam remembered the people standing, lining up to view the body. And she hated them for it. How could they do it, see him there and not scream? She remembered the impossibility of walking, of any kind of movement. She remembered what it felt like as she'd started, right there, to fade, disappearing against the words from the pastor, and the expressions of grief from the mourners. They made no sense anyway, those words, because nothing did. They might as well have been spoken in a make-believe language. Even the church itself was made up. It could have been a back alley, a condemned building, a house caught afire, a tin-roofed shack. Miriam faded and no one noticed, because everyone was wrapped up in their own world, their own sorrows, their own.

Which must have been why no one saw her, the pregnant teenager, fly, evaporate up out of herself right then, right there, in the presence of God and all those who were gathered. They didn't see it happen, there at the church, and they didn't see what happened after, what happened to Miriam in the days after the fading, after the burial.

People know that the shape of the days that come after should be amorphous days, disordered, sloppy, and frayed. They should be days without borders, without centers, without weight, without length. But they were not.

What came after—after the funeral and the burial, after the mourners and the hot meals left by friends and neighbors at the outside of the apartment door, after the hour or minute when Miriam eventually stopped looking out of the window to see if Bird was coming down the block, stopped checking around the corner and watching the clock for him, for he who had laughed and complained and sung off key, loudly—eventually after all of this was a time that went taut.

It was an uncomfortably neat sort of time. A time that came in quietly one unbearably bright morning nine days past the burial when Miriam woke with a surprising bout of nausea. She rushed to the bathroom and crouched, and then sat over the toilet and let it all come down and out of her. She heaved and gagged and her eyes were closed and these closed eyes held back the watershed of tears, the tears that, in the end, did not bring back Bird anyway.

But in abandoning that wide landscape of grief, Miriam abandoned Bird, and more than that, she abandoned who she had become, what she had learned and done in the time of loving Bird. She was different, this Miriam, from the one who flew out of herself that day in the church. Then, she was trying to fade out of this world and into Bird's. Now she accepted that there was and would never be again a Bird, and with that acceptance came a determination to leave behind every memory of him, every part of him she could. How else could she survive? It was a conscious decision in a sense, and then again it wasn't. It was more a decision made out of training, made from habit, this quickness to leave and not look back. Really, Miriam had no other way to go about things. Whoever had suggested one?

≈

Indeed, everyone from Mama to the pastor felt at ease with this new Miriam. The one without sound. The one who cleaned and made space for the coming child. The one who applied for state benefits and never missed a prenatal visit. The one who went to church with Mama and told people she was doing fine, the baby was growing well, no her back didn't hurt too much, and yes she was sleeping all right most nights.

Among themselves they commented on how good Miriam looked, very together, even as she entered her seventh and then eighth month of pregnancy and had only one pair of pants, two skirts, and three blouses to wear. But her hair was always neat and pulled back. Her skin shone. She told people that, yes, it was disappointing to have had to drop out of school, but once the baby was here she would get her GED and then a job. *Good plan,* she was assured by those who thought they were in the know. They patted her on the shoulder. They told her how strong she was.

Mama was the only one who even thought to press Miriam about how she was feeling. Was she *really* all right? Mama asked this, but only once. "Let's read from the Book" was her usual refrain. "Let's pray." And Miriam, out of respect, would sit there with Mama, lower her head and close her eyes as Mama did her best to anoint the two of them with prayer. But between Miriam's lack of response and, truth be told, her own exhaustion, Mama eventually gave up.

She gave up praying with Miriam, and she gave up asking Miriam how she was doing. Because when she thought about things in the sudden and sad quiet of that home, she thought making such inquiries was probably pointless, maybe even wrong. Mama knew, after all, what she had had to do in order to live to this age. She thought about the specific steps she had followed to get from one day into the next, from one minute into the next. Those steps did not allow for looking back, did not allow one to linger on what had been lost or what had never been given. To look back one ran the risk of falling, and there was no one to catch you if that happened. And the point was to live, which is what she told Miriam when she finally talked to her one afternoon over tuna salad sandwiches.

"Listen to me," Mama said suddenly. "That child is going to be here in a matter of days. I know things aren't the way they supposed to be. They don't be like that for most of us. But the thing is, what we got to do as parents, as people who been here longer, is make it a little easier for the next."

"I understand, Mama," Miriam had said.

"I ain't had nobody's easy life. Lost more than I can ever remember having. And sometimes, let me tell you, Miriam, you listen to me, I wanted to cry. I'm near seventy years old and still feel that sometimes. So it's things I understand that I don't always speak of. I know it ain't easy. But finally you got to let the hope of easy just go and think about what you need to do. How you can just be right. For yourself and most of all for that child."

"Yes, Mama."

Mama was in her own world now, a place she often went to when she started talking like this, in these monologues.

"You know, hard as I had it, I *still* had it better than my mama and daddy did. I always had me a job. I mean, wasn't no kind of great glorious work, but it was work enough that none of mine ever went hungry or without a home. That kind of thing happened to people, happened to my family when we was coming up. But my mama showed me how to clean, how to not fear hard work, and she saved enough money to get a bus ticket and she sent me up here to work for some relatives of white folks she knew down from around our way.

"Those white people paid me all right and they didn't fire me when I got pregnant, and like I said, it might not have been glorious work, but it kept us going." Mama let out a breath, and then continued, "I'm trying to tell you that if you just do what has to be done, and don't look at the should-a-beens and could-a-beens, you be all right. Them woulda shoulda coulda things—they'll drive you crazy and you'll wind up creating more problems than what you started off with. Just take each day piece by piece, detail by detail, and you'll get through."

Miriam nodded and Mama continued.

"Believe me, I know. You may not get through the way you want, and not the way that you deserve. But you'll get through, and that got to count for something. It'll mean that that baby you got inside of you, she might have it just a little bit easier. Just you make sure she's fed right, clothed, and got some education and sense. Other things will take care of theyself."

Miriam looked at Mama for a long time. Somewhere inside

of herself she wasn't sure she believed what Mama said. But Miriam, not knowing what else to do, just shook her head, and said, "Okay, Mama. Okay."

≈

The years opened and the years had closed like a thin screen door blowing against an insistent and steady wind. Mama died fourteen months after the baby girl Miriam named Aya was born. Miriam, straight-backed and perfunctory, organized the members of the congregation and buried the old woman with all the love and care they could summon, but surely not all that she had earned.

Miriam went on public assistance for a few months, finished her GED, and then took a job—the one she would hold for the next twenty years—as an office clerk at a small accounting firm. For a time she continued to live in the apartment she'd shared with Bird and Mama. But she hated it there.

As much as she tried to block out the silence, the voices that no longer lived within these walls but haunted them, she could not. Too many days she thought she heard Mama calling them to dinner. Then once she thought she saw Bird in the hallway, getting ready to say seductively, *Come here, girl. A brother needs a little love.* Miriam could not and would not tolerate that.

To survive, to survive for herself and for her daughter, Miriam recommitted herself to ridding her world of voices and vision. They were tyrannical, a torture, and surely they would kill her. She began looking for a new apartment, although it was difficult since her salary barely stretched across the distance from what she earned and what she needed to live on. Innumerable evenings after Aya was asleep, Miriam would go over her budget again and again.

She considered taking a second job, but a job on weekends would only really pay enough to cover the cost of child care. Miriam felt so hopeless so often that she wondered, and eventually came to believe, that the challenges she faced were some sort of payback. Revenge taken on a girl who had defied her parents, turned away from the teachings of her church. What other explanation could there be?

Miriam accepted the stark and narrow of what her life had become, and she comforted herself by coming back to God. By assuring God that she would do everything she could to instill His values into her girl; that she would never again veer from the rules, the teachings; that Aya would be given an opportunity to become the woman, the person, Miriam had rejected that night she kissed Bird in the street, and then, after, had refused to adhere to the dictates of her parents. Aya would be raised to be a righteous woman, a clean and pure and proper woman. Miriam would not allow her girl to follow the example of her life. She would be a new example. One of chastity. One of godliness.

The first of that effort, the one that came immediately after Miriam's return to the Church, was Mama and Daddy. One day after work, Miriam made her way over to their home, Mama and Daddy's. She had not seen the house in almost three years. She called the woman who sometimes baby-sat Aya, and asked her to pick the girl up at the day care center. "I have to work a little late," Miriam had explained, excusing her lie with the idea that no one had a right to be in her business.

After work she rode the train over to her once-upon-a-time home; in her head she practiced a fully rehearsed confession. She thought about how she would not ask them for help. She would only offer an apology, and ask for their grace. She would beg their forgiveness, God's forgiveness. As Christians, surely they would give her that, and maybe, maybe one day, they would love her again, and even love little Aya. In time.

Walking down the block she grew up on seemed both famil-iar and bizarre. *There's the corner store I always bought candy in, but has that house always been that color?* Her old street, her old neighborhood seemed like a place she visited once long ago: familiar yet only vaguely so. Still she walked, albeit with trepidation, past apartment buildings and homes, until she reached the door she'd once walked into and out of every day of her life. Her old life.

Miriam rang the bell, and heard heavy footsteps coming quickly to answer. The door flew open and a short brown-skinned woman of about thirty years old asked, "Can I help you?"

Miriam said nothing. She stared, completely baffled. *Did I stumble on the wrong house? No! There is our mailbox, our front yard with the crab apple tree.*

"Can I help you?" The young woman asked this again, a small measure of frustration singing the borders of the question.

"I . . . I . . . I'm looking for my m-mother," Miriam finally stuttered.

"Well, you have the wrong house, honey. It's just my husband and I living here."

"No! This is my house!" Miriam's voice grew more adamant. "I grew up here. I live here."

"Uh, no you don't. We live here and have lived here over a year. So I don't know what you're talking about."

"I grew up here," Miriam insisted, desperate to make this woman, this interloper, understand. "This is my house. The Rivers' house."

"Oh . . ." the woman nodded, finally recognizing the problem. "We bought this house from Mr. and Mrs. Rivers. That was the beginning of last year sometime. They moved down South." And then, surprised, she added, "I didn't know they had a daughter. You're their daughter?"

The words from this woman, a woman Miriam had never

seen before, a woman she would never see again, the words, the innocent, matter-of-fact, didn't they tell you, let me bring you up-to-date words, punctured Miriam. They slit her tongue, glued her teeth together, perforated her vision, paralyzed her limbs. How was she standing, how was her heart beating, and beating so quickly? Why did her body function when surely her mind was dissolving? Again. *Again.*

"Are you all right?" Miriam heard the woman ask, but of course there was no answer to this question, no known language to say what she felt, to say how she was, to explain, *This is what is happening on the inside of me.* How could there ever be a language for what we are not supposed to ever experience?

Miriam turned slowly, and opened the gate, and walked down the street, back to the subway station, back to her baby. And in the whole of that time, and in the time that came after, she refused to recall, or reflect, or wonder, or analyze. Why should she ask questions about things, why should she consider things to which there could be no reasonable conclusions? It would only make her insane. It would lose her in a labyrinth with no exits, pathways only, which look exactly the same, and offer no escape, none.

Nearly twenty years old now, and alone with a child, Miriam was clear about what she had to do. She had no choice. In order to drown out the terrible clamor of all she had lost and the chaos it had created, Miriam got back on the train, and picked up her child, and together they went back to their home.

And then, every day after, she scoured the papers until she found a small apartment advertised for a price she could afford. Eight Manchester Place. Miriam liked it because there was only one other tenant in the building. It would be a quiet place. A place where she could pray, where she could pull it all together. Where she could do it without distraction.

They moved, Miriam and baby Aya, after visiting the apartment once, and making a good impression on the landlord, who also felt sorry for the young and single mother. "I raised my sons alone," Mrs. Richardson commented to Miriam after the two had met and discussed the terms of the lease. "It ain't easy," she had said.

"No, ma'am. It's not," agreed Miriam. "But there are people even worse off than us. So I try not to complain."

"It's best. A good complaint never did nobody no good. Like you said, it's always somebody worse off in life. Complaining make you miss the blessings right in front of you."

For a moment Miriam thought to ask, *What blessings? What has been given to me? I can only think of what was taken.* But she thought better of speaking this truth, and so she simply responded, "Yes, ma'am."

After checking her work references, Mrs. Richardson gave Miriam a two-year lease, and within just three weeks, Miriam and her daughter had left Bird and Mama's home. She left it much in the way she'd left the home she'd been born into: taking only bare necessities. Only enough for basic survival.

Miriam and Aya arrived at 8 Manchester Place with all their possessions packed into a Volkswagen van that was driven by a man who worked for discount movers, and who knew, it seemed, everything about every neighborhood in Brooklyn. "Here," he commented, pulling up to the apartment building that stood on a street where Fort Greene ended and Bedford Stuyvesant began, "is a good place to live. No matter what it looks like. Don't worry about some of these buildings around here that's burnt out and stuff. This is a good place."

Miriam wished he would shut up. He didn't.

"Few years back is when it was some riots and things like that. It's why you see the abandonment. Bunch of shop owners left in that time. But this here, this is a community. I know. It got block associations, and people know each other. They look out. Even when they look like they can't look out for they own selves. They look out. I know. I got a lot of people over this way."

And in truth, the neighborhood really wasn't very bad. Manicured lawns interrupted the vacant lots, the abandoned shops. Still, once inside the apartment, Miriam realized how much work the space needed. She was not worried though; she could do it. Of that she was confident. The cleaning and the scraping, the painting and the laying of traps, hammering the nails back into the ancient floorboards. After six months, the apartment looked nearly as though it had undergone full renovations. It was a new place now, neat, and folded up, creased down the center. Miriam had done it all on a budget. She had done it reading books on home improvement. She had done it according to a schedule. She had done it despite exhaustion, and she had done it giving up even the idea of a life outside of work and the apartment, and missing dinner many nights, and losing time with Aya.

Most of all, she had done it without thinking what it would have been like had Bird been there: to scrape and clean and paint with her. Miriam never stopped long enough to wonder what if? Indeed, she never stopped long enough to even wonder could there ever be someone else to help her?

Finally it was all done, that which was needed to be done, but done without pride or pleasure. Miriam followed rules out of books, and never asked anyone for help, never reached out, never, never considered whether or not there could have been any other way. In the end she looked around at her clean and neatly appointed apartment, and told herself that it was enough. She told herself this again and again, and of course, eventually, that lie became the truth.

# 23.

Bird was not a household name there, in that household which his absence had so largely defined. When Aya asked her mother about her father, what Miriam said was "Your father was in Vietnam. He was shot," stringing together those two disparate events of Bird's life. She'd shown Bird's military photo as proof, and eventually the story began to take on a comforting place in Miriam's life. It was so much easier for her to think of Bird killed in action. Bird as a hero cut down while defending his troops. It was easier than thinking of how it really had been: Bird shot down in the street as though he were a large and vicious wild animal about to attack. Shot down without the opportunity to turn and say, *What's happening? I'm not doing anything wrong. I just want to work, to support my fiancée who's at home with my grandmother. We're about to get married, Miriam and I. We're having a baby. I'm going to be an attorney one day.*

But Bird, shot down as he was, had been left with no room for compromise. So Miriam had to make the compromise. This is what she told herself. Because after the killing there had been no apologies, there had been no protests. The world did not stop and recognize the monumental shift that had occurred the moment the policeman looked at Bird and did not see a human being, just a figure in black who needed to be stopped. He squeezed that trigger again and again; after Bird had fallen, the policeman kept squeezing, and then the earth went off its axis and no one anywhere seemed to notice.

The buses still ran, and the stores still opened and sold their goods. The sun still rose on the same side of the sky, and the streets were still littered with discarded pieces of people and the limitations of their lives. Nothing changed and everything changed and not one person Miriam had known back then started screaming, or kicking, or cursing, or questioning. Not even Mama. For a time after the shooting, Miriam would peek out from behind herself, searching to see if Mama, if anyone, was mad or even mildly annoyed. But no one displayed any sort of emotion Miriam could discern.

And then, of course, the baby came.

The baby came and Miriam knew from the beginning she could not tell her girl that Bird was one of hundreds of Black men shot by police in those post–civil rights, post–Black Power years. The years when revenge had been sworn out against man, woman, and child alike, because for almost two decades there had been rebellion.

For almost two decades Black people young and old had forced legislative change, and Malcolm X had encouraged vision change, and even Martin Luther King told the workers to lay down their tools. But most of all, there had been these nineteen-year-olds from Oakland to Brooklyn who had said enough is enough, and they brandished pistols against the tanks, and they tried to protect the places where they lived, the places where they hoped they would one day live. And they did not win that battle, and revenge had been sworn out, and once again the enemy was anything that moved.

This is why there was no real way to sort Bird out from among all of those bones, all of that ash and soot. No way to try to do that and also maintain sanity. So Miriam did the best she could to pick his remains out of the pile.

She told Aya a sketch of a love story ended by a faraway war, and Aya grew up thinking that her father was killed in a Southeast Asian jungle, that he died a war hero, that he died and it was too painful for her mother to talk about it.

She told her friends that story. How her parents loved each other, and how her mother still loved her daddy, which is why Mommy never married again. And the more Aya told the story, the more romantic it became and the more her father expanded. He became mythic in her eyes. Miriam could see that every time Aya mentioned his name. Every time she looked at that stiff military photo of a strong and intense seventeen-year-old, headed off to war.

The eyes that looked at that photo, that gazed so many nights into it, those were hungry eyes, the eyes of that girl. From the first time she saw it, and forever thereafter, Aya would stare into her father's picture that looked nearly like it could have been any young man, every young man, and she tried to know some piece of her father, and by extension, some piece of herself. Miriam could not stop Aya's hunger, Aya's searching, and so she would just turn away, tell her daughter it was bedtime now. Put the picture down and go to sleep. Aya always said, Okay, Mommy, but the next night the picture was there again. And then again and then again.

Even when she was only five years old, Aya wanted to know *exactly* who she was, *exactly* where she came from. Aya asked about grandparents (dead), can she see the grave (they're buried down South), can I visit (Aya, please, maybe one day, we'll see. Why don't you concentrate on life right now? Go do your homework, okay?). She did it, her homework, of course, because she really was a very obedient child, and she really did love her mother and want to please her.

But time and again Aya would look at her friends with their aunts and uncles and cousins and sisters and brothers and grandparents, and she would want, she would feel she needed more. Even if the more just came in the form of stories, of hazy or funny or disjointed memories from her mother, Aya *needed* them, and so she would push. But the more she pushed, the more Miriam shut down. She barricaded herself away from her child, and away from the pain of knowing she was unable to give Aya the very thing the girl so desperately needed—a father, a friend. Instead, she threw herself into that which was attainable: hot meals; lunch prepared and waiting for Aya to take to school; clothes clean and pressed.

With these things, Miriam never missed a beat, and she would block out the times she heard her daughter talking about her daddy with her friends. Aya talking about how he was a man who had saved hundreds of men, who gave his life for them, who threw himself on a grenade, who was fearless and handsome and strong.

Aya told her friends that all her dad wanted was to take care of his family, that he was about to be a great and rich lawyer, but the war got in the way, and when his country called, because he was so brave, he could not ignore it. For years small children would sit at Aya's feet and listen to stories about Bird. Not just war stories either. There was the time, Aya once explained in a hushed, slow voice, to a group of her friends who had gathered at Aya's for homemade cookies, that a big, mean dog escaped from its leash and came running toward a group of little children. "My daddy, this is before I was born, but my mom told me, anyways, my daddy grabbed that dog up by the neck!"

"And then?" the collection of eight- and nine-year-old children chorused.

"Well, all the kids were saved because of my daddy. And he was only about fourteen when this happened. But he was really *really* strong. Nothing could stop him!"

"Then how could he have gotten killed in the war?" asked

one particularly bright and inquisitive little girl. "How could the war get someone so strong?"

The question stopped Aya. It stunned her, really, though she tried to hold back the shock, and also the painful reality of that question. Instead she became indignant.

"My daddy made a choice because he was in charge. They didn't *take* his life. He *gave* his life. 'Cause of all the people he would save!!"

"I was just asking," murmured the little girl, who immediately furrowed her brow and began to pout.

"Well, if you would listen, then you wouldn't have to ask stupid questions like that." Finally Miriam interrupted the girls. "All right, all right. Time to go home. Aya's got to eat her dinner and get ready for school tomorrow."

Aya got herself together enough to say good-bye to everyone, including Angel. After they were gone, Miriam told her to come, sit down at the table and eat her dinner, and for goodness sake, stop telling all those made-up stories and start living in the present. The little girl ran into her bedroom crying. She reached under her mattress and pulled out the aging picture of Bird. And for a long time she stared into the quiet eyes of the man she had never known, the man who had helped create her. Miriam had followed her daughter, stood in her bedroom door, and watched Aya looking into the stilled eyes of her lost father. She'd thought, it was true. He *was* brave.

She let a few minutes pass, and then Miriam went to Aya and sat on her bed. Gently she took the photograph out of Aya's hands, and hugged her lightly. "Come on now, honey. I made a nice good meal for you."

Aya clung to her mother for as long as Miriam would allow, and then, prying her daughter from her, she said again, "Come on. Don't make yourself all upset. I made a nice good meal for you. Let's go eat."

Which they did. But later that night, when Miriam went into Aya's room to check if her daughter was asleep, she heard her girl whisper, "I love you, Daddy." Aya whispered this into the picture that could not whisper back, and then she kissed it. And then what was it that Miriam heard? It sounded so like Bird's voice saying "I love you, too." Miriam watched a little longer and saw Aya kiss the picture again. She hugged it against her heart, and she curled up on her bed, and she lay there just as quiet as she could be.

Right then, and right there, Miriam almost gave in. She almost lost herself in a sea of what could have been. What should have been. But she knew that sea was a rough and deadly one. She tiptoed away from her daughter's room, laid down in her own bed, and willed herself to sleep.

≈

"Stop it, stop it, stop it." Miriam shouted this aloud at the rushing tide of memories that had taken over her home, her mind. She shouted it so forcefully she startled herself. She began speaking aloud to calm herself down. "Okay, okay," she breathed, rising from the couch, trying to gather her mind back together, back into the small place she allowed it to exist.

Nearly running into her bedroom, Miriam rummaged through her closet and found her beige housedress, and threw it on. She pulled her hair back, and went into the bathroom to splash some water on her face. And then she did something that, despite all that had happened, was still completely out of character for her to do. Miriam grabbed her keys and went downstairs to see Althea.

Althea was relaxing, watching a game show, when she heard the knock at the door. Who in the world could that be, she wondered. It wasn't the downstairs buzzer going off. It was the actual front door to her apartment someone was knocking on, which meant that it had to be someone already inside the building. But the only person inside the building was Miriam, and it certainly wouldn't be her. Althea was thinking this just as she opened up the front door and saw Miriam standing before her. Her pretty brown face was twisted into a knot. "Miriam?" Concerned, Althea furrowed her brow. "Miriam, come on in."

Miriam walked silently into her neighbor's apartment. She had not been in here since the day of Aya's funeral. She thought then that she'd never set foot in this apartment again. What for, she'd thought.

"Sit down," Althea offered, moving aside pillows on the couch. "Let me get you some water." Miriam shook her head.

"You want some tea then? What can I get you?"

Miriam shook her head again, and finally said, "Nothing. Nothing."

"What it is then?" Althea asked softly, taking Miriam's hand.

Miriam kept shaking her head, until finally tears welled up in the sides of her eyes. "It's so unfair," she whispered at last.

"I know, I know."

"Not just what happened," Miriam continued nearly inaudibly. "But no one's even going to be punished."

Althea, like Miriam, had seen the news about the police not being indicted. "They never are," she commented, matter-of-factly, thinking this would offer some sort of comfort to the grieving mother. It did not. It didn't help Miriam to know that Aya would not be treated any differently from so many others, that this was just the way things were here. And she could have predicted what Althea would say next.

"But you know they may get away with it in this life, but they ain't gonna get away with it when they got to go to the next."

*That's not good enough,* Miriam thought. Instead what came

out was a look, a vacant look. A look that said she'd gone again, back to a place where no one could find her. That's what Althea thought as she looked at her neighbor.

Just then the buzzer rang. "Now who's that?" Althea asked, not really expecting a response and not waiting for one. She walked over to the intercom. "Who is it?" she called into the speaker.

"Dante!"

"Oh!" Althea buzzed him in, and heard him run through the hallway as though he was running from a monster. He'd done that since he was a boy, and since he was a boy, she would throw open her door, and exclaim, "Dante! Boy, don't run like that! You gonna break your neck like that one day." Today was no different, at least not in that respect.

"Hey, Auntie!" Dante bellowed out as soon as his aunt opened the door.

"Boy, slow down! And bring it down a little. I have company," Althea murmured, opening the door wider, revealing Miriam's still figure, sitting on the couch.

"Oh. Oh." Dante cleared his throat and stepped all the way into the apartment. "Hello, Ms. Rivers." Miriam turned her body toward Dante, but not all the way. "Hello, Dante."

"I ain't mean to interrupt anything," he began awkwardly. "I just, when I was here last week, I had left my credit card. I left you a message, Auntie. You got it?"

"I did. And I got it. I put it up someplace in my room. Wait here a minute. Let me go find it." Althea walked away talking to herself, wondering where she'd left the darn thing. And if he could have, Dante would have followed behind her. The last thing he wanted to do was sit here with Ms. Rivers. What was he supposed to say to her? How was she doing? He knew how she was doing: bad. Had to be. On top of everything else that had happened, all over the neighborhood people were talking about how the police got off.

*Knew they would.*

*It still ain't right.*

*Right ain't never been part of it.*

*It should be.*

*Lot of things should be.*

That's how the conversations were going. Anger watered down and down until it became frustrated acceptance. People grumbled, *If ten people were killed by the cops in a year, one story made the news. Ain't nobody got time to protest everything. Just got to try to stay out of their way.*

In the year before Aya was killed, a young Black medical student was shot fourteen times by officers who said he fit the description of an armed robber they'd been looking for. Despite the outrage and protests, those officers weren't indicted either. After that the local paper ran a twelve-week series on the life of police officers, the difficulties and challenges of it. And after that, an off-duty cop intervened in a gun battle between rival drug dealers. The dealers got away, but the cop was wounded when he pushed an elderly woman out of the line of fire and saved her life. At a press conference the mayor said if he could, he'd give the officer a purple heart. The mayor had said, his voice quivering with emotion, that officer was a hero. Then he said, truth be told, all our cops are.

Two weeks to the day after that statement, Aya was killed.

This was the story behind the story. This is what everyone in the neighborhood knew but no one said. They knew they should have been angrier, they should have done more than simply agree to help bury the child, but what good would it do? What good did it ever do? Folks went back to work, to school, to the corner even as there was a sense inside them that it was all wrong.

Surely that sense was shared by Dante as he shifted uncomfortably on the couch next to Miriam. He looked over his shoulder several times, wishing his aunt would hurry up and get back in here. After an interminable five minutes, Althea came back into the living room, victoriously waving the credit card.

"Here you go," she said with a smile.

"All right," Dante nearly exclaimed, jumping up from the couch. "Let me be out then." He turned to Miriam, lowered his voice, and offered, "Uhh . . . you take care of yourself, okay, Ms. Rivers?"

"Thank you, Dante," Miriam answered. And then to her surprise, but more to his, Miriam added, "Dante, may I speak to you for a moment. Privately."

He wished, Dante did, that there was some way, any way, out of this, but he couldn't think fast enough. He did say quickly, "I do have this appointment I'm late for," but then he added, "Yeah. Sure."

"Althea, do you mind? Would you excuse us for just a moment?"

Althea was confused. What could Miriam want to talk to Dante about? And then she thought that Miriam probably wanted to thank him for carrying the coffin, for getting his boys together to help. "Of course not. I'll be here."

Dante and Miriam stepped out into the hallway. He was thinking the same thing Althea was, that Miriam just wanted to say something again about him carrying the coffin. He stood there in the hall, waiting for Miriam to say her peace, wondering how hard this time must be for her. Softly, he asked, "Is there something I can do for you, Ms. Rivers?"

"There is, Dante. I want you to understand, first, that I thought about this." She didn't tell him she'd only thought about it for the last few minutes. "And it's not that I'm crazy. I just need to make myself feel safe."

"I don't understand."

"I need . . . I need a gun, Dante. I need a gun," Miriam repeated with slightly more confidence. "Would you get me one?"

Dante was shocked. This was the last thing he thought Miriam would say. He began shaking his head vehemently. "Oh, I can't help with that, Ms. Rivers. I'm sorry. I mean, I understand how you feel—"

"That's not true."

"Okay, it's not true. But I understand the feeling safe thing. I *really* do. But, Ms. Rivers, I'm trying to do a different thing these days. You can get one through, you know, regular ways, and—"

"They take so long."

"I hear you, Ms. Rivers. But you know what I'm saying? I'm trying to start a business and I just, you know, you understand, I just . . . I just . . ."

"Thank you anyway, Dante. I understand. Please don't mention this conversation to anyone."

"Oh, ain't no doubt about that." Miriam turned and walked back into Althea's apartment, while Dante stood there, in total disbelief.

Althea smiled as Miriam walked back in the door. "Come have your tea, Miriam. It's getting cold." Miriam sat down and sipped the lukewarm beverage. She had to get out of there. Why had she come down in the first place? There were things she had to do. No time to waste feeling sorry for herself. She had responsibilities. Responsibilities as a mother.

"Althea," Miriam began, "thank you so much for the tea. I'm going to go back upstairs."

"Are you sure?" Althea needed the company more than Miriam did. "Did Dante say something to upset you?"

"Oh, no, no. He's a very sweet young man. It's just that every now and then, it's hard, so hard, to be, you know, alone. But then as quick as that comes, being alone becomes all I can be. I know that doesn't make sense but—"

"Well, none of this does," Althea said, truly understanding, she thought, her neighbor's struggle. "I'll be here, anyway, if you need something else."

"Thank you, Althea. Thank you for everything." Miriam said this and then disappeared through the door, into the tiny and closed world of her apartment.

≋

*This is the home that is not a home, but a place to store. To store clothes and food and boxes and books and electronics and linens and time and people and people and time. Beneath carpets, behind chairs, in closets, under layers and layers of white, white paint. People and time and memories that are no longer distinguishable, no longer unique, individual. They are unformed now, running together, running apart. They are messy, leaving prints, like some sneaky animal that creeps in through the night window marking up the floors, the walls, escaping out before the sun, and you never are a witness, never, ever catch the thing. Still you know it's been there.*

≋

Miriam had done her best, with the painting and the furniture, the new sheets, and things sent to storage, to remove all traces of Aya from the apartment. She couldn't live with the dents Aya left in chairs, the stains she'd left on rugs. She couldn't live in a place if everywhere were Aya's things but nowhere was Aya.

Of course her best attempt had failed. That painted-over wall there by the kitchen was still the wall Aya used to lean against as her mother made dinner. Aya chattering, about school, or a poem, or some new outfit she wanted to buy. That wall was still Aya's wall, and Miriam was staring at it.

It made her remember Bird's anger. She thought about how she didn't understand it then, but it was so clear now. Not only the broad terrain of it, but how it got there, why it grew. In the face of too much loss, too much effort gone unseen, unrewarded, what else but anger? What else but rage and bitterness? Miriam could feel these two emotions she'd never before allowed herself to taste, burning in the back of her mouth, waiting for her to swallow them. She swallowed them.

It was new to her, and she disliked its burn. But it was what she had now before her, so she drank it and drank it until her eyes glazed over, glazed so you could see through them, and they could see through you. Every muscle in her body went so tight, it was awkward to walk. From the living room to the bedroom, where she put on her clothes. Blue slacks, a gray shirt, black walking shoes. She went into the bathroom to throw water on her face.

She had to get out, go out, be in a completely new and differently environment. A park, a movie, better yet, church. She had to get going or else she might kill someone. This is how she felt when she opened her front door, when she saw it, the package, unaddressed and unlabeled except for her name, Miriam, scrawled across the front. She did not wonder what was inside. She knew what was inside. Miriam picked up the package, took it into the apartment, opened it up, and got herself ready, knew exactly where she had to go.

# 24.

Two hundred miles from Brooklyn, New York, up Interstate 87, onto and through routes no one ever remembers, behind a mountain with no name, over a bridge that is just ten yards long, there is a town. It is an old town, a generally ignored town. It is a town that is not unlike its once upon a time people; the ones who are left to live out their days in the sort of nursing homes that seem to believe people outgrow the need for dignity and respect. No proper hygiene or food, no loving touch or intelligent engagement, no regular outings or visits, no future, no past. That's how the town was, left alone, left slumped over.

Wagner's ice cream, Brownie's diner, St. Joseph's Church, the U.S. post office, the sheriff, Bones Pub, Rite Aid, and McDonald's. Then an abandoned movie theater with a dark marquis, closed now for four and a half years. There was the supermarket and gas station, the volunteer firehouse, and Dr. Richards's office, and then that was it. Two minutes of town stretched out over two thousand acres of land.

That's Oak Street, the one drag that runs through Waterkill. And if you know Oak Street, then you know Waterkill, with its population of 5,830 people. And Waterkill, with its all-white citizenry. Its citizenry who for years have lived under the harsh boot of poverty, but who have come to believe that now, at last, they may find a way to breathe easy again.

For the last twenty-five years, Waterkill had been a community of laborers without labor. Many of the people lived in dilapidated trailers. Luckier families lived in homes that had been passed down through the years. Grandparents to parents, parents to children.

Still, those old family homes cried out for new roofs, new shingles, a fresh coat of paint, some reenforced steps. Even as the people began working again, home improvements did not rank high on the list of what had to be taken care of. There were loans to repay. There was food to buy. So Waterkill, even with its newfound revenue, sagged in the center, appeared old beyond its years, looked like the landscape of nightmares, the backdrop to the most violent, the most frightening of horror movies and campfire ghost stories.

But here was the difference between it and the towns you would most likely see in a slasher film: The main thing the town was known for, the main source of its revenue was not an old college sitting high above on top of a hill; in Waterkill there were no female co-eds running naked around the showers, screaming for their lives. In Waterkill, the only women who could be found screaming for their lives, the only women who could be found high atop a hill, were the women who were dressed in stiff polyester green skirts and tops. They were women who spent the majority of their days piled one on top of another, in six- by eight-foot cells. Cells that, only a few short years ago, had been built for one, but now, unbelievably, were housing two. Cells with no windows, unless you counted the bars that looked out into the cell block. There were windows in the cell block.

The women confined to the correctional facility in Waterkill, New York, were considered to be among the most dangerous in the state. This is what the information supplied by the Department of Corrections reported. The department even said that some of the women were considered the most dangerous in the nation. But the people of Waterkill loved these women. These women who brought them jobs. These women who were helping to ensure that the loans were repaid, that the houses were not foreclosed upon.

One captain, a veteran in the department who had recently been promoted and transferred to Waterkill, even said, and it was quoted in a newspaper, "Listen, it wasn't never an inmate I didn't like. Every inmate I ever met has helped keep a roof over my head, and food in my kids' stomachs. So there might be one or two who mess up your day here and there. But so what? At the end of the day, they don't bother me neither."

It was in this place with this man, this captain, that Miriam Rivers calmly prepared herself to live for the next two, and possibly six, years. That was the minimum time she would have to serve for reckless endangerment and the criminal possession of a firearm. Community sympathy, and an excellent attorney brought on board by Miriam's former boss, had ensured her acquittal of the most serious charge: the attempted murder of a police officer.

On the day the prison bus pulled into the grounds at Waterkill, and Miriam was taken—hands shackled to a waist chain, feet bound by leg irons—into the room where she was stripped and cavity searched, the voice of the judge who sentenced her, and the voice of the judge who had set Aya's killer free, were as distant as her daughter's laughter, as long ago as the grin and inquisition of the girl's wide eyes.

Miriam was not worried about, upset over, or disheveled by the time she was facing. Not by the amount of time, or by the injustice of it. Miriam had done the best she had known to do. Raising Aya, and attempting to avenge Aya—in her heart,

Miriam was eased by the knowledge that she had done her best. And she pulled that around her, and it barricaded her more effectively than even the forty-foot stone walls of the prison.

≈

It was a Monday morning at about 8:30 when Miriam marched blankly into the barren prison room where the women— mostly Black, some Latina, a couple white, and one Asian— were told to line up for the search. One of the women brought in with Miriam complained, "Goddamn, they just looked up our pussies on Rikers. Y'all like the way our pussies stank that much?" The woman shouted this at the three guards who were there with them. They ignored her, everyone did, including Miriam, who stood absolutely still, and did not speak and did not move.

One guard, a woman, a fifty-five-year-old grandmother, eventually glanced passively at the angry shouting woman. But then she turned away from her and simply went into her routine. She told each woman there that she must:

*Strip.*
*Everything off. I mean everything.*
*Fingers through your hair.*
*Lift your tongue.*
*Turn around.*
*Lift the bottom of each foot.*
*Right one, then left.*
*Now bend over.*
*Spread your cheeks.*
*Stand up.*
*Turn back, facing me.*
*Lift your right breast.*
*Now the other.*

*Now arms up, overhead.*
*Stand with your legs open.*
*Wide, like this. Over the mirrors on the floor.*
*Right.*
*Now, squat directly over the mirror.*
*Squat down farther.*
*Now cough.*
*Now stand.*
*Okay, we're done for now.*
*Get dressed.*
*You have three minutes.*

Throughout the whole of the process, the women grumbled and griped, every last one of them. Except Miriam. Miriam was humming, almost singing. She was thinking about Aya, and she was thinking about Bird, and the sound she was making, if any had cared to listen closely enough, and of course no one did listen closely enough to recognize it, was a dirge.

But it was a dirge unlike other funeral dirges since the deaths Miriam had known had not been natural deaths. Deaths you could come to terms with. Deaths you could go through a series of emotions with. Go from denial to anger, from anger to confusion, from confusion to at last acceptance. To some sort of peace. This had not happened for Miriam however, because really, Aya and Bird did not die. Only Mama had died.

Mama had slipped from life, but only after she had lived. Mama had lived the way so many people Miriam had known through the church had lived. Fully, often painfully, but they had lived. They had held down jobs. They had eeked out some sort of retirement. For some, there was also a home they had finally come to own, and furniture they had kept and cared for. For others they'd left behind the car that had taken them on short weekend trips and daily errands. There were the children they'd seen grow. Grow and then go on to make more children. More and more of them.

But what had Aya ever been able to know of these things? What had Bird?

Both of them had been buried before they had ever spent time in a job they liked, or at least one that promised a pension at the end. Aya and Bird had both been buried before they'd finished college; in fact, Bird never had had the opportunity to begin. And buried, both of Miriam's loves, before they'd owned cars; Aya had never even learned to drive. Buried before a wedding, before the birth of a child, before the crystallization of even a single dream. They'd been buried before they walked on a shoreline just as the day pushed in. Buried before they'd ever taken a walk in the woods. Buried. Before, and before.

So it was a dirge Miriam was humming, almost singing, but a dirge unlike other dirges, because these had been two deaths where no one had died. They had been killed. And there was a universe of difference between dying and getting killed. One seemed proper, the fitting end, unavoidable. The other was a reprehensible toying with the natural order of things. That was the difference, and it required acknowledgment. It required something to say it was wider. Something to say it left behind a space that was greater. A space that had no beginning, no ending, and Miriam was humming, almost singing into it, that vast nothing, and the space did not sing back. It tugged at Miriam's voice as though it was some great magnetic. The boundless space where nothing made sense and nothing was fair, tugged and yanked as though it wanted, as though it needed to snatch up and keep all that teetered at the edge of its uncompromising field. It tugged and yanked, trying to take the very last bit that Miriam had left to offer.

And all through the initial search, through the cell and uniform assignments, through her first meal, and her first night, and then the next and then the next, Miriam continued to hum, almost sing, in a voice, with a soul, that grew weaker and weaker. But it was all she had—that specific dirge. Even as she knew it could take her to the other side of sanity, she would not stop.

Because despite what many people thought—that Miriam Rivers had passed into the frenzied world of the insane on the day she took that gun and went out to shoot that cop—indeed the woman was quite lucid. Miriam was aware of everything that had been, aware of everything that was. She knew where she was now, and she knew why she was there. She knew why she had made the choices she had made. She knew. She knew. And she could prove that she knew. Miriam Rivers could show anyone, anyone who cared to see, the places on her body that were cut and scarred until they looked like a frantic, complex map across her skin. She could show people the bruises, even the ones just below the surface. The bruises that changed color, the bruises that never faded, the bruises that grew uglier and uglier. Miriam could show the organs, the muscles, and limbs swollen out of usefulness.

Here was the arm that hung slack on her right side. It was the arm where Aya was once cradled. Once this arm was the place of comfort from which Aya could latch on and drink from her mama. Be sustained, entirely, completely, from her mama. But it wasn't only this arm.

Miriam could show people her hand. Here was the hand that was clenched into a fist that could not be pried open. Not all the way. It was as though it had been crippled by the worst arthritis, that hand. That hand which was the one that should have grabbed Bird back on the night he stormed out of the house, stormed out angry. It was the hand that should have snatched him back as she cried, Baby, where you going without me? Stay.

It was also the hand that should have reached out and grabbed the truth out of the air, and told it to her daughter. That was the disorder that crippled Miriam's limbs, her body, her soul. But worse of all, it was the hand that, if she dared force it open, would reveal how there was now nothing left for it to hold. Miriam knew that. She knew, although she never said, because in all of her life, from the beginning of her life, who had really wanted to listen to it? Who ever wanted to hear a story all the way through? Not her parents or Joan or Mama, or even Bird when the days got hard. But even if she never spoke, and even if there was no one who would ever be there to hear, she knew, Miriam did, every detail, every one.

Yes, this woman, this Miriam Rivers, was sane. Because unlike all the faceless, nameless people who have been driven mad by whatever terrorists had taken over their lives, unlike those who had drifted into an alternate universe believing that there, at last, they might be able to embrace some degree of safety, Miriam knew no such escape. She knew exactly why there was the awful sound of crackling and burning always inside her head. She knew why her arm did not work right. She knew the reason for her disfigured hand. She knew the reason why she walked so slowly, so heavy. She knew.

She knew as the days of her incarceration began to stack up and her first night in prison became her first week. Her first week became her first month. Her first month became her first two months, and so on. Miriam knew. That's why she hummed, letting the humming pull her apart from herself. Eventually she even thought to become that crazy lady who sang to herself. If she became that, then she wouldn't have to know any more. Then she could just get lost in that strange wrapping of prison time, and perhaps they would never, ever let her out. Yes, that's what she wanted.

And then there came a night.

～

There came a night when it was unbelievably cold outside and the heat had gone out throughout the entire prison. And as the guards huddled together beside portable space heaters, the women, the prisoners, whooped and carried on and complained, until realizing it was useless and all they could do was crawl into their bunks and burrow beneath blankets and layers and layers of clothes. The cold prison became a quiet prison, except for the bodies shivering so intensely you could hear it. You could hear the rattle and chatter of teeth and bone. But other than that sound, it was quiet. It was so, so quiet. And Miriam, there on the top bunk, fell into a deep sleep. The kind of sleep that seems it could last years, and then longer.

But it did not. Moments after Miriam fell into her sleep, she felt a hand touching her hair. At first she thought she imagined it, and so she did not move, she did not open her eyes. But then the hand was still in her hair. Miriam's eyes finally opened. And she could not believe what she saw.

Sitting there, squeezed onto that tiny top bunk, was the luminous and beautiful brown face of her child. Miriam sat up, shot up. What was she seeing? What was she seeing? She reached out for Aya, and Aya reached back. Without a word between them, they embraced. They embraced long and they embraced hard.

"Baby. Baby. How are you here? How did you come here? I don't understand."

"I was always here, Mama."

"What do you mean, baby? I haven't seen you in so long.

Where've you been? How could I not have seen you? Why am I just seeing you now?"

"I don't know, Mama."

"It doesn't matter. It doesn't matter. It only matters that you're here." And then realizing suddenly where here was, Miriam said, "Oh God, Aya. Do you know what I've done?"

"I know, Mama."

"Oh God." Miriam hid her face in her hands. "I thought you were gone. I thought you were gone forever. And it was so bad. There was so much I hadn't told you. So many things left unsaid. I don't even know where I could begin, where I could end . . ." Miriam had to grab hold of the side of her bunk in order to keep speaking. "For so long, all I have been able to think about was, when was the last time I told you I loved you? Do you know, I couldn't remember, Aya," Miriam stuttered in a voice burdened by shame. "Oh God, Aya, I'm so sorry."

"I'm not mad at you, Mommy." Aya leaned her body against her mother's, into it.

"I never . . . I never . . . wanted you to see the inside of a place like this again. After, when you had to go to that place . . . to the Hall . . . I told myself while you were gone all these things. I had failed you. Should have made sure Dawn's mother was home. Should have done so many things. And while you were gone I promised myself I was going to watch you, really watch and make sure that never again. And I tried so hard to watch, to make sure you were in school. Ask about your assignments. But now," Miriam sobbed and was nearly incomprehensible, "I've dragged you here myself. How could I do that to you?"

"Mommy, don't cry. I understand. I understand things I didn't before."

Miriam shook her head, "What do you mean?" she asked, her words interrupted by sobs.

"I just understand things now, Mommy. I understand you. And now that I understand, it's better. It is."

Miriam stared at Aya, still confused, but desperate not to be. "I know there were things that I didn't share with you. There were things I didn't even want you to have to understand. It was best, Aya. People said, Let things go, move on. Don't drag your girl into a mess you created. I wanted the best for you."

"I know you did. I know how hard you worked."

"I loved you most, Aya."

"I know that now, Mommy. Can I tell you something?"

"Anything," Miriam wept.

"Your parents loved you most, too. They didn't know things. They didn't know."

"What are you saying, Aya? What are you saying?"

"I'm saying what I know. What I know now. They loved you most. Even if they couldn't make you know it. People only do what they know, what they've been taught. Sometimes, this is what I learned, Mommy, we have a chance to learn more. When we learn more, we can do more. Not everyone gets that chance. But some of us do."

Miriam's sobs shook her loose, shook her breath from her lungs, her nostrils, her heart. But she never felt more alive.

"I learned things, Mommy, and I understand now. And it's better." Aya looked into Miriam's wet eyes, and whispered, "Mommy, can I sit in your lap, Mommy? Just for a second?"

Miriam, unable to speak, nodded at her daughter and opened her arms. She opened her body. Wide. Finally, she whispered, "I didn't want you to carry what wasn't yours to carry." Aya nodded as Miriam let that big girl, that grown girl of hers crawl up into her. Crawl up into her in a way she'd never allowed. At least not past the age of five or six.

But Miriam thought now how that decision had been the wrong decision. And she let that girl sit in her lap, curl in her lap, cry in her lap. And she held that girl, she held her tight, tight, and she thought, *I'm gonna hold her right here. Hold her until I can't hold her no more.*

And she tried to do just that. Miriam's thighs and arms went to sleep, holding that girl, but it made no difference. Miriam held on. She held on all through the night, as the moon shifted position, as the crickets sang and then went silent, she held on. And so did Aya. And they said I love you. They said it a thousand times, and then a thousand times more.

They said it until the sun began to creep up on the horizon, and Aya looked up, and ever so lightly, pulled away from her mother, and whispered, "Mommy? Mommy? I have to go now."

Hearing those words, Miriam's whole body reacted almost violently. "No! No! You can't leave! Please. Please. Listen, I'll be better. Listen, I can't lose you again. Please, Aya." Miriam's words stumbled out in staccato.

"It's not my choice," Aya tried to explain. "I don't want to, Mommy."

"Where are you going to go?" Miriam implored, trying to insert logic and reason into a negotiation process that did not really exist. Still, "Who will take care of you? You can't just leave! Not again, baby, please."

And Aya, having no desire to defy her mother, sat there. She didn't say she'd stay, she didn't say she'd leave. She just sat there in her mother's arms, until a voice from the corner of the cell called out, "It's all right, Miriam." And it was only then that Aya rose, took her father's hand, and disappeared against the ringing of the prison's morning bell. Miriam sat up, and saw the light drifting in from across the cell block. Slowly, she lowered herself off the bunk. She could not avoid the wild flux that she was, that she'd become. All at the same time, Miriam was confused and clear, joyous and deeply sad, at peace but also agitated. Despite the unimaginable weight of these emotions, despite the way they bloated her, Miriam made it over to the gate. She could feel her legs shaking, but she nevertheless stood there. Stood there to be counted.

≈

Minutes and minutes after the count had been cleared and all of the women had gotten back into their bunks for the last hour before chow was called, Miriam was still standing at the gate. Her cellmate, Barbara Mayfield, who was in her ninth year of a twenty-five-year sentence for killing the husband she'd sworn was about to kill her, stared at Miriam. She thought to ask her, What the hell is wrong with you? Why you standing there like an idiot, but then thought better of it.

The two had exchanged very few words since they'd been assigned to the same cell five weeks earlier. Miriam was quiet all the time, only ever saying that which absolutely needed to be said. She never answered any of the prying questions Barbara asked; she only looked past that irritatingly inquisitive face and acted as though she couldn't understand English. Barbara was certain her cellmate was crazy.

"Maybe they got her on them new drugs," Barbara told her friend CeCe.

"I ain't never seen her come down to where I work at in the infirmary to get nothing," CeCe replied, authoritatively. "I think the bitch just crazy."

"You got to be out your mind if you gon' pull out a pistol at the police station," Barbara had agreed.

"'Cause if you gon' do some crazy shit like that, all I wanna know is why you gon' do it with a twenty-two? What you gon' accomplish with that *but* get a bust? She lucky that police stopped her when he did. Otherwise she'd have a body, and wouldn't never be able to even think about getting out of here."

"I heard she ain't even know how to shoot if she'd had the chance to actually do it."

"She crazy. You know crazy people always find a way to figure shit out. She'd have shot that ass if she hadn't been stopped."

If crazy was the consensus then that was fine, because it meant that eventually people left Miriam alone to wander through her days, doing her work assignment, which was laundry, and walking alone in the yard, humming to herself.

The humming was the main reason Barbara didn't ask Miriam why she was still standing at the gate now ten minutes after the count. Because at the gate, Miriam wasn't making a sound. None of that annoying humming to herself she so often did. It bothered Barbara to no end, but the few times she'd asked Miriam to stop, the request had gone ignored. She'd learned to live with it, but she hated it. So if standing at the gate was going to keep the crazy lady quiet, Barbara figured her celly need never sit down, lay down, nothing.

Miriam, however, wasn't even aware that she was standing there as long as she had been. She was awash in her own thoughts, awash in Aya. She was trying to figure out if it had been a dream or if it had been real. It seemed so real! It had to be real! And maybe, maybe Aya would come back again. Miriam prayed for it.

And Bird. Was that too much to ask for? That he come, too? And if he did, what would they say to each other, all these years in between them. Did he hate her now, for not protecting their girl? Would he know of and review the last twenty years, pick apart Miriam's decisions, tell her where she went wrong?

Where did she go wrong? She thought about how methodical she'd been. How everything had fallen apart, or else completely evaporated. She'd tried so hard to do what was best. She'd tried so hard to work, to provide, to put the past in the past, to only see the future, to save her money, to push Aya toward college and a career, to set a standard, to set rules. But it hadn't worked, it hadn't saved her baby.

So there, in front of a gate that caged her into a tiny cell, Miriam Rivers—thirty-eight years old, a childless mother, a convict, an enigma, and a woman who was now living her life facing a hole so great, so wide, so magnetic that it could have easily swallowed the whole of her, and some might have argued that it did swallow parts of her—began to pull.

When Miriam first began pulling, she was thinking of Aya. Aya in her lap saying something about understanding—that understanding was better. Aya, in her lap, feeling closer to her than even when Miriam had carried her in the womb. Miriam allowed this feeling. She allowed the feeling, and she pulled. Miriam pulled at what was left of herself, and to herself she cried out to Aya, and she said, This is for you, for when you come back, so I will be here, all the way. And I will never let anything happen to you again.

And the more she pulled, the more she saw what she was getting back, the stronger she felt, the more encouraged she felt. She pulled, and there was the moment she decided to leave her parents' house, a seventeen-year-old filled with love and possibility and hope and a clear sense of defiance toward a world that wanted to hand her to herself, preassembled, predetermined. She saw her seventeen-year-old self and remembered how once she had rejected that notion. She remembered.

And she remembered living with Bird, and what it was to be in a family where you could stretch out your soul. Making love with Bird, the reach and stretch of his touch, of their touching. After Bird was killed, when Miriam was convinced she was being punished by God and her parents, all she wanted was to ensure that their child never knew the pain she had known. That's why she tried to block it all out, but now it occurred to her she must have been wrong. Because in blocking out the pain, what else was kept on the other side of the wall?

Strengthened by this thought, Miriam pulled, and she would not stop. All day until the day was gone and it was night again, and she was alone, laying down on the top of her bunk, Miriam was still pulling, but suddenly it occurred to her that while she may have started pulling for Aya, now she was doing it for herself. She was doing it for the woman she was right then, locked up there in the prison, and for the girl who was once sixteen and wanted, more than anything, to be seen and heard and loved for the soul of who she was. As beautiful or ugly as she might have been, as wise or as ignorant, it did not matter. What mattered was that she wanted to become known in the world as a woman, fully a woman, bursting at the seams with experience and hurt and joy and confusion and desire and anger and laughter and breath.

She thought about Bird and Aya and the police, and the lies, and the years lost, and the years stolen and all of that silence, all the things she never said, and for a moment it occurred to her that she had lost everything, ruined everything. That her opportunity to fix things ended with Aya's shooting. It occurred to her that this realization, the one to speak, needed to come before Aya was killed, when her daughter was still here and alive. But the thought that followed immediately was that *she* was still alive—she, Miriam—in a prison, yes. Without her child, without Bird, but alive, and with herself. Could that mean something? Miriam wanted to find out. She continued to pull, to tug, to yank and snatch, and she did not stop until she was laid out, all of herself, sweating and exhausted, but victorious. Holding on to herself. Victorious.

Just after, there in that windowless cell where Aya had come only the night before, something else happened. Something incredible, a miracle perhaps. Miriam heard her daughter's voice calling out to her from the long ago dining table, the one in the apartment at 8 Manchester. The one beneath the spider plant and window.

"Mommy! Listen to this. Listen. I want you to hear this poem."

And Miriam could hear Aya reading the words of her favorite poet, Sonia Sanchez,

*I shall become a collector of me / and put meat on my soul.*

"Isn't that beautiful, Mommy?!"

"Yes, honey," Miriam had said then, only half paying attention. As she so often did, Miriam had quickly moved back into the details of her life.

But here and now in this barren place, in this place of no light, a place consumed by rules so numerous that they wound up canceling themselves out, Miriam heard the poem, its words, its meaning, and at last she heard the wonderful sense of discovery in her child's voice. And that hearing was a beckoning. It called Miriam home to herself, and now, now, she could not, she would not, refuse it. Miriam walked, slowly, even uncomfortably, but unhesitatingly into all the rooms of her house.

The next morning, when Miriam came out of her cell with all the other women who lined up and then marched over to the mess hall for powdered eggs and soggy french toast, she was a different woman, although no one noticed this immediately.

But Miriam was different, and in her pocket was a piece of paper on which she'd written down the lines of the poem.

With a tray of food in her hands, Miriam walked over to where Barbara was sitting with CeCe and two others, and she asked, "May I sit here?"

Barbara nearly choked on her food. She couldn't believe that Miriam was trying to be . . . how would you call it . . . *social*? Not knowing what else to say, Barbara simply replied, "Yeah." She could not imagine why today Miriam seemed to want to be with them, but in truth, she felt a little special that this odd and infamous woman, this woman who had gone to kill a policeman because the police had killed her daughter, this woman whose story made the news, this woman, Miriam Rivers, had chosen them, chosen her. And so despite the rumors of her insanity, Barbara not only said, "Yeah," but she also moved her tray over, trying to make room.

Miriam sat down and didn't say anything at first, and then, after the others had finished staring at her in disbelief, and had gone back to their discussion about the last episode of "All My Children," Miriam turned toward Barbara, and said softly, "Can I tell you something about my daughter?"

"Umm," Barbara began, uncertain about how to speak with Miriam. The table fell silent. "Yeah," Barbara continued. "Sure. What?"

"My baby liked to read. She liked poetry, and Aya, my daughter, used to read me her poems. I don't remember all of them. I don't really remember any of them." Miriam paused and the space shrunk, went uncomfortable for a minute, awkward. But just as Barbara was about to give up on her, about to turn away, Miriam continued. "I remember . . . I remember one line from a poem. It was 'I shall be a collector of me / and put meat on my soul.' I remember. My daughter read that poem to me."

Barbara wanted to dismiss this woman, this Miriam Rivers,

as crazy, because who talked like that? Who would say this sort of thing over powdered eggs in a prison mess hall? But the fact was that what this woman said, the words themselves—they were not crazy. They were, well, truthful words. They were truthful and they were useful and, in fact, they were sort of like the words that Barbara herself had uttered all those times she'd wanted to leave that no-good ass nigga.

Barbara knew that no matter what her past had been, when this bid was done and over with, she was going to run her own life, put meat on *her* soul. She knew she'd spent too much time putting meat on the soul of men who didn't deserve it, who didn't deserve anything from her. So she understood exactly what this Miriam woman was saying, but that wasn't the point. The point was why did she speak that way here, in the mess hall? The point was no one said thoughts like that out loud. At least not like that. Out loud you could say, and Barbara had said, Niggas ain't no good. And she would say, Ain't no nigga getting close up on me like that again. Believe that shit.

What Miriam was saying was the same thing, really, only more beautiful, more clear. So what to do, what to say in the face of this? Barbara stared for a while, and then said,

"I hear you." She hesitated and then added, "Let me see a copy of that poem." CeCe and the two other women at the table couldn't believe what was going on. They didn't know if they should get up and leave, or if they should stay.

"That's all I have. Just that line. It's all I remember," explained Miriam. And then, "Maybe in the library they have the book."

Which is how it began. How Miriam and so many other women began to reveal the secrets that had kept them twisted, limping, half-blind, teeth coming loose, hair falling out, blood thinned, lungs waterlogged, imaginations drawn and quartered.

It all began when Miriam and Barbara went to the library later that day to look for a book that had that poem inside of it. But nothing was there. Only romance novels, a few legal books, some murder mysteries. So with nothing else, no poems between them, they began to talk. Really it was Miriam who began to talk, to tell on herself, to tell all the secrets. She told everything. She told it like it happened. She told it from her childhood to Bird, to running away, to getting pregnant, to Bird being killed, to her dying her death after that killing, to Aya, and the silence, and rules meant to sort out the confusion, the rules that failed her, how she had failed herself, and now Aya was gone and she was here. But if she was going to be here, then she was going to be here all the way. That's what Miriam explained.

And after days of Miriam telling, days and days of it, Barbara became less willing to cling to her own secrets. She became less willing because she saw pieces of herself in this woman who had once seemed so different from her, so odd. She saw pieces and she even thought she saw the way to gather and put those pieces together.

So when CeCe, who was starting to feel left out, asked, "What y'all be talking about all that time?" Barbara told her to "Come on. Come talk with us." And after a while these three would walk the yard, talk in the yard, talk in the mess hall, talk wherever. And when the three became five, they decided to form a group that wrote their own poems about the things they'd seen and come to know. Then they invited others to join.

And some women pretended that they did not hear the invitation.

And some women simply turned and walked the other way (some women ran).

And some women talked bad about the crazy lady who had once up and tried to shoot the police (some women complained about her to the police).

But then there were some women who listened.

And those women, trembling in defiance and fear, began to collect, examine, and compare the various and scattered fragments of their own bones, the outlines of their own bruises, the measure of their own scars, pick back up their own knocked-out teeth. And those women who did that, either quietly or loud, began to tell. They told the way Miriam told. They told everything.

They told all they had ever choked on, or up. All they'd ever had to escape or confront, the streets they'd known, the strolls they'd taken, the men they wanted when they didn't know better, the men they wanted when they did, the women they loved and touched. The women they didn't. They told everything they'd ever sniffed, smoked, or swallowed, everything they'd dreamed or had forgotten to dream.

They told about the children they lost, or gave away, the children who had been stolen. They told about the parts of their own selves that had gotten snatched up and stolen—in the blinding light of day, in the presence of God and people—they told about the thefts of their own fingers, and hands, a leg taken here, an eye gone there. Gone.

These women, they removed the patches and prostheses, the makeup, and the wigs. They stopped holding in their stomachs and painting their nails fire red, and in this state, laid bare before themselves, they told.

And some told it in poems.

Some told it by scratching it into bathroom walls.

Some told it in newspaper and magazine articles.

Some told it in letters back home.

Some told it in clemency applications.

Some told it all the time: to the sisters in the laundry room, to the sisters in the mess hall, to the sisters in the law library.

Some told it to themselves, sitting alone on their bunks.

And some, the ones who could, told it on Saturdays or Sundays when their daughters came from miles and miles away to lean into their mothers' breasts, and to eat microwave popcorn and processed fish sandwiches and call it a meal, and to try to stitch together a semblance of a mother-child relationship.

Some women told their daughters that they wished there was a place they could send them. A place where they were going to be loved the way they deserved to be loved. A place where the romance of life surpassed the romance of movies and songs, of television shows and books. But if that place existed somewhere in this time, in this country, then it was a hidden place. And until it got found, what they had, all they had, was a place in themselves. The women told their daughters this.

What you mean? many of the daughters asked.

And the mothers said, each in her own way, and each at her own pace:

You have to love you right. That's all you got. Even when everybody else is bent on loving you wrong, and wrong begins to look like it's not *that* wrong, you got to love yourself right. Especially then. And you got to do it in public. You got to do it where everybody can notice and say, That girl there? She love herself. She love herself like she teaching a class in loving herself. Like the whole world everywhere is her student, and they depending on her to be exact, precise, and creative in her teaching. That girl there? She love herself good because she love herself with imagination. Matter of fact, I saw her do it with a morning stretch.

Well, I saw *her* do it in a song.

I saw her do it with her walk.

I saw her carve it into rings and wear it on every finger.

I saw her string it into a line of colored glass beads and wrap it twice around her waist.

I saw her tattoo it on her ankle, and let the picture wind up her leg.

I saw her cornrow it all long down her back.

I saw her weave it into her hair with golden strings.

I saw her throw it into the stew at the very last minute. She said it was her mother's secret ingredient.

I saw her do it on the train one time. She did it with a smile and a motion. She slid over and made room for another girl. It was a girl who got on the train with a scowl on her face, but did not leave that way, now that room had been made for her presence.

After these visits with their daughters, and after the discussions in the mess hall, or laundry, or on the court in the yard, many of the women would come to Miriam and tell her all the things they'd said, all the things they'd heard. And Miriam listened to these many testimonies.

She never rushed anyone's story. She just listened like the mother she was, like the mother she'd become, and sometimes she held a shaking hand, and sometimes she hugged a woman very close to her heart, but always when they were done speaking Miriam said the same thing.

She said, "Please, just keep talking. Keep telling it. Especially to your girls."

Miriam told them they had to say their stories, the things they knew, the puzzles they'd fit together despite the missing pieces. She told them they had to say the stories from the front of them all the way to the back. Tell them from the side, and tell them at an angle. Tell your daughters everything, whoever they may be, wherever you may find them. Tell the daughters who came through you, and tell the ones who came another way.

Tell them before they have a chance to slip out the front door, out through your fingers, out and you have lost that once-in-a-lifetime moment to hug, or hold, or kiss, or warn, or remind, or tease, or touch, or savor, or save. Them. Save them.

Call out, Baby! Wait. I have something I have to tell you.

Come back.

Come back.

*Aya.*

Since 1990, at least 2,000 people have been killed by law enforcement in the U.S.

Most of those people were Black or Latino.

Most were unarmed.

# Acknowledgments

I want to gratefully acknowledge all the people who took the time to read, in whole or in part, various versions of what finally became *Daughter*: Autumn Amberbridge, Akissi Britton, Kimberly Elise, Zayd Rashid, Robin Templeton, Beulah Trist, and Eric Williams. Your belief in my work has been the very thing that made it possible.

Equally important in allowing the work happen, has been the practical and absolutely essential support I received from Jean Stewart, and Robert and Rosemary Singh. Their care for my daughter gave me the freedom to work with a peace of mind that is borne only of genuine love. Nisa and I both thank and appreciate you.

Victoria Sanders, and all the members of her team, especially Imani Wilson, continue to deserve particular acknowledgement for quelling, with incredible grace, my all too regular bouts of insecurity and *artiste* drama. You know this means you're stuck with me forever.

The women of Scribner, Nan Graham, Susan Moldow, Rachel Sussman, and most recently Alexis Gargagliano, have provided me with a home that truly respects literature. As a young woman, it was literature that, without being hyperbolic, saved me. I am therefore grateful to be in the presence of people who understand its absolute necessity in the world, and I am most grateful of all to my editor, Gillian Blake, who understands what I try to do best of all. She's understood it even when I haven't, and never fails to challenge me when I need to be challenged. With her clear guidance, insight, and love, I was able to complete this book during the first two years of my daughter's life. No matter where she is, she will always be my partner in this work.

My ability to write this book at this time in my life was made possible, in no small part, by the support I've always received from my colleagues at *Essence* magazine. While across the board, the people I work with are among the best people anyone could ever hope to work with, there are some who have extended themselves to me in extraordinary ways: Susan L. Taylor, Patrik Henry Bass, Nicole Saunders, Imani Powell, and Penny Wrenn. I hope that each of you knows the value you hold in my life, and the place you have secured in my heart.

Finally, three weeks to the day that my daughter was born, and about six weeks after the idea of this novel was born, I sat down to interview Katiadou Diallo. I didn't know then the first thing about motherhood; Mrs. Diallo had to show me how to hold my baby. The measure of her elegance and dignity as a parent and as a woman, was defining for me as I began my journey—both as mother, and as a writer who was creating a picture of what motherhood could become. I am certain I am a better mother because of my engagement with Mrs. Diallo, as I am equally sure I've written a better book.

# A SCRIBNER
## READING GROUP GUIDE

### DAUGHTER

#### DISCUSSION POINTS

1. In *Daughter*, Aya Rivers, a vibrant but mischievous teenager, tries to be obedient but has a hard time, particularly "when she [comes] across a rule that [doesn't] fit into her life" (page 4). Discuss the notion of rules as a theme that resonates throughout the novel. How do rules factor into the lives of Miriam and Aya? In what ways does following the rules backfire?

2. As a child, Miriam "was loved, yes, but hers was a childhood defined by the church, and by her mother's restrictions and protection" (page 62). Examine the parallels between Miriam's and Aya's childhoods and upbringings.

3. How is Miriam, as a parent, the product of her mother and father's attempts to do things "just so"? Were Maud and Fred successful as Miriam's parents? Was Miriam successful as a parent to Aya?

4. Up until Miriam meets Bird, she is a silent and respectful girl who never really asserts herself or her point of view. She tells Bird that "if you say how you feel it's either considered complaining, not being grateful for your blessings, or else not being in control of your emotions" (page 101). Discuss the themes of silence and voice. How does Miriam eventually use the voice that has been locked within her for so long?

5. Aya, seeking to define her identity, is naturally curious about her absent father. Miriam, attempting to shield her daughter from the bitter truth, tells Aya that her father died in Vietnam. Do you think Miriam should have told Aya the truth about Bird? How might have Aya's understanding of past events potentially affected her future?

6. Devastated by the loss of her first and only love, Bird, and her only child, Aya, Miriam seeks to avenge her daughter's death by opening fire in a police precinct. Are you surprised by this sudden turn of events? Is Miriam justified?

7. Growing up a lonely child, Miriam forges a strong and binding relationship with God. How does prayer and faith factor into Miriam's life? Ultimately, does she break her pact with God?

8. An underlying theme of the novel is the impact of police brutality on families and the community at large. How do you reconcile the fact that both father and daughter are victims haphazard policing? Considering the high levels of police antagonism, is it a startling coincidence or a probable occurrence?

9. The novel *Daughter* sharply focuses on familial relationships, in particular, the raising of daughters. The narrator states: "Aya would be raised a righteous woman, a clean and pure and proper woman. Miriam would not allow her girl to follow the example of her life" (page 218). Do you think Miriam and her parents would have been as strict and restricting if they were raising boys instead of girls?

10. By the end of the novel, Miriam encourages the women at the Waterkill facility to "say their stories, the things they knew, the puzzles they'd fit together despite the missing pieces" (page 259). Discuss the importance of passing on stories and sharing histories. How does Miriam eventually fit her puzzle together in spite of the missing pieces?

Joyce Ravid

**asha bandele** served as features editor and writer for *Essence* magazine and is currently a Revson Fellow at Columbia University. She is the author of *The Prisoner's Wife* and a collection of poetry. She lives in Brooklyn, New York, with her daughter.

**Look for more Simon & Schuster reading group guides online and download them for free at www.bookclubreader.com**